THE LAST MAGAZINE

MICHAEL HASTINGS was a contributing editor to *Rolling Stone* and a correspondent at large for BuzzFeed. A onetime correspondent for *Newsweek*, Hastings covered the wars in Iraq and Afghanistan, as well as the 2008 and 2012 U.S. presidential campaigns. Hastings was the author of three books: *I Lost My Love in Baghdad*, *The Operators*, and *Panic 2012*. He died in 2013. A winner of the George Polk Award, he also posthumously received the Norman Mailer Award for Emerging Journalist.

Praise for *The Last Magazine*

"What a novel it is! Tenacity and perseverance were the qualities that helped Hastings become a star reporter for *GQ* and *Rolling Stone*, and they inform the novel's narrative, creating a story as engrossing as it is believable. While the characters are not always likable, they are unfailingly engaging. And the breakneck pace of the narrative is so unrelenting, it makes you wonder if Hastings lived as he wrote."

—*Newsweek*

"Even from the grave Mr. Hastings has demonstrated anew an ability to reframe the debate. The novel . . . reads as vivid archaeology that reveals much about the present moment. . . . The milieu of the book paints a picture of a tree house where like minds connive and look for an opening. But far below them, there is the sound of sawing—steady and implacable. The tree will fall. . . . Remarkable."

—David Carr, *The New York Times*

"[*The Last Magazine*] is fast and funny and humane. When I put it down, it called to be picked up again."

—Dwight Garner, *The New York Times*

"[Hastings's] keen eye for the creatures of the New York media universe focuses on the fabricated lifestyles of that world's desperate inhabitants. Here, no one is immune. . . . The suffering amid the insufferable is comic gold, and Hastings had no time for heroes. The world he created is filled with lost boys stamping their feet for validation. This could be the perfect summer bro comedy. Paging Judd Apatow!"

—Mark Guarino, *Chicago Tribune*

"A convincing account of the perils of war—and of the journalistic wars of an institution under siege from New Media. . . . *The Last Magazine* remains a loving account of a profession Hastings believed was honorable and tried to honor. Only the guilty have something to fear."

—Paul Wilner, *San Francisco Chronicle*

"Surely Michael Hastings would have savored the taste of revenge had he lived to see his first novel, *The Last Magazine*, published. . . . The humor throughout is searing . . . entertaining."

—Sherryl Connelly, *New York Daily News*

"Remarkable . . . Hastings, the novelist, reminds one at times of the early Robert Stone."

—*Booklist*

"A messy, caustic, and very funny satire . . . A ribald comedy about doing time in the trenches and the bitter choices that integrity demands."

—*Kirkus Reviews*

ALSO BY MICHAEL HASTINGS

Panic 2012

The Operators

I Lost My Love in Baghdad

The
Last
Magazine

A NOVEL

MICHAEL HASTINGS

A PLUME BOOK

PLUME
Published by the Penguin Group
Penguin Group (USA) LLC
375 Hudson Street
New York, New York 10014

USA | Canada | UK | Ireland | Australia | New Zealand | India | South Africa | China
penguin.com
A Penguin Random House Company

First published in the United States of America by Blue Rider Press,
a member of Penguin Group (USA) LLC, 2014
First Plume Printing 2015

P REGISTERED TRADEMARK—MARCA REGISTRADA

THE LIBRARY OF CONGRESS HAS CATALOGED THE BLUE RIDER PRESS EDITION AS FOLLOWS:

Hastings, Michael, date.
The last magazine : a novel / Michael Hastings.
p.   cm.
ISBN 978-0-399-16994-6 (hc.)
ISBN 978-0-14-751618-3 (pbk.)
1. American periodicals—Fiction.   2. Journalism—United States—Fiction.
3. Periodicals—Publishing—United States—Fiction.   I. Title.
PS3608.A86147L37   2014   2014006271
813'.6—dc23

Printed in the United States of America
10   9   8   7   6   5   4   3   2   1

Original hardcover design by Meighan Cavanaugh

to Brent and Molly

The
Last
Magazine

INTRODUCTION: WHY I WRITE

My name is Michael M. Hastings, and I'm in my twenties. I'm sitting in a studio apartment on the Lower East Side in Manhattan. Second floor, overlooking Orchard and Rivington. There's snow dropping by the streetlights. It's three a.m., and I just got off work.

My magazine has a policy, a little item in the fifty-seven-page Human Resources manual called the "outside activities clause." It prevents employees from publishing journalism without the magazine's permission. That could apply to writing books like this one. So I want to say right now: This is fiction, it's all made up.

This book is a story about the media elite. Maybe you're interested in that world. I have the cc's and the bcc's and the reply-alls. Three years' worth, from 2002 to 2005, time- and place-specific, a very recognizable New York, at least for now.

I do have themes, too. Love, in a way, though it's not my love, and I can't say I understand it too well. Not murder, at least not in the whodunit sense. No ghosts or supernatural horrors or serial killers. Sex, yes, I have a bunch of sex scenes. There's war in the backdrop, looming and distant and not real for most of these characters, myself included.

Maybe I'm talking genres, and maybe the genre is *corporate betrayal*.

Including the big decision that the entire media world is so interested in: Who and what is left standing?

It'll take me about 300 pages, approximately 85,000 words, to get to that. By turning the page, you're 1 percent closer to the truth.

PART I

The Intern

1.

Morning, Tuesday, August 20, 2002

What's our take?"

That's Nishant Patel talking. He's the editor of the international edition of our magazine, available in eighty countries.

"It's a real genocide. We got A.E. Peoria there, got some great reporting. Guys on horseback burning a village, cleansing the place, poisoning wells. An interview with the IFLNP rebel leader."

"And?"

"Uh, we'll be talking about the genocide, that the UN called it that, great detail, how the catastrophic—"

"That's not new."

"The genocide?"

"Yes."

"It's new, it only started last week—"

"We've read it before."

Nishant Patel is hearing story pitches for next week's magazine. Tuesday mornings, ten a.m., in the sixteenth-floor conference room. He sits at the head of the table, thirteen swivel chairs in length. The section editors sit around him.

"It's an on-scener," continues Jerry, the World Affairs Editor. "Horseback riding, the rebel leader's got a motorcycle—"

"What are we saying? To have spent thousands of dollars so Peoria can land at an airport in Khartoum, tell us how hot and sunny it is, and bump his head in a Land Rover so we can read what we've already read in the *Times*?"

"Nishant, the *Times* only did one story on it—"

My job as an intern—or as a just sort of promoted intern—is to sit in the meetings and write down the story list, divided into the proper sections, with a note on how long the story might actually be. Length is measured in columns. There are approximately three columns to a page, about 750 words total, depending on photos. It's a rough list that changes throughout the week. On Tuesdays at ten a.m., I have to make a best guess at what stories are most likely to survive.

Jerry's story on the genocide is already on deathwatch.

The other editors are looking down, shuffling reading material, pretending to take notes. It's not proper etiquette to gawk at a drowning man. And if another section editor does speak up, it won't be to rescue Jerry. It will be to throw a life preserver with the intent of cracking the drowning man's skull so he sinks even quicker.

Like so:

"You know, Nishant," Sam, the Business Editor, says, "you're right. That story is stale. I saw a report this week that showed the fastest growth industry in East Africa is mobile phone sales. Up like eight hundred and thirty-three percent from two years ago. If that's going on across the continent, that's a story with regional implications."

Sam emphasizes the word "regional."

Nishant Patel nods.

"An outsourcing angle too," says Sam. "Americans outsourcing to the Indians, the Indians outsourcing to the Chinese, and the Chinese outsourcing to the Africans."

"Who are the Africans outsourcing to?" Nishant asks himself. "A great question. Yes, get Peoria to talk to someone who sells mobile phones there."

I write down the potential story: Mobile Phones/Outsourcing/ E. African Genocide (Peoria, 3 Columns).

Next up is Foster, the Europe Editor.

"The Islamic Wave Recedes. We have numbers showing that Islamic immigration is dropping. A huge drop, off a fucking cliff. Fears of Islamophobia? Unfounded. Townsend is writing from Paris."

"My sense is that the Islamic wave is cresting," says Nishant.

"Exactly. The Islamic Wave Is Growing. The numbers don't tell the whole story. Other factors that aren't being looked at show a real significant increase. Townsend can get that in by Wednesday."

"That sounds fine, yes," says Nishant.

"Cover: The Global Housing Boom," says Sam for Business. "The most expensive house in the world was just sold for two hundred fifty-three million dollars. It's happening everywhere."

"Good, good," says Nishant.

"Didn't we just do that story," says Jerry from World Affairs, but Nishant has moved on.

"We're reviewing three women novelists," says Anna from Arts & Entertainment and Luxury Life. "All are writing about ethnic marriages—I mean, they are, uh, beautifully written, and they take place in these settings that are just, really, they're about the experience of two cultures and how—"

"Fine, fine, but let's cut down on the novels."

"We have our story on Space Tourism," says Gary from Sci/Tech. "Our crack intern Hastings is working on it."

"Who's Hastings?" says Nishant.

Let me say that my heart—well, I like the attention. After working over the summer as an unpaid intern, I'd been hired as a temp just last week. I'd never had my name mentioned in a meeting before. Nishant Patel is about to see me for the first time. His gaze trails nine swivel chairs to his right. The eyes of Nishant Patel are deep brown, a set of chocolate emeralds that a profile writer for the *New York Herald* said were like an Indian Cary Grant, his lashes fluttering in sync with his melodious voice, British with a hint of the refined castes of New Delhi—the voice of an internationally flavored school tie.

"Thanks, everyone," Nishant says, and stands up.

Everyone thanked stands up too, and walks along the sides of the conference room, passing by the great big windows that look across 59th Street to a massive construction site of dual glass towers in Columbus Circle. Our competitor, the other weekly newsmagazine we call Brand X (and they call us Brand X), is getting ready to move into the towers when construction is complete. Brand X, as usual, is following our lead. We were here first. (You can also see an apartment building on Central Park West where everyone says Al Pacino lives.)

I step out into the hallway, and as I'm walking away, I overhear a brief exchange. I look back to see who's talking.

"Professor Patel," says a voice in the hallway with a southern drawl.

"Mr. Berman," Nishant Patel says.

It is the first time I see them side by side, Nishant Patel and Sanders Berman, sizing each other up.

2.

Tuesday, August 20, 2002

Magazine journalist A.E. Peoria is kneeling on top of a 1994 Toyota Land Cruiser in eastern Chad. It's night, and he's up on a small hill to get reception. The engine is running so that the electronics he has plugged into the jeep stay charged. A.E. Peoria is swearing. He believes that his Uniriya mobile satellite phone must be pointed 33 degrees southeast, and that should make it work.

The Toyota Land Cruiser is making a beeping sound because the keys are in the ignition and the door is slightly ajar. It's actually more like a dinging sound than a beep, and Peoria would close the door but he needs the interior ceiling light from the car to see what he is doing. His seven-inch black Maglite, which he usually would be gripping in his teeth, has run out of batteries. Or so he thinks.

Before climbing onto the roof of the Land Cruiser, he had tried to turn on the flashlight. When the light didn't come on, he checked the batteries to make sure the + and – were correctly in place. Unscrewing the top, he saw that the two double-A batteries inside weren't the Energizers he'd purchased at the Dubai Duty Free Travelers' Shop and Market at the Dubai International Airport. These were batteries with Chinese characters on them, the word MAJORPOWERY in pink English.

Someone had switched his Energizers for MAJORPOWERYS.

Why hadn't the person just taken the flashlight—that would have made more sense. Why did the thief bother replacing the Energizers with dead knockoffs? The thief either was trying to be clever and/or knew him, swapping dead batteries so he wouldn't notice the difference in the flashlight's weight. The prime suspect, he reasoned, was his translator, David D. Obutu from N'Djamena.

"It's dark, man, don't go up there. It's stupid shit," David D. Obutu had told him twenty minutes before Peoria had decided to drive the Land Cruiser to the top of the small hill.

"I have to get reception to check if there's anything from New York."

"Stupid shit, man. You have a light up there they can see for fucking kilometers, man. They'll start shooting again."

"They haven't shot in three days. I should be okay. I'll do it quick."

"It's some stupid shit, man."

"This *is* stupid shit. I'm here to do stupid shit. I'm not asking you, I'm just telling you."

"The villagers aren't going to be very happy with you."

"Fucking villagers have more to worry about than me checking my email for twenty minutes."

That was how he'd left things with David D. Obutu, translator turned battery thief.

Now kneeling atop the Land Cruiser, Peoria understands why David D. Obutu didn't want him to go up to the hill. Obutu knew he'd need his Maglite. When the Maglite didn't work, he might check the batteries. David D. Obutu's motives, A.E. Peoria thinks, were not pure. His motives were not to protect Peoria's well-being, or the well-being of the village (really a refugee camp), but to prevent the detection of the theft.

Still, magazine journalist A.E. Peoria knows that Obutu did have a point, even if it was secondary to hiding the double-A rip-off—kneeling atop a Land Cruiser at the crest of a hill next to the refugee camp that had been victimized, in the strongest sense of the word, by various tribal/warlord/bandit factions in the previous weeks, was stupid shit. Especially with the door to the Land Cruiser left slightly ajar.

He had thought he'd need the light for just a few moments—a minute at most—while he plugged the Ethernet cable connection into the Uniriya, then booted up his laptop, then aimed the Uniriya in the appropriate direction to pick up the satellite signal.

But the fucking thing isn't working, and he needs the light on as he keeps trying different angles and different settings.

It is doubly bad, MAJORPOWERY bad, because now the screen on his laptop adds to the illumination.

Ten minutes I have been fucking around with this thing, A.E. Peoria thinks.

He feels like he is being watched. What is that kind of feeling anyway? How does that work?

Sitting cross-legged, Native American style, on the roof of the Toyota Land Cruiser, he can see the tent village/refugee camp to the west and to the east he can't see anything clearly but knows there is a border. He sees that about one hundred of the refugees have crowded together near the bottom of the hill. It's so dark he knows people are there only because they are a mob of blackness, and he thinks this might be taken as a reference to skin color, but it's actually a reference to the fact that the gathered crowd has just taken on a shadowy shape. They are watching him; he is entertainment.

He uncrosses his legs and kicks the driver-side door shut. The interior car light stays on a few more moments, then turns off.

The dinging, too, ceases.

He decides to use his laptop screen for light, which is annoying because the dial that adjusts the angle of the Uniriya satellite modem is very small. The digital glow, even after he opens the laptop like a book, flattening it out so that he can get the screen close to the dial, isn't very helpful.

The laptop and the satellite modem are tethered together by a blue Ethernet cable, making the movement even more awkward. Other wires come down off the car through the rolled-down window on the driver's side to stay charged in a contraption hooked into the Land Cruiser's cigarette lighter. The cigarette lighter is rarely used for lighting cigarettes anymore, A.E. Peoria thinks.

What is that noise?

Oh, it's just a new dinging. It's his laptop making the new dinging noise, no longer the car door, which means the software for the Uniriya is trying to "acquire" the satellite, *ding, ding, ding*.

He presses the mute button on his laptop so it stops making the dinging noise. He's sweating and worried and very much discomfited. That fucking David D. Obutu. The country to the east, where the refugees came from and where the attackers came from, looks very flat and peaceful and serene and unthreatening—though admittedly he can't really see much of it in the dark. And A.E. Peoria knows that scenery in this region is not a good way to judge the chance of catastrophic violence occurring at any moment.

Satellite found. 123 bps.

Is that a whistling?

No.

He gets on his email. The web browser allows him to pull up his account, and there's the email he's been waiting for, the story list from some kid named Michael M. Hastings. Must be an intern.

He sees the list:

Cover: Global Housing Boom
Nishant Patel on TK
Rise of Islam In Europe?/townsend
Mobile Phones/Outsourcing/E. Africa Genocide/peoria
The Swedish Model
TK Columnist on Financial Scandal
Three Novels on Exile
Space Tourism

Mobile phones? Out fucking what? What moron wrote up this story list?

He refreshes his screen, and there's a new email from Jerry, the World Affairs Editor.

Hey A.E., the story is on for this week—just going to make it more of a business story pegged to a new report about the increase in mobile phone sales across Africa. Would be good if you interview a mobile phone vendor or talk to some Africans about their use of mobile phones. What colors, styles? What kind of brand? How many phones do most families have? How much do the phones cost in USD? What are the Chinese really up to? We'll have an intern here call the authors of the study, so no need to worry about that. We'll wrap your on-scene reporting lower down in the story. Can file thursday ayem? many thanks, j

A.E. Peoria is about to hit Reply, about to cc the entire top editorial staff. He gets only to the words "Jerry that sounds like" and doesn't

get to "absolute bullshit" when he notices that the crowd that had
gathered to watch him from the bottom of the small hill has dispersed.
To move silently away, in a herdlike fashion, as if sensing an earth-
quake or a thunderstorm or some kind of major weather or geological
event. He listens closely. There is actually a deep and frightening
whistle. He understands that perhaps a mortar shell or a rocket is on
the way. Right when he thinks that, he hears a very loud boom and
grabs his laptop and satellite modem, and while flipping the screen
down, he hits Send by accident and falls off the roof of the Toyota
Land Cruiser. He protects his laptop, falling on his back, but the
Uniriya satellite mobile modem, which looks like a gray plastic box,
falls on the ground next to him. Peoria scrambles to his feet and
opens the door to get back in the car and the overhead light goes on,
and he thinks, Oh fuck, fuck me, this is stupid shit.

He slams the door and puts the Toyota Land Cruiser in reverse
and starts driving down the hill, thinking he should try to get back
to the refugee camp. The electronics he had been charging in the
cigarette lighter are tangled on his lap, and the interior of the car is a
fucking mess. He feels liquids, like spilled water bottles or something.
Ka thunk, ka thunk, ka thunk. Without a seat belt, each twenty-foot
stretch on the dirt path down to the village sends him up high in his
seat. He keeps bumping his head. Finally he gets to the bottom of
the small hill and stops outside the tent that he and David D. Obutu
are sharing. David D. Obutu is standing outside the tent and smiling
and shaking his head.

"You lucky the Ibo tribe can't shoot RPGs for nothing," David D.
Obutu says.

"That was an RPG? I thought it was a mortar."

A.E. Peoria and David D. Obutu smoke a cigarette.

"We have to get back to N'Djamena tomorrow. We need to go to
the market and talk to someone who sells mobile phones."

"No problem. Everyone in Chad has mobile phones now. Two years ago, nothing! Now we are all talking on the mobile phones. Makes a good story—I worked with Granger from *USA Today* last week, and we did a big report on how Africans love mobile phones. Big business. Fucking Chinese."

"That's what I hear. Did you take my fucking batteries?"

3.

Afternoon, Tuesday, August 20, 2002

My desk is on the sixteenth floor, at an intersection of cubicles and two hallways, a listening post for office gossip. Every day, the section editors gather on the other side of my cubicle wall before going out to lunch.

Today, Jerry is the first out of his office, then Gary, then Anna.

"Want to come to the Crater with us?" Gary asks me.

It's the first time I've been invited, suggesting I may not just be another temp, replaced each season.

The Crater is two blocks west from the office, on 57th Street. It's cramped and greasy, an atmosphere of frequent foodborne illnesses. We're at a table in the corner underneath framed pictures on the wall of unknown famous people who have dined there and have taken the precaution of bringing aspirational publicity shots, signed with Magic Marker, made just in case.

"Ask for the burger well done if you're going to get a burger," says Jerry. "Nishant is really getting to me."

"Did anyone read his book?" asks Anna.

Jerry and Gary don't say anything. I wait a second.

"I read it," I say.

"What did you think?"

What did I think of Nishant Patel's book? It doesn't matter what I think of his book. I bought the book to find out as much about the boss as possible, not for any particular love of the subject matter. Reading it gave me insight into his thinking, insight into who he was or at least what he pretended to think. It was preparation for the moment, assured by probability, when I would be stuck in the elevator with him and I could say, "Gee, Mr. Patel, I loved your book, especially Chapter Seven, where you talk about transparency and corruption."

"I thought it was good," I say. "Especially the parts about transparency and corruption."

"What's it about again?" says Jerry, who makes a point not to pay attention to anything Nishant Patel–related that does not directly affect his stories or mood or job security. "Outsourcing, right? That fucking bastard."

"Uh, sort of. It's really about benevolent dictatorships."

The editors are listening to me.

"Benevolent dictatorships. How, you know, democracies evolve, and how they really take time to evolve, and so, though human rights activists like to push for changes really quickly, stability is preferable to quick or immediate change, and expecting immediate change, you know, is really, really a folly. Illiberal democracies. You know, like Tiananmen Square was a good thing, because look at the economic growth of China, when a democracy there could have really fucked— sorry, excuse my language—really slowed everything down."

"What countries does he talk about?" says Anna.

"Oh, you know, the Middle East, China, Indonesia, Pakistan, the, uh, warm countries. But America too, and he makes this kind of interesting argument that the problem with our government is that it's too transparent, that it should, I guess, be a little more secretive—that the transparency sort of paralyzes us and prevents good decision making."

Jerry isn't really listening to what I'm saying.

"He's just getting on my nerves," Jerry says.

"He might not be with us much longer," says Gary.

"No way—he's staying," says Anna.

There are three competing Nishant Patel tea-leaf readings. (1) Nishant Patel might accept some kind of government position at the NSC or State. (2) Nishant Patel might accept some kind of position in academia, president of Princeton or something—considered the most unlikely, as he has already spent much of his time in academia (Harvard, Yale, Ph.D., youngest professor, youngest editor of *Foreign Relations*, etc.). (3) And this is the juiciest: Nishant Patel is a contender to take over the domestic edition of *The Magazine* after the editor in chief retires. The EIC is named Henry and he's been EIC for seven years, and seven years is the historic average for EICs.

"They're not going to give him EIC. That's what Berman is being groomed for," says Jerry.

Sanders Berman, official title Managing Editor of *The Magazine*, ranked number six on the *New York Herald*'s "Top 20 Media Players Under Age 38."

"Why do we keep coming here?" Jerry says, looking at his chicken potpie.

"It's cheap," says Gary.

"Do you guys like Berman?" I ask.

"Ummm," says Jerry.

"He's okay," says Gary.

"Don't really know him," says Anna.

"Have any of you read his book?" I ask.

The Greatest War on Earth. A book about World War II. It's currently competing with Nishant Patel's book on the national bestseller lists. I've been keeping track of whose book is up and whose book is down.

"I'm thinking of reading it," I say.

The editors give a smile, condescending.

"How old are you?" says Gary.

"Twenty-two."

"Twenty-two."

"So young," the three, in unison, say at the table.

"I remember when I was twenty-two, walking around, change jingling in my pocket," Gary says. "Got the assignments I wanted, the jobs I wanted. No responsibilities. Just wait for the disappointments."

The check comes, and Jerry says he'll pick it up and expense it—it's only $43.37, but he likes to stick it to the magazine when he can.

"Man, Nishant is getting on my nerves," says Jerry. "I've got to quit."

Out on 57th Street, cabs and delivery trucks don't slow at the Eighth Avenue crosswalk, and Anna tells me that Jerry has been saying he's going to quit for fourteen years.

4.

Wednesday,
August 21, 2002

Space Tourism.

I'm excited about this story, and I've been working on it for two weeks. The story is pegged—"pegged" is a news industry word—to an American centimillionaire who's scheduled to go up in a Soyuz rocket in Novorossiysk, Russia, on September 14. He'll be the seventh private citizen to make the trip to space, and the private company, working with the Russian government to send him up, is called Orbital Access Inc. Orbital Access Inc. has one industry rival, Great Explorations, and they aren't very friendly. The two CEOs are quoted in most stories on the subject explaining their two different business models on monetizing the "nascent space tourism industry."

I'm supposed to do an interview by phone, in fifteen minutes, with a businessman, an engineer who lives in Colorado and is designing a space hotel. I'm preparing for the interview. I had printed out a stack of clips about the gentleman two days earlier, and I'm trying to find those pages. They are somewhere in the vicinity of my cubicle, but I am very messy, and there are stacks of newspapers and magazines and Post-it notes and binders and folders left open and creased at the spine.

I start to dig for the papers, throwing open the metal cabinet drawers underneath the desktop, tossing and shifting piles of eight-by-eleven sheets.

My cubicle is in a process of fossilization. The process, as far as I can tell, began when the magazine started to rent space in this building in 1987. None of the interns who have sat in this cubicle has ever completely removed all of their belongings. Decaying bits of personality, deposits of forgotten headlines, inexplicable artifacts.

I've been getting the sense lately that someone, perhaps the Mexican cleaning service woman or the Polish cleaning service old man, is messing with my documents and cleaning my desk for me when I go home, so the papers could really be anywhere.

I pull open a drawer where I think the stack of papers could be.

Inside is a pile of comic books, with a graphic novel on the Palestinian territories on top of the stack, and I assume these are from four interns ago, because that was when A.E. Peoria started his career at the magazine. In this very cubicle. He'd become a star foreign correspondent, and it would make sense that a star foreign correspondent would be reading comics about war.

Tossing through another drawer, I find a green construction helmet and a gas mask with a broken rubber strap—I date this find to October 2001, after the terrorist attacks in New York convinced Human Resources to provide protection from chemical and biological threats targeted at media organizations. The construction helmet and gas mask are on top of a manila folder with notes from a story about the Supreme Court's 2000 decision to make George W. Bush president; those notes are piled on another folder, red, with photo caption information about the Balkans, notes on a graphic illustration breaking down population levels and ethnicities in the ratio of numbers killed in Bosnia-Herzegovina, Croatia, Serbia, etc.; there are lots of spelling mistakes and red pen on this document.

Underneath the folder is a pile of back issues, the newest one dating from 1996, working backward at uneven intervals to 1991. Whoever chose the issues to collect in this pile was making some kind of time capsule point or editorial critique. All the headlines on the covers either contain the word "new" ("The New Happiness," "The New War on Drugs," "The New Normal," "The New Hollywood," "The New Aging," "The New Parent Trap") or end in a question mark ("Did the President Lie?" "The Candidate to Beat?" "Is the Globe Warming?")—and sometimes have both ("The New Mystery of Mary Magdalene: Can Science Tell Us What History Can't?"). According to this compiler's count, marked by a yellow Post-it, either a question mark or the word "new" was used more than thirty-nine times in that five-year stretch.

What catches my eye is another Post-it note, hand-scrawled, on the last issue in the pile. There is no question mark or word "new" in it, so I wonder why it's there. The date says January 3, 1991. There is a picture of a desert and an American tank. "The Vietnam Syndrome," blares the headline.

This story is famous in the magazine's lore. It was written by none other than Sanders Berman while he was finishing up his final year at Tulane. Quickly flipping through the other issues, I see that a good 90 percent of them carry the Sanders Berman byline—it dawns on me that I might be sitting in the exact same cubicle that Sanders Berman once sat in, though I find that hard to believe. Legend has it that he was only in the cubes for three months before he got his own office, before he was made the youngest editor of the National Affairs section of *The Magazine*. Perhaps I am sitting in the cube of Sanders Berman's old assistant?

I place the "Vietnam Syndrome" issue on top of my desk—I'll get to this soon—and continue my search for the papers, when I'm distracted again.

Did I mention where *The Magazine*'s TVs are? It's a matter of some dispute, as there's a shortage of television sets. For some reason, most of the sets are on the fifteenth floor, where the production and photography staff are, not the news reporters. This helps the fifteenth floor follow important sporting events on Saturday, like the Kentucky Derby or March Madness. But in the southeast block, near me, there is only one television shared by sixteen cubicles—it's on a swivel attached to a column.

The column is outside Nishant Patel's office. The TV hangs over the three cubicles surrounding the column, and those three cubicles are manned by Nishant Patel's three assistants: Dorothy, Lucy, and Patricia. The highest person in the hierarchy of the three assistants is Dorothy, and Dorothy has been at the magazine for three decades. Dorothy does not like to have the volume of the television set on. Dorothy always puts it on mute.

So it is a fluke that in my search for the Space Tourism papers, I turn around 180 degrees to catch the BREAKING NEWS ALERT on MSNBC.

The vice president of the United States, Richard B. Cheney, is standing at a lectern, speaking to men and women in military uniform. You know what Dick Cheney looks like, so I won't waste time on that, and I can't hear what he's saying. Luckily, MSNBC has taken what it thinks are the most important themes in his speech and keeps scrolling them across the screen while he speaks.

VP CHENEY: IRAQ HAS CHEMICAL WEAPONS

VP CHENEY: IRAQ IS PURSUING NUCLEAR WEAPONS

**VP CHENEY: WE CANNOT ALLOW
IRAQ TO ACQUIRE WMD**

My phone rings and I pick it up.

"Michael M. Hastings."

"Mr. Hastings, this is Douglas Dorl, from Outerlimits Hotels."

"Mr. Dorl, great, thanks for calling me back. Is this a good time?"

"I called you, yeah."

"Great, great, great."

I spin back around, and though I'm not entirely prepared to do the interview, I do remember the list of questions that I more or less wanted answers or quotes about.

"Oh, so, uh, when will the space hotels be ready?"

"If our models are correct, we hope to get the first space hotel in orbit by 2015."

"And, uh, what, are, the, uh, challenges, to, uh, this?"

I have a tape recorder hooked up to the phone and press Play/Record, so I'm not too worried about listening that closely.

"Customer confidence."

"What do you mean?"

"We have to avoid catastrophe. Look at the airlines. The first national airline began in the early 1930s. But it took years of proving to the consumer that it was safe to fly. Almost didn't—an accident in 1938, a crash over the Alleghenies that killed forty people, almost ruined the airline industry as we know it. There's a reason for that. There was a law in Congress trying to ban air travel! Can you believe that? So I'm talking bulk. We need to have regular tourist space flights, at cost, at a price point people can afford. One tourist flight blows up, and we're sunk as an industry. Funding dries up, the public won't have trust in us."

"So, your hotels, um, how expensive are they to build?"

"Cheaper than NASA."

"So is that like a couple hundred million?"

"We think we can do it for a couple hundred million. Hell, a new hotel that just opened in Las Vegas cost one hundred and twenty million, and that's on Earth."

"Right, right."

Phone tucked under my ear, typing what Douglas Dorl is saying, I peer over my shoulder at the television screen, and VP Cheney is still talking.

VP CHENEY: U.S. MUST TAKE ACTION, NOT APPEASE

"And how much a night, do you think?"

"Between three thousand and ten thousand a night."

"Does that include travel cost?"

"Goes back to what I was saying—making an economy of scale."

"Right, right. Tell me more about your company, how you founded it, why you're interested in space."

This is a throwaway question to get him talking—I'm distracted by the news on the television set, and I'm not as focused as I should be on what Mr. Dorl is saying: As a kid watched the moon landing. Worked for NASA. Designed a part of the shuttle. Enjoyed the film *The Right Stuff.*

Then I catch sight of the TV screen again.

Sanders Berman is on, as a guest, giving analysis.

"Okay, great. Yeah, thanks, um, if I have any follow-up questions, mind if I give you a call?"

"Be my guest."

I hang up the phone and walk quickly two cubicle rows over.

"Hi, Dorothy, mind if I turn the volume up? Sanders Berman is on."

"Ohhhhh, Sanders Berman," she says, her tone suggesting a familiarity with Sanders Berman, years of anecdotes about him that she's not about to share with me.

I kneel on the desk of one of Nishant Patel's three assistants and hit Volume Up once.

Sanders Berman is discussing what Vice President Cheney just said.

". . . certainly," Sanders Berman answers.

"Sanders, now, you're the expert, you're the historian, give us some historical idea of what you make of the vice president's speech."

"In 1940, President Franklin Roosevelt gave an underlooked address to a Lions Club in Decatur, Illinois. Now, no one pays attention to that address today, it's been overshadowed by the 'Day of Infamy' speech after Pearl Harbor. But what I hear in the vice president's language, in his somber delivery, his cadence, the timbre of his voice, is what FDR said in Decatur—he's quietly preparing the American people for what clearly is a dangerous and imminent threat. I suspect the discussion, going forward, is not going to be a question of *if* we should go to war in Iraq, but *when*. The vice president is warning of a great evil we face. It's not Japan or Germany; it's Iraq, Iran, North Korea. It's the 9/11 terrorists, a great evil. Of course the audience here is the American people, but there's also a second audience—our allies—and this is a call to the Winston Churchills out there, a warning to them that we need them, and I hope they will stand on our side."

The door to Nishant Patel's corner office opens, and he walks out.

"Dorothy, can you have Patricia bring my lunch?"

"Yes, Nishant," Dorothy says, and she stands and looks over the cubicle wall at Patricia, a thirty-seven-year-old Korean woman who lives with her family in Queens. Patricia is deaf in her right ear and blind in her left eye.

"Patricia," Dorothy says, "can you please go get Nishant his lunch."

"What, Dorothy?"

"Patricia, Nishant's lunch," she says.

Dorothy sits down, Patricia stands up, and Nishant Patel asks, "What are you all watching?"

"Mike turned the volume up, Dr. Patel," Patricia says.

Dorothy looks at me.

"Vice President Cheney, I think, just sort of said we're going to war in Iraq," I say.

"Oh, yes, of course, I had heard that the vice president was going to do that. I had dinner with the undersecretary in Washington on Monday."

Nishant Patel walks around the corner of the cubicles and looks up at the TV, just as the cable network is about to cut to a commercial.

"Mr. Berman, a pleasure as always," says the host. "*The Magazine*'s managing editor and also author of *The Greatest War on Earth: The New History of World War Two*," says the host, holding a copy of Sanders Berman's book.

I'm not looking at the TV; I'm looking at Nishant Patel. He winces when the MSNBC host bangs Sanders Berman's book on the table.

"We'll turn the volume down right away, Nishant," says Dorothy.

Nishant Patel goes back in his office. I go back to Space Tourism.

Three hours later, I get an email forwarded to me. It's a forward from Dorothy, forwarded from Sam, who forwarded it from Nishant Patel.

Subject: Fw: Int'l story list change
From: Dorothy
To: International Staff

See below from Sam/NP, dorothy

Subject: Int'l story list change
To: Dorothy

From: Sam
Subject: Int'l story change

All, we are going to go with a new cover this week. "The Case for War?"

Dropping sci/tech and Mobile phones.

Subject: [blank]
To: Sam
From: Nishant Patel

Change in cover. See me in my office. np

It's 5:30 p.m. and the editors are leaving the office. Gary stops by my cubicle.

"Hastings, you're off the hook for Space Tourism this week."

5.

Friday, August 23, 2002

Thirty-four-year-old magazine journalist A.E. Peoria sits in first class right now, right fucking now, just sits down, and there are two women standing over him. DBX to JFK. One has a tray of hot hand towels, and she gives him one and smiles; the other has a tray with a variety of liquids: booze, waters, juices—sparkling water, nonsparkling water, tomato, mango, grapefruit. Peoria takes three glasses—sparkling water, grapefruit juice, and wine—and he gulps them down and starts to pat himself down, rubbing the tiredness from his eyes, the days in the African bush getting soaked up in the warm hot towel. He removes the towel from his face and the three glasses have already been taken away, replaced with a four-page menu.

He didn't have to suffer the indignity of finding the menu in the seat-back pocket.

The flight attendant is asking him if he'd like something else to drink, and he says, "Yes, give me a gin and tonic," and as he is scanning the menu—whipped summer squash, couscous, goat cheese and beet salad, Asian wheat noodles with shrimp, a seven-ounce grilled flank steak, potatoes and chicken curry, and more, and flambéed ice cream and rice pudding and bread baskets with thirteen different kinds of bread and a cheese plate with grapes and orange slices and bananas and cheese and apples and olives—he gets the gin and tonic delivered to him, and it's in a glass glass.

Another indignity avoided: the woman—what a fucking angel—is unscrewing the cap of the small bottle of gin and pouring it into his glass and mixing it for him. Even as the cabin doors close, everyone in first class is still talking on their mobile phones, and even as the plane is taxiing, people are still talking on their mobile phones and the stewardesses are letting it happen, until the last possible moment, when they ask them, politely, to please finish their conversations, as we are about to take off.

Politeness, no glowers or glares, politely requesting that you turn off your mobile phone. They are treating him like some kind of human being up here, not an animal that needs to be prodded and kicked in the seat.

Eight hours or more and the magazine gives correspondents a first-class ticket. Until he became a star foreign correspondent, a roaming-the-globe international affairs reporter, he had flown first class only once. Sixteen, visiting a friend in the Bahamas for spring break, an upgrade. That wasn't real first class. That was Delta domestic first class. This is real first class, and real first class makes him wonder how he had ever traveled in economy/coach class without developing a severe class hatred. When did economy become coach and coach economy anyway? He thinks it was around 1997. Must have been an advertising or marketing study. *Coach* is a respectable word, he never thought anything was wrong with *coach*—stagecoach, almost classy-sounding, or even *coach* as in a bus, where everyone has an equally comfortable or uncomfortable seat. *Coach* is an equal opportunity word, a normalizing word. *Economy* is a word for "cheap."

Cheap.

It's another way, he thinks, the mix of liquids giving his thoughts the appearance of great profundity, for the airlines to subtly rub it in the passengers' faces that they are screwed in life and made bad decisions every step along the way and are forced to pay attention to money, forced to pinch pennies.

The airlines, he now realizes, had been trying to make him feel bad his entire life, or at least since 1997.

For years in coach, with the rest of the fellow failures, he had gotten off the plane last. This meant that he'd had to walk past the first-class seats and business-class seats. Before getting to the first- and business-class seats, he had to go through at least two or more cabins of economy.

Economy always looked like shit after a fourteen-hour flight. It looked like a bunch of preschoolers had been stuck in a fallout shelter. Empty plastic water and juice cups, tangled headsets, ripped plastic bags, crumbs from never-go-stale biscuits, bright blue thermonuclear fleece blankets, weird puke smells, torn packaging, yes, lots of shredded plastic and mutilated packaging, as if a scarce amount of resources had been consumed in a frenzy.

The flight attendants didn't bother with cleanup in coach—no, they wanted the evidence of the savagery on display. And by the time the disembarking economy passenger got through the coach wasteland, the single business-class cabin was a relief and went by in a blur. It wasn't so obvious that a major shift in socioeconomics had taken place. In fact, the business-class cabin seemed designed to ease the shock that those traveling in coach would have experienced if they'd just stepped directly from coach to first class, from one socioeconomic sphere to the other. Like letting a bum into the country club. Yes, that would have been too much of a shock, that might have backfired. Best to use business class as a buffer zone. The airlines wanted you to know what you were missing, but they didn't want to spark any social revolts, any impromptu pummelings, anyone to take a protest dump on an aisle seat.

So Peoria would walk through business class and see nine seats per row instead of twelve, and this wasn't too jarring, and then when he got to first class or, on some planes, just got a glimpse through the curtains ahead, there were only six seats—and what big and comfortable-looking seats they were. And where was the evidence of a fourteen-hour flight?

The evidence, Peoria now knew, had been quietly picked up and cleaned along the way by these angel flight attendants. Angels pushing dangerous and embittering illusions without rubber surgical gloves to protect their hands from economy-class parasites and filth. The evidence of the disgusting humanness of adults locked in a capsule of recycled air and sleep breath and hunger had been erased and sterilized even as the first-class passengers were getting off the plane. Even as the first-classers were exiting, the flight attendants, an entire team of them, would rush to perform an instant cleanup. It gave the passengers in economy, who had to pass through the cabin before deplaning, the unconscious impression that perhaps they were truly savages at heart, truly disgusting people who deserved to sit side by side in the cattle car, making a mess of their environment, using thin polyester pillows, hauling luggage with rolls and rolls of clear plastic tape and big handwritten notes with foreign names and impoverished zip codes, digesting single-serving chicken and beef on a single-page menu.

All of this, all the service, the high-touch service that had taken over his thoughts, had been so engrossing to him that he hasn't even bothered to look at who he is sitting next to or any of the other people sitting in his first-class cabin.

He is sitting next to a woman.

Two hours, four gin and tonics, and he is looking out the window of the plane.

Why so emotional on night flights?

Hour three and a half and he goes to the bathroom and snorts the cocaine he bought in Dubai on the twelve-hour layover.

Hour five, he is going to the bathroom, and he is talking to the woman.

"It's so rare to sit next to a pretty woman my age in first class," he says. "Usually they can't afford it or they're with some older rich guy."

The woman nods, and across the aisle, there's an older rich guy who smiles at A.E. Peoria.

"Oh shit, is that your boyfriend?"

Hour seven, there's a knocking on the bathroom door, a glowing sign that says PLEASE RETURN TO YOUR SEAT, with a little figure of a dickless man and an arrow.

"Sir, are you all right?"

Wobbling, A.E. Peoria opens up the bathroom door, which folds up like an accordion, and he laughs at this, and the pretty stewardess woman who gave him the menu and poured what he estimates to be five out of his seven drinks is standing there.

"You're the one who gave me that menu! Thank you, thank you. You're Miss Five-out-of-Seven, Miss Laila. 'Laila' is Arabic for what?"

"Look how much legroom I have," A.E. Peoria says, returning to his seat.

"I always wanted an electric chair as a kid, one of those electric La-Z-Boy chairs where I could move it around like this," A.E. Peoria is saying while he adjusts every control on the seat. There are sixteen different ergonomic portions of the seat to calibrate, five just for the upper torso and seven for different leg positions. How do you even describe all of these positions? Stretched, outstretched, slightly stretched, partially stretched, a quarter partial stretch, a half partial stretch, three-quarters partial stretch. He would need to resort to math to describe all the things his seat could do.

"You know what I like about first class," he says to the older man, who is now sitting next to him, having changed places with his girl-friend or wife. "I like that there's no evidence that I'm drunk. If I was back with the fucking beasts and vampires back there, sucking the fucking marrow from bones, you know, if I was fucking back there, there'd be all these little bottles in front of me because the service back there sucks and there's no way I could have even had that many drinks because the service is slow, so it's like a catch-22, you know?"

Hour nine.

"You don't fucking know what I saw out there, man. You don't fucking want to know what I saw. Heads on pikes."

Hours ten and eleven.

"Hey man, fuck, sorry dude. But here's the thing. Here's what you're missing. Don't worry about getting sleep and rest. I've been thinking about this, and the irony is, if you travel a lot, if you do a lot of travel, it's ironic, because nowadays . . ."

A.E. Peoria pauses.

"The irony of international travel is that you spend as much time or more time going nowhere as going somewhere. You spend time sitting in the same fucking place."

He pauses again.

"Even right now. You can't even tell that you're moving."

Hour twelve.

The stewardess hands A.E. Peoria an immigration card, and this reminds him to take one more trip to the bathroom, where he flushes the small and empty plastic bag of coke down the toilet after ripping it and licking the insides so he can numb his gums.

A car is waiting for him at the airport, and when the driver asks for directions, he tells him to bring him straight to the office, to West 57th Street. He wants to talk to someone, whoever the motherfucker was who killed his story.

6.

Saturday Night,
August 24, 2002

Saturday night is closing night. By three on Sunday morning, the new issue is electronically transmitted to seven printers across the continental United States and twelve printers in different regions across the globe, where it is printed, tied in stacks, put in the back of delivery trucks, and distributed to newsstands and delis and bookstores, or shrink-wrapped and mailed to 2.2 million subscribers.

I treasure Saturday nights. The sixteenth floor clears out around three or four p.m., leaving a handful of editorial staffers, whose job it is to make sure all the stories, captions, pull quotes, photographs, and tables of contents make their way safely through the gauntlet of copy desk to make-up to production, to catch errors that might have slipped in along the way.

My role on Saturday night is to be available in case there are any last-second changes the correspondents want to put in the stories. They call me, I pull the story up in the computer system, and I make the changes. I'm the liaison between the correspondents in the field and the editors in New York, who by Saturday night are at home.

It's mostly downtime. The waiting begins mid-afternoon and ends between eleven p.m. and one a.m., when I get the word from the production staff that I can leave.

I've found comfort in waiting: the empty floor, the vacuuming, the dark offices, a warm feeling, a feeling that I am part of something *bigger than myself,* a dedicated servant to the magazine.

My friends tell me that it sucks that I have to work Saturday night. I don't mind at all—I have no problem working Saturday nights. I would not want to be anyplace else.

But what to do during those seven or so hours of waiting.

Get to know *The Magazine.* I want to learn as much detail as I can about the lives and careers and personalities of the people who work in our little universe. The histories, the disputes, the controversies, the raw copy sitting in the computer system—to know the real story of the stories. To know how the magazine got started, stretching back to 1934, its evolution and many incarnations, and to understand the different factions at work today.

Red Notes are a function in the computer system (called Agile). They allow editors and researchers and copy desk employees to ask questions by writing them in the actual file of the story. They are like the Track Changes function in Microsoft Word. Rather than simply delete something, the editor can write a Red Note so the changes can be seen by the person looking at the file but not by the reader when it finally gets published. The editor uses Red Notes to put questions in the text that the correspondent or writer has to answer, like so: <<this attribution okay?>>

The most important Red Notes are at the end of the story. These are the Red Notes that editors, on each level of the editorial chain, use to give praise. Or don't.

To know who is up and who is down, you have to look at the Red Notes.

I have access to all the stories in the domestic and international editions.

I can see all the Red Notes. I study what changes have been made and how they have been made and why.

I read the Red Notes at the end first. The praise in Red Notes is an indication of the star power of the writer or reporter, how valuable they are to *The Magazine*.

Nishant Patel's story "The Case for War?" is being published in both the domestic and international editions. In the international edition, it is the cover story. In the domestic edition, it isn't the cover story—the cover this particular week is about autism and twins.

I open the story, file name int0114, and scroll to the last page.

Four editors have signed off on Nishant Patel's essay.

```
<<magnificent, thought provoking. Sure to
get us out front. excellent work Nishant//
jeff>>

<<superbly done. compelling, challenging,
deceptively entertaining. i second
jeff//nh>>

<<amen. you've blown us all away again with
your elegance, style, and fresh thinking.
this has national magazine award written
all over it. the greatest piece yet on the
argument for war. you've outdone yourself
mr. patel, many thanks.//sanders>>

<<couldn't agree more. a fluid, engaging,
comprehensive, persuasive, groundbreaking
```

```
essay. puts our competition to shame. glad
to have you here raj//henry>>
```

The effusiveness is not unusual. The effusiveness is what a figure like Nishant Patel would expect from Red Notes. What it means on this story is that Henry the EIC took the time not only to read the story but also to actually type a Red Note himself.

Alone, perhaps, this wouldn't mean much. Out of context, it might just seem the norm. But I contrast Red Notes on Nishant's story with Red Notes on the next story.

I open the essay Sanders Berman wrote this week, file na0214.

It is about FDR's speech in Decatur, Illinois.

I skip to the bottom of the page.

There are two Red Notes. Only two.

```
<<impressive, sanders//tom>>


<<excellent timing//nh>>
```

There is no comment from Henry the EIC. Again, alone, this wouldn't have much significance. Henry the EIC is a busy individual. He doesn't have time to read all the stories, so you could easily dismiss the non–Red Noting as an issue of scheduling and time management. But if you are a savvy user of Agile, you know that by clicking on one of the drop-down menus, a list of every user who has opened and made changes to the document is available. (For my Saturday-night readings, I use the "read only" function so my username, mhasti, doesn't appear on this list.) And sure enough, on the list is Henry the EIC's username, heic.

Which means Henry the EIC read Sanders Berman's column and didn't say anything.

He didn't leave a Red Note.

A shift in the power balance is occurring, not yet seismic but clearly felt.

I hear a loud banging on the glass doors down the hallway. Not unusual. Means someone has forgotten their company identification.

I get up from my cubicle and walk down the hall, past the men's and women's rooms, to the set of glass doors.

I jump back, slightly shocked.

A face is pressed up against the glass, mouth like a blowfish, the full weight of the figure propped up by the door.

The eyes on the face above the gaping mouth are closed.

The eyes open. Bloodshot, one thick eyebrow arching.

"You going to let me in," says the person. "It's me, A.E. Peoria. I fucking work here."

"You might want to step back," I say.

A.E. Peoria, in the flesh, stumbles back.

I pull open the glass doors.

"Where the fuck is he and who the fuck are you," A.E. Peoria says.

"I'm Michael M. Hastings, but I just got hired on—"

"Mmmmm, Mike Hastings . . ."

I am holding the door open; A.E. Peoria has yet to step through.

"You sent the story list."

"Yeah, I did this week . . ."

"Sh . . . Sh . . . Sssssshhhhh."

There are two bags at A.E. Peoria's feet. His eyes are opening and closing as he rocks back and forth.

"It's not your fault, it's not your fault. You can get my bags, right, bro?"

A.E. Peoria walks past me, zigzagging and pushing off from one wall to the other.

"Watch the—"

On his third sequence of zigzagging, he pushes the door to the men's room. The door swings open easily, and he falls through, losing his balance. His legs are sticking out in the hallway. He groans.

I run up beside him.

"Here you go, let's get you to your office," I say, as his blowfish mouth is now half on the white-tile floor of the men's room.

Kneeling, I notice we are not alone in the bathroom—someone else is in there. I can see his shoes underneath the blue stalls. The shoes are pointed at the toilet bowl, not away from the toilet bowl, which means this person is either urinating standing up in the bathroom stall or doing something else. Whoever's toes, they have frozen still. Whoever it is, he's waiting to see if he will have privacy in the bathroom again.

"Thanks for the help, bro," says A.E. Peoria, getting up, then saying, "I don't need your fucking help, bro."

A.E. Peoria stumbles off down the hall, toward his office. I follow him to make sure he doesn't fall again. We get to his office and he throws himself into his chair.

"I gotta check my email," he says, sitting in the dark.

I flick on the light switch and go back to get his bags.

I pick up the bags. As I'm turning around, the door to the men's room swings open slowly and a head peeks out.

I freeze, carrying A.E. Peoria's baggage, a duffel bag and a North Face hiking backpack slung over my shoulders.

It's Sanders Berman.

This is the closest I've ever been to Sanders Berman, and I can now tell you what he looks like in person.

Sanders Berman looks like he got his wardrobe from raiding Mark Twain's closet.

"Mr. Berman," I say, "I'm Michael M. Hastings. I work in international, saw you on MSNBC, really fascinating what you were saying."

Sanders Berman shoots his eyes back and forth and he wipes his mouth. What is he wiping from his mouth?

"It's okay to call me Sanders," he says. "What are you doing here so late?"

"Oh, I'm here late every Friday and Saturday, making sure the magazine gets put to bed."

Sanders Berman looks at me.

"Going somewhere?"

"Oh, these are A.E. Peoria's bags. He just got back from eastern Chad, covering that, uh, mobile genocide there."

"That was Peoria on the floor?"

"Yes, he tripped."

Sanders Berman is wearing a bow tie and is hunched over slightly—he's a thirty-seven-year-old trapped in a sixty-seven-year-old's body, and from what I've read about him, he's been trapped in a sixty-seven-year-old's body since puberty.

"Did he hear anything?"

I don't quite know what he's talking about.

"I think he heard a lot, I mean, he was in Chad for, like, three weeks, so I'm sure he heard a lot."

Quizzically, Sanders Berman nods.

"It's been one of those days," he says.

"Really honored to be here, Mr. Berman," I say as he walks down the hall.

I wonder if I made a bad first impression. Fuck, I think. But I start to get a bit giddy, having finally introduced myself to Sanders Berman.

In one week, I'm now on the radar of the two really important men at the magazine. It is strange, though, Sanders Berman being here so late. I've never seen an editor that high up stick around to this hour on a Saturday.

Lugging the baggage, I go back to A.E. Peoria's office. He's not there. I put the bags down and walk back toward my desk, where I find a much more awake and lively A.E. Peoria sitting in my cubicle.

"I'm checking my email," he says. "This is my old cube. It's nostalgia. It's like instinct, me coming and sitting back down right here."

A.E. Peoria is wearing green work pants with extra pockets and black leather hiking boots. He doesn't look cool. I had this idea in my mind that because he was doing cool things, like traveling to eastern Chad and whatnot, and because he had kind of a cool byline, A.E. Peoria, no first name, that he would look more striking, more tall, dark, and handsome. Can't judge a man by his byline apparently. He's short and sort of dark, but he would not be mistaken for handsome, I don't think, unless we lived in a world where people who looked like pudgy gnomes were considered handsome. He does, though, have a bundled, intense energy around him, even while he is completely shit hammered.

My phone rings.

A.E. Peoria picks up.

He covers the mouthpiece.

"What's your name again?"

"Mike Hastings."

"Mike Hastings," Peoria says into the phone.

"Excellent, that's fucking excellent, bro."

He hangs up.

"That was production. We're free to go get a drink."

7.

Early Morning, Sunday, August 25, 2002

I have a disorder," says A.E. Peoria.

It's two a.m. and we're sitting in O'Neil's Irish Pub and Tavern on 55th and 7th Ave. It's sort of shitty, but it's upper Midtown we're talking about, shabby since the 1950s. There aren't too many good places to go in upper Midtown at this hour. We're in a strange late-night dead zone. The nightlife in New York is to the north of us, to the south of us, but right here, it's lame places like O'Neil's Irish Pub and Tavern, a default location that seems to cater to tourists who don't have a good guidebook or the courage to go farther than five blocks from their hotel.

"CDD," he says. "Have you heard of that?"

"Is that like OCD?"

"Maybe it is. Want to take a shot?"

"No, remember, I don't drink."

"Really? That's fucked-up. Are you one of those Mormon interns?"

The Magazine had a special relationship with Brigham Young University, which meant Mormons had three guaranteed internship slots a year.

"I mean no offense if you are a Mormon."

"No, it's not for religious reasons. Moral reasons."

"What?"

"Moral reasons. When I drink, I lose my morals."

I'd been saving that line, thinking it was a clever way to parry questions about my nondrinking, but A.E. Peoria doesn't appear to find it funny. My clever lines rarely pay off in context of the conversation. The last time one worked was in AP History class in twelfth grade. A girl sitting in front of me was debating with another girl how to pronounce the word *schedule*—was it "sked-u-al" or "ssshed-u-al"? The girl asked me to weigh in. I did. "What ssshoool did you learn that at?" I asked. Meaning "school."

"That's good, man. Good for you for not drinking."

"Thanks."

"I'll take two shots then, one for you, one for me."

He orders two shots of tequila.

"Fuck I haven't slept in a while. What day is it?"

"Saturday."

"That's why not one of those fuckers was at the office. I got my date and time all wrong—it's all fucked-up. I'm something like six and a half hours ahead, which means I'd be just waking up, but I was in Thailand before Chad, and that's like thirteen hours ahead, and I went back four hours and never really adjusted to that, so I don't really know what time it is."

"I think it's two-thirty."

"Two-thirty for you, but for me I'm talking about."

A.E. Peoria, four-year veteran, with just over a six-figure salary as a staff correspondent. A.E. Peoria, living the dream. How did he do it? Like a sponge, I want to know.

"How was Chad?"

"Intense," he says.

The bartender puts two shots of tequila down in front of us. I thank the bartender and ask for a club soda. The bartender passes me a club soda and puts down a slice of lemon and a saltshaker next to it. A.E. Peoria licks his lips, licks the salt, throws the shot back, his blowfish mouth widening. He coughs and his eyes water.

"Cheers," I say, tilting my club soda in his direction.

"Ahhhhhahahhahahhahahahh," says A.E. Peoria. "That's better."

Here's what I know about A.E. Peoria. I got most of this information from the Meet the Staff link on *The Magazine*'s website and the rest from an online profile of him from a recent alumni newsletter posted on the Internet. I know he started at *The Magazine* in 1998. I know that he spent his early twenties working for a midsize newspaper in Virginia. He left the midsize paper and traveled across the country on a Greyhound bus. He talked to the passengers along the way, bag ladies, scratch-ticket junkies, blacks and whites and Hispanics, single mothers en route to visit deadbeat convict lovers housed in the federal and state prison system; dreamers, degenerates, dopers, hippies, whores, keno players, bingo fanatics. He wrote a book called *Desperation Points West*. I'd checked the book on Amazon, and its sales ranking was #1,934,987. It got one review by *Booklist*, a five-sentence critical summary that called it "disappointing" and said, "Hoping to hear from voices of America's economically deprived, we instead are treated to monologues from the painfully unaware narrator. . . . *Desperation Points West* points nowhere." Shattered by the absence of the book's reception, Peoria spent the next eighteen months in Cambodia. It was his magazine work there that got him back on the fast track. "There's nothing like seeing a field of skulls while listening to AC/DC's 'Thunderstruck' in a jeep full of ex–Khmer Rouge to give you a new perspective on life," he'd told his alumni newsletter. He got hired during flush times at *The Magazine*, and they outbid a competitor to bring him on staff as a roving-the-world writer for the international editions.

"Are you going to drink that?" he asks me, looking at the shot of tequila.

"No, I don't drink," I say.

"Oh that's right, a Mormon."

A.E. Peoria snaps up the other shot, quenchingly.

"I have a disorder," A.E. Peoria says again. "So I'm not going to be apologizing for this. CDD. Have you heard of it?"

"Is it like OCD?" I ask again.

"Yes, but reverse. Compulsive disclosure disorder. I have no filter, my shrink says. I don't know boundaries, I'm always revealing very personal and intimate details about my life, and there's nothing I can do about it unless I want to get on medication, and I just don't want to get on medication right now because I would have to give up drinking, and it's just not time for me to give up drinking."

I nod.

"See, right there. I don't even know you and I'm telling you I have a mental disorder and I don't want medication and I see a shrink. Blows my fucking mind. But I'm aware of it now, you know? I'm aware of it, and that's good progress, right?"

"Sounds like great progress."

A.E. Peoria orders another shot of tequila.

"How old are you, Hastings?"

"Me, I'm twenty-two."

This bit of information always has impact, and I don't really understand why. Age isn't a big deal to me (yet?). For most of my life, I've always been the youngest one at the table, and it's something I've come to expect, maybe take for granted. I can't imagine that when I'm older I'll ever ask that question.

"You're just a fucking baby, bro," says A.E. Peoria. "Let me tell you something about the magazine. The magazine is shit, but it's great for someone your age. You have to get out of the office. The office will steal your soul. The lights in the office—you've looked at them? Those fucking energy-efficient fluorescent things, the dimpled plastic, all of that, it's like it's radiating soul-suckingness. It's radiating deadly soul-destroying, like, radiation, and it will fucking kill you if you don't get out. You really want to end up like Jerry and Sam and Gary and all those guys? Fuck, I mean Gary and Jerry are cool, but shit, you really want to end up like them?"

I nod.

"Know what I should do? I should write up tips, a tip sheet for a successful career. You'd like that wouldn't you?"

"Yeah, that'd be great. I mean, I wanted to ask you, how did you end up—"

"How did I become A.E. Peoria," he says.

"Right."

"Never do the job you have—do the job you want to have. I kept asking for more when I was at the *Fairfax Gazette*. They wouldn't give it to me, so I left, and I wrote this book—maybe you heard of it, *Desperation Points West*—and then I went to Cambodia. Cambodia— let me say this: There's nothing like riding in a jeep with ex–Khmer Rouge in a field of skulls listening to AC/DC's 'Thunderstruck,' the wind blowing, high on hashish, to give you a real perspective on life."

I nod, and he starts nodding too.

"But I don't know if I'm hard-core enough. I really started to question that in Chad. Like Townsend."

A.E. Peoria reaches in his left pocket, then his right pocket, then notices that he placed his mobile phone down in front of him next to a bowl of popcorn, provided free of charge by O'Neil's Irish Pub and Tavern.

"Oh shit, I should go see my girlfriend. What do you think? I think I might love her. I gave her six orgasms. Big orgasms, huge orgasms. I'd never given anyone so many orgasms before. But I don't know if she's top tier, do you know what I mean? I want a top-tier girl, and I think she might be second tier."

Realizing the conversation is wrapping up, I try to think of any other questions I want to ask.

"I mean, how exactly did you become a foreign correspondent?"

"Look, I'm not going to lie. The job is fucking great. But it's also shit. I mean, my career is shit. Look, what have I done? Okay, so I wrote a book? So fucking what. Okay, so I've covered stories in thirteen different countries? Big fucking deal. Okay, so I'm only thirty-four and I've accomplished things that most people won't do in their entire lives. Okay, so I'm probably, give or take a few thousand, one of the highest-paid journalists my age in the country. None of it means shit."

"Well, I mean, you did write a book. How many people can say that? And like you said, you're only thirty-four."

"Yeah, I did write a fucking book. I guess that is pretty elite. Fuck, I really have to go. What do you say, time for one more shot?"

His phone vibrates.

"Oh shit, she just sent me a picture of herself. Here, take a look at her."

He slides his mobile phone to me on the bar as the bartender pushes another shot of tequila in front of him.

I snap open the mobile phone, and there's a surprisingly clear digital picture of A.E. Peoria's girlfriend. It's an impressive feat of self-portraiture. From knees to face. Shaved to drooping. Nimble fingers. Lips, a toy.

"She got cleaned up yesterday," says A.E. Peoria. "Timed for me. She's great like that, you know? She doesn't like to fuck on the day she gets waxed because her vagina gets irritated. But look at that—she has a really wet pussy. That ever happened to you? Very adventurous. She calls that one in her mouth the Contender. She's a little on the heavy side, you know, and she likes it doggy style the best. They have a name for that. I think it's like Dirty Sanchez or something. Six orgasms I gave her—incredible. She's a writer. She even does ghost-writing for *Penthouse* letters, but I don't think that's going to last much longer with all the porn on the Internet."

"You're a lucky guy," I say as he takes his phone back and stands up from the bar.

"What's your number? I'll send it to you," he says.

A.E. Peoria punches in my number and tries to send the photo.

"Thanks, man, I appreciate it."

"Bro, I'm fucking drunk. It's really amazing that you don't drink. I have a lot of respect for religions, though I think they're bullshit. Want to share a taxi? I'm going uptown."

"I'm heading downtown."

"I'm expensing all of these drinks tonight, fuck *The Magazine*. We deserve it."

I follow A.E. Peoria outside, and he ducks into a cab and shuts the door, and in the four seconds the courtesy light stays on after he closes the door, I can see his blowfish mouth has already opened to give directions and likely more to the taxi driver.

Seventh Avenue at 3:25 a.m. on a Sunday in August is hot and damp, wafting the smell of trash. Most of the cars are yellow taxis. The storefronts are shut, except for a few bars, chalkboard signs not yet dragged back inside, and the unnatural glow from twenty-four-hour corner delis shining through the temporary-looking but perma-nent plastic walls set up to protect the fruits, vegetables, and flowers. I wonder how those flowers sell. I decide to walk a few blocks before hailing a cab myself.

I wake up at 10:35 a.m. and leave my apartment to get iced coffee. I spend the day watching television.

On Monday morning, I take the F train to work. I stop at the newsstand underneath Second Ave. and Houston to look at *The Magazine*—"Autistic Twins" is the cover, but over the logo, on what's called the roofline, it says "Iraq: The Case for War?"

Exciting times, I think.

TOWARD A MORE CYNICAL PROTAGONIST

We're about fifteen thousand words into the story, a good seventy thousand more to go. Adjust your schedule accordingly. If it took you thirty minutes to get this far, that means the running time for the remainder is, oh, four more hours.

Let me offer some preemptive criticism.

I see that I'm setting myself up as the coming-of-age protagonist, a naive and excited twentysomething hero named Michael M. Hastings, unleashed on the world, loose in the big city. Wet behind the earlobes, bright-eyed and puppy-tailed, the universe my own clambake.

But how *could I ever have been so naive?* How can anyone be naive these days? What's my excuse?

How could I have expected anything else besides what happened? The eventual disillusionment, the disappointment, the subtle corruption. Shouldn't I have seen it coming? If I'm a cliché, shouldn't I have been aware of why I'm a cliché—because my life story, my pattern, has been told and retold over and over again, the future for me was already written? Is it excusable to feel what I eventually feel—betrayed, disappointed, wronged, and upset by how *The Magazine* treated A.E. Peoria?

Aren't we in a new age? The end of naiveté?

I grew up reading media satires, reading about the corporate culture, massive layoffs, and polluted rivers, reading about censored stories and the national security state, our imperial sins, FBI investigations into masturbation in the executive office, reading Noam Chomsky and Howard Zinn and Tom Wolfe and Pat Buchanan and Hunter S. Thompson—what else could I have expected from *The Magazine* besides what I saw? I grew up reading Holocaust literature at the beach, Gulag literature on winter holidays, Vietnam memoirs on spring break. Histories of Gentiles and Jews and Germans playing poker and swapping wives at Los Alamos. The rap music I listened to was about dealing crack and dropping Ecstasy and cunnilingus. The television programs and films a constant stream of irony and mocking. How could all of that not have prepared me for the human condition, in the most extreme possible circumstances?

Isn't it somewhat preposterous, looking at the character that I'm presenting to you, for me to feel let down by the world? Isn't that narrative arc just a little tired?

Maybe that's the genius of it, then: because it is tired, it's easily recognizable. You can relate to me. And even with the knowledge of how the world works, we don't really know it until we see how the world works ourselves. Secondhand information doesn't do it.

Until your own hopes and dreams are shattered, or just slightly cracked, shouldn't you be allowed a bit of innocence?

I don't know. Maybe that's the growing-up part. Maybe I was just going through the motions, maybe I knew the fall was coming all along.

Anyway . . .

I'm going to give my past self a more cynical edge, whether or not I actually had it at the time.

I've taken a week off from the magazine to finish writing this. It's still snowing.

8.

Wednesday Evening, October 23, 2002

The signs are up all over the lobby, in the elevator, in the cafeteria on the twenty-first floor, right outside the elevator doors on the sixteenth. The signs are big blown-up pictures of different scenes from World War II, and every picture—Stalin shaking FDR's hand, the flag show at Iwo Jima, seven slightly out-of-focus dead bodies floating up to the shore on Omaha Beach—has the big name under it: SANDERS BERMAN.

"You going to this thing?" Gary asks me, leaning up against my cubicle.

"The Berman thing?"

"Yeah."

"I was thinking about it."

"I'm going up now, you want to come?"

"Sure."

I prepared for Sanders Berman's book party accordingly. I read his book, *The Greatest War on Earth*. If I am in the mood to be cruel, I'd say his book does really well at nourishing our national myths. It's a real comfort, reading his book. It gives you a real warm feeling about that whole time between 1939 and 1945. A real black-and-white-photo wholesomeness to it, a breast-fed narrative of good versus evil. A time, thankfully, when there wasn't much ambiguity. Or at least that's what he's selling and that's what people like to read about, and Sanders does a good job at throwing around words like *tragedy* and *Holocaust* and *Stalingrad*, and does a real good job at making us all feel special about it.

You can say I'm something of a contrarian here, but I guess my reading list on the Second World War is a bit different—more *Thin Red Line*, memoirs from Auschwitz and Hiroshima, *The Battle for Moscow* and *Life and Fate*—stuff that when you read it, you don't come away feeling particularly enamored with the greatness of human beings and the exceptional nature of the American character. "Fuck my shit," is how war correspondent Ernie Pyle put it at the time. "That's what war adds up to."

So fuck my shit, *The Greatest War on Earth* reaches number one on the bestseller list, so Berman must be doing something right, and there's nothing wrong with admiring success. Can't argue with success, can't argue with this book party on the twenty-second floor to celebrate the success that he's having.

"I'm just going to use the restroom," I tell Gary, using the word *restroom* because I'm never really comfortable, at work or at home, saying things like "I have to take a piss"—or "a leak" or "drain the lizard" or "shake hands with the wife's best friend."

I push open the door to the restroom and hear what sounds like a retching, a *hughghghg*. The noise stops right when the door is in midswing. I can always tell when someone is standing still in his bathroom stall. It's as if by actively trying not to make a sound, he's making a silent dog-whistle-like noise that triggers a well-honed lavatory sixth sense—probably a survival instinct from when I was a little kid and public bathrooms were always a potential danger zone, booby-trapped with lurking perverts.

Walking up to the urinal, I glance down at an angle and see the same pair of shoes, pointed to the toilet, not away from it, that I saw a few months back on the night with A.E. Peoria.

I start urinating (or, if you like, I use the urinal, make water, piss, etc.), and it lasts about thirteen seconds. I probably have more left, but I'm a tad nervous with Sanders Berman standing behind the blue panel five feet to my left.

I flush. The man behind the stall flushes. I zip up; I don't hear a corresponding zip-up. I turn to take the three steps to the six sinks and six mirrors; the door to the stall opens, and there's Sanders Berman, taking his own two steps to the sink.

"Mr. Berman," I say, tapping the pink soap container screwed into the white tile just below the mirror. "On the way to your book party now."

"I'm running late," says Sanders Berman, and he's not so much washing his hands as looking in the mirror and wetting a brown paper towel and wiping his face, primarily around the mouth.

I think it might be best to wait it out, to let the water keep running, to take even more time so he finishes his cleanup first and leaves. Or should I finish washing my hands right now and leave first?

Leave first, I think, but in the seven awkward seconds it takes me to make that decision, Berman has turned off his sink, and we're both tossing crumpled brown paper towels into the steel wastebasket built into the wall next to the door.

Gary doesn't act surprised when he sees me coming out of the bathroom with Sanders Berman, and he cracks a joke.

"We're going up with the right company," Gary says, and all three of us walk through the glass doors on sixteen. I push the up button on the elevator, and we're in that waiting time when, really, it's proper etiquette for Sanders Berman to start asking Gary, a senior editor, questions about how life is going for him, etc.

But with the pressure of having a book party, I guess, Sanders Berman doesn't fulfill that etiquette duty, and as we step into the elevator, *bing*, I take up the slack.

"Really enjoyed your book," I tell him. "I'm a big fan of World War Two."

"Oh, thank you," says Berman.

"Hastings is the rising star in international," Gary says, getting in on the act. "He does great work—if you ever need another researcher, you should ask him."

Sanders Berman looks at me, nods, and says, "I'll keep that in mind."

Mercifully, we've arrived on the twenty-second floor, and both Gary and I say, in chorus, "After you," and Sanders Berman goes first, and Gary and I do what's proper and just hang back for an almost imperceptible split second so Berman can walk into the room on the twenty-second floor without us.

It's a good thing we do, because when Sanders Berman enters the dining hall, the crowd gathered inside starts to clap.

Gary and I look at each other—dodged a bullet there.

9.

Book Party, Five Minutes Later

The twenty-second floor is called Top of the Mag. A catered dinner is served to the staff there on Friday nights, the late nights at the magazine. It's classy, with nonindustrial-strength carpeting and rich, glossy brown-paneled walls. The best part is the view. For that brief moment on Friday, I feel like I'm part of the big time, one of those Captain of the Universe types, with a view of Central Park and Columbus Circle, breathtaking and unmolested greenery all the way to Harlem.

It's also where the magazine hosts events like this one.

Framed posters of Sanders Berman books are up on the wall, with pictures that I have seen before in history books but not pictures that I've seen in the context of the promotion of his book—the USS *Arizona* going down in Pearl Harbor, VJ-Day in Times Square, Churchill on some podium.

Gary and I head to the bar, something to do, and I get a club soda and he gets a Coke.

"You owe me one," says Gary.

"Thanks. No, that would be great, doing research for him."

"It'd be a real feather in your cap."

Gary often talks to me about feathers in my cap. Now, it isn't about the good of the magazine that Gary tells me to get as many feathers in my cap as possible—because I don't know anyone who hates the magazine as much as Gary does. He hates it, really detests it. Thinks it's a total piece of shit. "You don't think I don't think about quitting this fucking place every day of my life," he told me last week. "You don't have a mortgage, you don't have kids, you don't have responsibility, just walking around, the change jingling in your pocket"—he likes to tell me that, that I walk around with change jingling. But we do get along, and he wants to help me out in my career as much as he can, by assigning me that Space Tourism story, for example, or by putting a good word in for me with a guy like Sanders Berman.

Gary and I stand next to each other, sipping our nonalcoholic beverages, watching other people socialize.

There are some noticeable absences. Where's Henry the EIC? Nishant Patel? Every other bigwig is here, including Tabby Doling, the daughter of *The Magazine*'s owner, Sandra Doling, who, when she was alive, also owned a big newspaper in Washington and nineteen other media properties around the country, including local television and radio stations.

"That's Berman's source of power," Gary whispers to me, talking about Tabby Doling. "Her mom is the one who discovered him. Way back in the early nineties. I think he was still in school. She put that story of his, the famous one he did . . ."

"The 'Vietnam Syndrome'?"

"Yeah, that's the one. She put that story on the cover."

At that moment, a semicircle of people starts to form, the employees and famous and semi-famous guests (Kissinger, Stephanopoulos, Brokaw, etc.) step away, leaving Sanders Berman, Tabby Doling, and Delray M. Milius in the center. Milius holds up his glass and taps it, chinking and bringing silence to the room.

Delray M. Milius is doughy-faced and five-foot-seven, and I don't mention his height pejoratively, as I'm only five-foot-nine, and I've never put much stock in how tall somebody is in relation to their character. I know big pricks and little pricks, as I'm sure we all do. He's Sanders Berman's right-hand man, his hatchet man, if you will, or if you believe the story—and I believe it because it's true—he's "that glory hole ass gape cocksucker." I don't choose those words lightly, or to offend homosexuals, some of whom are my closest friends, but because those were the words that Matt Healy, a correspondent in the magazine's Washington, D.C., bureau, put in an email, accidentally cc'ing the entire editorial staff. This was back in '99, before my time, and when email mistakes like that were more common. It was also back when Healy was in New York. After that email, he was sent to DC in a kind of exile, while Delray M. Milius leveraged the potential sexual harassment suit to get a big promotion to assistant managing editor, where he's twisted Sanders Berman's bow tie ever since.

As you can probably guess, Milius isn't too popular at the magazine. There's a strong anti-Milius faction, and within this faction, there's always a running bet about how long Milius is going to last—this time. He's left and come back to the magazine five times in twelve years. "Don't let Milius bother you" is the conventional wisdom in how to deal with him. "It's just a matter of time before he wakes up one morning and just can't get out of bed and quits again. Paralyzed. By depression, fear, anxiety, who knows—it's happened before."

Delray M. Milius keeps tapping the glass.

"Thanks, everyone, for coming to Sanders Berman's celebration," Milius says. "I especially would like to thank our esteemed guests. Without going on, it is of course, and has always been, an honor to work with Sanders, and those of you who know him know that this success is the perfectly natural result we would have expected. But without going on, Tabby Doling would like to say a few words."

Tabby Doling is bone-thin, rail-like, brown hair held in a pretty coiffure. She's maybe sixty.

"When my mother first met Sanders, he was a senior at Tulane, and she was there on a speaking engagement. What, Sanders, you were still in seminary studies?" she says.

"God and war, my two favorite subjects," Sanders says.

Everyone in the room gives a nice and expected laugh.

"Sanders is a prize, and I'm very pleased so many of us are here to recognize this, especially my guests—"

Notice the word *my*. Tabby Doling's thing is that she's friends with a bunch of famous and important people, media types, heads of state, Academy Award winners from the '70s. Though she's partial owner of *The Magazine*'s parent company, on the masthead she's listed as "Special Diplomatic Correspondent," which is kind of a joke, because that would lead readers to assume there are people above her in the hierarchy, which there are not—she even has a floor to herself, the notorious twenty-third floor.

Tabby is one of those people who, if you bring up her name in conversation around New York, you'll most likely get three or four really great anecdotes about. Everyone who's met her has a moment to recount, told with the bemused acceptance that if you're that rich and that eccentric, it's par for the course. Gary's Tabby Doling story, for instance, is that he was standing in the hallway on the sixteenth floor when he heard a knocking on the glass; someone had forgotten their ID. When Gary went to answer it, he saw Tabby through the glass and decided to make one of his customary jokes. "How do I know you're not a terrorist?" he said, as if he wasn't going to let her in. And she responded, "I'm Tabby Doling," with a real flourish and emphasis on both her first and last names. Gary thinks that's why he got passed over for the domestic sci/tech gig and has been stuck in international. That's a pretty low-level story, too, not one of her best.

I don't know her at all and haven't spent time with her, which isn't surprising, as she has a $225,000-sticker-price Bentley and a driver I always see idling outside the entrance on Broadway for her—though she did say hello to me in the hallway once, so in my book that's a plus. She keeps talking about what a wonderful man Sanders Berman is, and everyone agrees and claps and laughs when appropriate.

I'm looking over the room, and I notice that most of the people look more or less like they're up here for a reason—because they're supposed to be—or are here because they're the kind of name that goes in a New York gossip column, which is great for Sanders Berman's book, because the gossip items, whatever they will say, will also mention *The Greatest War on Earth*. I'm not telling you anything groundbreaking or new, but it's good to explain a few things every once in a while.

There is one guest, a man, I'd say sixtyish, who would stand out less if he weren't planted back in the corner against the glossy brown paneling. I've never seen him before, which isn't that unusual, but he's wearing a baseball cap—the baseball cap says "POW/MIA," and so I think, If he's wearing a baseball cap, he probably works in the mailroom.

Sanders Berman starts to speak, a perfunctory address, and the book party—and the "party" part of book party is a bit of an overstatement, as there's not really much partying; a more accurate phrase would be something like "mandatory book gathering"—starts again.

The guy with POW/MIA is still planted there, and I end up next to him.

"How long have you been with *The Magazine*?" I ask.

"Not with the magazine, son," he says with a southern drawl. "That's my boy up there."

"You're Mr. Berman's father," I say, for lack of anything better.

"That's right."

Times like this are when it really pays off for having done so much research and reading about my colleagues. I did get around to reading the "Vietnam Syndrome" story, and in it there's a reference, in, like, the sixteenth paragraph, to Sanders Berman's father, a "Vietnam veteran." It stood out because Sanders Berman is never one to write about his personal life; I think that's the only reference to his personal life I've seen.

"That's great that you could make it up to New York," I say.

"He didn't ask me here. I don't think that boy wants me here. I'm here because I'm trying to save him," he says.

"Right, of course," I say.

"Did you know that Sanders, and that other one, Nishant Patel, are members of the Council on Foreign Relations?"

"That's right, I did know that."

"Did you know that Tabby Doling's mother, Sandra Doling, used to meet every year in Germany, a little something called the Bilderberg Group. Freemasonry, you know?"

"Yeah, I've heard of the Bilderberg Group."

"What does that tell you?"

What it tells me is that rich people like to hang out with rich people, and that guys who fancy themselves foreign policy experts like to hang out and talk about foreign policy, but I know he's looking for a more History Channel "Conspiracy Revealed" insight. The problem with talking conspiracies is like the problem with talking religion: you're either preaching to the choir or arguing with the inconvincible.

"You were in Vietnam," I say.

"I was. Phoenix Project. Air America. Blackest of black ops. Over the border, Cambodia, Laos. I drink because of it. I'm angry because of it. I killed people, and I don't say they were innocent—no one is innocent in this fallen paradise. I always told Sanders that killing and war are man's most horrible things, the most deadliest things. I will admit that it takes a lot of courage to kill like I have killed, and I made that clear to Sanders, but now here he is, hobnobbing with the Illuminatos."

"Illuminati?"

"Illuminatos, more than one. Hispanics influence nowadays. You know, Davos?"

"I see what you mean. So, you're from the South?"

"Rolling hills, bootlegging country, hollows. I haven't set my eyes on the boy in years, he doesn't visit much, but I tried to teach him as best I could. We're right near Chickamauga, and every weekend I would take Sanders out and let him loose, to teach him what it means to be afraid for your life, dress him in camo from the Army/Navy, face paint, and we'd play the special ops kind of hide-and-seek. He teethed on the KA-BAR. I think I failed, though. Look at him now."

I'm no Jungian, but the thought does occur to me that Sanders's loving embrace of Apple Pie and all that starts to make more sense after meeting his father and getting a glimpse of the kind of twisted upbringing in the American dream he was apparently subjected to. Rebelling in reverse—growing up under the PTSD fringe, when he was bombarded with all sorts of ideas about the bullshittingness of our national myths, it makes sense that he'd want to immerse himself in national myths, and in fact, start to believe in the exact opposite of what his father told him.

I'm sort of looking for a way out of this conversation when I see A.E. Peoria walk in, head straight to the bar, and say loudly, "No shots? Wine only?" And as Papa Berman keeps a running commentary on the insidious nature of his son's current endeavors—*The Greatest War on Earth* is published by Simon & Schuster, SS, the name of the elite Nazi unit, and Simon & Schuster is owned by CBS, and "CBS" backward is "SBC," and "SBC," in Greek letters, is the exact same sequence of letters engraved on the inside brass door knocker at the secret society, you guessed it, Skull and Bones, on the Yale campus in New Haven, the location of an underreported 1913 meeting where J.P. Morgan and some Jewish guy devised the illegal income tax— A.E. Peoria breaches etiquette by bumping up next to Tom Brokaw and Henry Kissinger, who is short, no comment, and they are talking to Sanders Berman and Tabby Doling, and even from thirteen feet away I can hear what he's saying—"Chad . . . *Penthouse* letters . . . where do you think I should go next?"

For five minutes Peoria stands there, before abruptly twirling around and leaving from where he came, and I hear Sanders Berman say, semi-uncomfortably, "That's a magazine foreign correspondent for you," and they all laugh at Peoria's expense.

By this time, I'm swept back toward Gary, and I ask him, "Did you see Peoria?"

"That was ugly," Gary says.

"Yeah, I think he was pretty drunk," I say.

"Hastings, you have ambitions to be a foreign correspondent, right? Just remember, really, do you want to end up like Peoria? I mean, he's a cool guy and all, don't get me wrong—but he doesn't have a home or a family or anything, and there'll come a time when you'll have to ask yourself, do you want to end up like that?"

10.

After the Party

Magazine journalist A.E. Peoria is in a career crisis. The crisis of what to do next. *Thirty-four, thirty-four, thirty-four.*

A.E. Peoria likes to say that he doesn't trust anyone who loves high school, and he especially doesn't trust anyone who loves college. He likes to say that the twenties are a time in life when things are uncertain and still painfully anxious, the twenties are rough, and he is suspicious of anyone who enjoys their twenties too much. He likes to repeat that it's the thirties, the fourth decade in life, when you really get that perspective and finally get that comfort of who you are. The thirties are when you begin to understand limitations in life, a time when the things that stressed you out so much in your twenties don't seem as important anymore. This is what he likes to say when he is invited to speak to young people at colleges and high schools: that by the time you reach thirty-two-ish, the childish dreams of childhood, the teenage illusions, and the stresses of the overreach of your twenties fall into their appropriate place in the memory bank.

Then why, he wonders, am I in a career crisis yet again?

He thinks it's the inverse proportional response to his CDD. It is the silent CDD. He is always compulsively disclosing and dissecting in his mind *to himself.* He has no control over it. He doesn't quite have the science to back it up, but it is this theory of his.

He cannot stop thinking about his career. What is *career*? There is no time to search for a meaning, because meaning cannot be found until the question of career is put to rest. Why is career always in crisis? It is a looping crisis. It is the crisis of reaching goals. The crisis of setting goals then reaching goals then setting more goals and reaching more goals. The crisis of five-year plans and ten-year plans and other evil baby boomer inventions. He cannot escape this vicious looping circle of career thinking. It is never far away from his mind. It's always there, career, he's always thinking about it, analyzing, plotting, planning, worrying, fretting.

He likes to think of himself as Icarus, probably because that's the only Greek myth he can remember accurately without the aid of a search engine. The only Greek myth that, after reading Sophocles and Euripides and all the other one-named Greek pederasts in school, he can remember and draw a detailed meaning from that he can relate to life today.

Icarus flies too close to the sun after his father gives him wax wings, and then the wings melt and Icarus falls into the ocean, maybe the Mediterranean, so it's not that bad, beats the North Atlantic, but he falls into the ocean and he drowns. A.E. Peoria likes to think of that myth and say to himself, or others if he's on drugs: Fuck you, father. Fuck you, Icarus. I am Kid Icarus, like in that Nintendo game from 1987, leaping from free-floating graphic structure to free-floating graphic structure. I fly too close to the sun and crash into the goddamn ocean! But I know how to swim, I know how to swim, I know how to swim to shore, and when I'm on the beach, I look at the sun again. The sun as it is drying the saltwater from my skin. I yell out to the sky, "Fuck you, Sun! I'll be back! With a new set of wings, just you wait, you shining, spotty-flaring, cancer-causing fuck."

Maybe it is New York.

A.E. Peoria likes to think maybe it isn't him, maybe it's this place, this city. New York, Peoria knows from reading Evelyn Waugh, is a city where "there is neurosis in the air which its inhabitants mistake for energy."

Couldn't say it better myself, A.E. Peoria thinks, could not say it better myself.

The city of New York is always causing this career crisis. An insidious conspiracy to remind him on every block about the state of his career.

What other reason for glass skyscrapers, glass windows everywhere, all this glass that was erected and positioned so that you cannot escape your own reflection—he is always getting himself bounced back at him in glass, as if whoever designed these glass buildings likes to keep putting him in his place. Look at what you're wearing.

The word *career*, A.E. Peoria knows, because he looks it up, comes from the Latin *carrus*, or "wagon," via the French *carrière*, or "road." A person's progress and general course of action through life or through a phase of life, as in some profession or undertaking. Success in a profession, occupation, etc. A course, especially a swift one. Speed, especially full speed. A verb meaning "to run" or "to move rapidly along." Careering, rush. "My hasting days fly on with full career"— John Milton. A third definition, *career*, a racecourse, the ground run over. Fourth, falconry, the flight of the hawk. "Careering gaily over the curling waves"—Washington Irving. Archaic: to charge ahead at full speed.

Rushing ahead at full speed on his life's vocation, in control, out of control, a little of both.

Up until when—recently?—he had viewed the path of career unimaginatively, like some kind of long hallway in a poorly designed international airport, where the architects seemed to have gotten great pleasure making sure that every connecting flight was mathematically at the farthest point away from any other point in the terminal. A long hallway, low music, beeping golf carts with oxygen tanks. As if the architects had taken to heart Zeno's paradox of never being able to cross a room and so designed an infinitely divisible hallway between points A and B at each transit underpass.

In his imaginary career-fantasy metaphor, there are those who are curiously choosing to walk the hallway, those who are standing to the right on the people mover, and those who are walking on the left of the conveyor belt, rushing along. That third lane was the lane he thought—from the age of twenty-eight to thirty-four—he was finally on. At some point he had jumped over the hand railing where he'd been walking, paused for a brief moment, and then he'd stepped on the fastest track, a track that he had just been watching other people use, as if it had been protected by a thick plastic barrier. And he was cruising along on this fast track, thinking, I did it, I am finally on the fast track, I'm going to catch my flight—but until when—recently?—that feeling changed.

A.E. Peoria had always thought of himself as lucky, and this luck, he felt, made him somewhat superior to other people his age. It was not the luck of good things happening to him, but the luck that he could always say, "I know what I want to do with my life. I'm lucky."

A.E. Peoria never questioned that he wanted to be a magazine journalist. Had always known it. Even when it was rough during his twenties, when all of his wandering and drifting college classmates were anguishing in this kind of existential variety of what to do. I just don't know what I want to do, his friends would tell him, and that was something he could sympathize with sort of, but not completely. Because if the conversation continued, he would always say, "I'm lucky, I've always known what I wanted to do," and they would respond, "Yes, you are lucky. I wish I always knew what I wanted to do."

Peoria, though, was getting worried that maybe he wasn't lucky anymore. Maybe he'd made a grave mistake by becoming a magazine journalist. Maybe it wasn't what he'd always wanted to do.

So, in his office—though the career crisis wasn't limited to his time in the office; how he wished it was limited to his office and not his bedroom, his bed, his showers, his jogging, his dinners with his girlfriend, his phone conversations, his commute, how he wished it was just limited to his office!—he had started for the first time to think about other careers.

He looked on the CIA website. He looked at Harvard Law School. He looked at SUNY Upstate Medical University. He looked at NASA. He looked at MCATs and LSATs and GREs and the Foreign Service Exam. Film school. He looked at job openings with small newspapers in places like Malone, New York, and Yaak, Montana. He looked at business school—Stern, Wharton, Stanford. He looked at financial aid documents. He looked at everything, and he fretted about everything. He looked at doctoral programs and master's programs and technical institutes in TV/VCR repair and forensic criminology. Dental school. He looked at intensive language programs for Urdu and Arabic and Russian and Spanish. He looked at teaching English in Katmandu and microfinance initiatives in Ghana. Those professions seemed so much simpler—doctor, lawyer, astronaut, accountant, linguist—professions where the path to success was clear. Why had he stupidly chosen to be a magazine journalist—now, that was a career with pressure! That was a career with stress, with uncertainty. How much simpler life would be if he were a brain surgeon or a physicist or designed helicopters for a defense contractor—a simple, stable career path with a well-defined destination, so much easier than this constant and vicious battle he was in with himself over this New York magazine media world he lived in. Those were careers with real skills, real sellable skills. What skills did he have?

Diagnose what? Consult on what? Fix what? No, he could gather information half decently and present that information half decently, but it was always other people's information, others' doings, always the observer—to make a career out of observing other careers, what did that say of him?

His girlfriend, to whom he had given six orgasms, had given him some of her Xanax, and that helped some.

Thirty-four, and never had a book party!

So, A.E. Peoria, door to his office closed, window shades clinched, drunk as fuck, pale light from the computer screen zebra-ing his face, is considering a change in careers, drastically, when he sees that another magazine has been delivered to his desk, the middle-highbrow magazine that Henry the EIC once clipped a cartoon from. He flips open to a story called "A Professor in Exile," and it's by a guy he's never heard of before but who seems very serious, and this guy's byline is Brennan Toddly, it's fifteen thousand words, very detail-oriented and persuasively reported from the halls of northeastern joint conferences and the cloistered monklike apartments off Ivy League campuses, leather-bound bookshelves, dust, reported with a forcefully humorless I-narrator, laying out in genius fashion the case for war against Saddam Hussein and Iraq, and predicting that the war will happen, needs to happen, within six months.

A.E. Peoria forgets about his career crisis and starts to make his own phone calls, all his anxiety relieved because he gets a urinary tract–like tingling that a big career-making story is on the way, something he can really sink his teeth into. He starts to think about the ways he can make sure that when this future war does start, he's in place to cover it. He sees the fast track again and its name is Brennan Toddly.

Before he gets too far, he passes out and falls asleep, curled underneath his desk, the book party six floors above him temporarily forgotten.

11.

Friday, October 25, 2002

D*ing.*
        I get an email, and it shoots me up in my swivel.
Nishant Patel. No subject.

come by my office np

Do I reply? Or do I just go?
I hit Reply.
My fingers freeze over the keys.

Dear Nishant . . .

What else? How formal do I make it? Or should it be as informal
as Nishant Patel's? Am I at a stage where I can write "ok" and put my
own initials: "ok/mmh"? Or do I need to sign off with at least my
first name?
        Five minutes pass.
        How deferential do I need to be? I freeze. Does Nishant Patel
understand the impact of an email from a boss? To see his name in
my inbox, to see it, and to think, How am I going to answer this?

Does he realize how much time it takes to compose a response? I want to choose the words perfectly. I am still at a stage where I think people are going to actually read my email somewhat closely, and there's all sorts of etiquette issues that will probably just disappear in the technological informality of communication that seems to be heading our way. No punctuation, no salutations, no goodbyes, just initials and shorthand and all caps or no caps.

I come up with:

Dear Nishant, I will come by now, if that's okay.

Sincerely,
Michael M. Hastings

I get up from my cubicle. I walk toward his office. The door is closed.

I stand next to Dorothy's cubicle for permission from her to go in.

Dorothy and Patricia are in dueling phone conversations. They aren't talking to each other. They seem to be in endless negotiations with other people's assistants. "Dr. Patel will call Mr. Rose back," says Patricia. "Yes, Dr. Patel called Mr. Rose and now Mr. Rose is calling Dr. Patel back."

The unknown figure on the end of Dorothy's line is acting pushy, and Dorothy is saying, "We very much understand how busy the Ambassador is, and I'm sure you can understand how busy Nishant is, and we appreciate Mr. Holbrooke's call and we're sure to find a time later this afternoon or tomorrow?"

Dorothy hangs up.

"Patricia, mark down that Nishant has a call to Holbrooke tomorrow," but Patricia doesn't hear Dorothy, over the cubicle divider and with that deaf ear. She just knows that Dorothy has commanded her to do something, so she says, "Yes, can you please hold, please hold, yes, is this Mr. Rose's office, this is Dr. Patel's office, please hold for a moment," and she covers up the mouthpiece with her hand and calls over to Dorothy, "What, Dorothy? What, Dorothy?" and Dorothy snaps, "Tomorrow, one-thirty, a call with Holbrooke's office," and Dorothy looks up at me.

"Yes, Mike?"

Dorothy, though aging, was once a real knockout, single but with former lovers who were diplomats and war correspondents, and weekend getaways with captains of industry and nights in the late sixties and early seventies in the West Village. She lives for the magazine now, and she is the gatekeeper, both physical and electronic, to Nishant Patel, the magazine's number-one or -two most valuable commodity, depending on who you ask. I'm lucky because Dorothy likes me, because if Dorothy doesn't like you, you have to wait in line.

"Hi, Dorothy, Nishant—I mean, Dr. or Mr. Patel asked me to come by."

Dorothy smiles, and nods.

"One second."

Dorothy stands up and says to Patricia, teaching her, "Patricia, we know the rule. If you have 'former' in your title, then we return the phone call in twenty-four hours. If you are current, then we return the phone call in six hours or less."

"What about Mr. Rose?" says Patricia.

"For TV, one hour or less," says Dorothy. "Go ahead and knock, Mike."

I knock on the closed door, and I hear the slightly accented British lilt of Dr. Nishant Patel, and he says, "Come in," and as I walk in, he's on the phone. He points to a seat in front of his desk.

I sit down.

Nishant Patel is in a corner office. There are hundreds of books, mostly his books, and they are all in different languages. German language, French language, Portuguese language. Spanish. Dutch. Italian. Indonesian. The books line the shelves and are neatly stacked on every free flat surface, tables, coffee tables. There are two couches and three chairs and a ledge on the window to sit, if he's having a meeting with everyone in his office.

Nishant Patel's legs are crossed, and he leans back in his Executive 3000 black swivel chair, perfectly tailored tan pants riding up to mid-ankle to reveal lightly patterned argyle socks, probably from Paul Smith, which are a perfect contrast to his brown Gucci loafers, going up to his thin waist and off–powder blue Ermenegildo Zegna dress shirt, knotted green silk cuff links from Bergdorf Goodman, silk Brooks Brothers–looking tie, though probably not Brooks Brothers, probably something a few steps above that, like Thomas Pink, hair cut and effortlessly styled every two weeks by the Grooming Lounge.

He's turned at about forty-five degrees to my right, his left, tilted a precise sixty-seven degrees backward, talking on the phone.

". . . Yes, it was an interesting meeting. . . . The undersecretary invited us there—Kaplan, Friedman, Haas, Brennan Toddly, a number of others from the Council on Foreign Relations. Oh, he wanted to get our opinions, our ideas. No, it was all very off-the-record. . . . We're not allowed to say anything or mention it in our columns. . . . No, Berman wasn't invited. . . . To convince us, and it was quite, quite convincing. I have to go. I'll be taping the show tonight, but I should be home after dinner."

Patel gently hangs up the phone and turns toward me.

"Hastings, thank you for coming. I need you to do research for my column this week. Have you seen this story?"

He tosses a copy of the middle-highbrow magazine on his desk, folded up to a story by a man named Brennan Toddly.

"Have you read this?"

I haven't read it, but nod yes, because I have learned that this magazine is the only one that the editors at *The Magazine* read on a regular basis—certainly, they never actually read our magazine, unless it is to see who got in the magazine that week and who didn't.

"He quotes an Iraqi man in there, and he cites Kenneth Pollack's book *The Threatening Storm*. Call Pollack and the Iraqi man, and have them say basically what they say in that story."

"Sure, Nishant, no problem."

"My column this week, to give you an idea, is going to go further than I had in my last cover story. I left my argument open—the case for war? Now I am going to answer the question. I will be making the argument primarily for national security reasons, but also, humanitarian reasons. We cannot forget about the Iraqi people, et cetera. You follow this stuff, don't you?"

"Of course, of course," I say.

"I'll be writing tomorrow afternoon, get it to me before then."

"Okay, Nishant, no problem."

And he doesn't say "Dismissed," but he does re-angle his chair, forty-five degrees back to the left, and hits the intercom button and tells Dorothy to get him the host of the TV show he's going to be a guest on tonight.

Taking the copy of Brennan Toddly's article with me, I go back to my desk, nervous and excited—getting to do research for Nishant Patel.

This is the big time.

12.

Two Hours Later

B efore I look at the Brennan Toddly story, I want to find out who Brennan Toddly is. There is a Wikipedia entry for him, a single paragraph:

> An author of three books, two nonfiction, one fiction.
>
> 1989: *A Peaceful Village*—an account of a Peace Corps building effort in Uganda. (Out of print.)
> 1996: *The Typewriter Artist*—a novel. The main character is a writer who lives in New York. He is a mild depressive and everyone ignores his work. (Out of print.)
> 1999: *Awash in Red*—a personal journey of self-discovery, as the author struggles with whether or not to remain a socialist.

I find out that Brennan Toddly, according to his bio, spent two years at *The Magazine* in the mid-nineties, has been the recipient of a number of government grants, and seems to have landed at his new magazine just this year. An impact hire, to be sure.

I power-read the story. It is impressively full of nuance. A representative paragraph:

> After the panel discussion, I made my way backstage, where I encountered Kanan Makiya. I introduced myself to Makiya. He invited me to his home for tea. We walked across the campus yard, where a new class of coeds had just arrived, playing Frisbee and hacky sack. Easy, carefree thoughts. The opposite of what Makiya was thinking. "This is what Iraq was like when I was a child, before I had to leave," he told me. "You Americans are finally paying attention. You must finally take action." Three hours later, I had left his office, a bladder full of sweet chai, convinced. But the arguments with myself would continue.

I call the university where Makiya is living out his exile and request an interview for a Nishant Patel column.

For Kenneth Pollack, I call his publisher and ask for a copy of his book *The Threatening Storm* to be sent over. It is getting so much attention, thanks to the Brennan Toddly story, that the publisher tells me they are doing a rush second printing of it. But he says they'll messenger me a copy and get Pollack to phone me later this afternoon.

Now I wait.

A blur of a human being passes by my cubicle, high-pitched voice trailing.

"Sanders, Sanders, Sanders."

I jump up in my seat to see the human comet. I recognize the man calling Sanders. It is Matt Healy, Chief Investigative Correspondent, based in DC.

Healy broke *The Magazine*'s (and the country's) biggest story in the nineties, the Pentagon Paper of Blow Jobs, that whole business with President Clinton and Monica Lewinsky. Without Healy, the nation might never have known the details of things like cigar vaginal penetration. Then where would we be? Well, the Internet would have solved that problem within a few years anyway.

Yes, there is no doubt in the mind of anyone at the magazine that Healy is the closest thing the magazine has to its own Woodward and Bernstein, rolled into one. A regular Neil Sheehan—revealing the past decade's version of Watergate, but easier for most to imagine, as it just involved a slightly chubby chick, infidelity, and a hard-on. The evolution of American journalism: three decades coming full circle, a source with the name Deep Throat leaking information about the chief executive's illegal behavior to investigating the actual mechanics of deep-throating a chief executive. There's no need to even point out that Healy himself isn't exactly a model citizen of marital behavior—the "ass gape cocksucker" email about Milius, for instance, a couple of divorces, smoking crack, rumored affairs, the whole deal—but of course, Healy never had the chance to lie about it under oath, in a grand jury, so ethically speaking, the magazine is in the clear from charges of hypocrisy.

Healy is pigeonholing Sanders Berman, right outside the men's room. A real bulldog type. Three spiral notebooks on his person. Two flopping out of his back pockets, one in his hand.

"We should make it a cover, a cover," he yells. "Three sources—CIA, DOD, the VP's shop—are all saying and confirming it. They are saying the links are there, they are saying there are links. Al Qaeda in Baghdad!"

Healy rushes off down the hall, his points made.

Sanders Berman comes wandering away from the men's room, as if in a daze, like he's just been hit by a dust storm.

I take the chance.

"Hi, Sanders, how's everything?"

He stops.

"Oh, hi—Walters, is it? Everything is good."

"Hastings, yeah, that's great, that's great. Yeah, I'm just researching Nishant's column for the week."

"What's he writing on?"

"The case for war, really coming down for it."

"He is? Darnit, that's what I was going to write this week."

I start nodding.

"I just had dinner with Ken Pollack last night. I was going to quote him, too."

Sanders Berman touches his bow tie. He puts his elbows up on my cubicle, a gesture of familiarity. He sees that I have the Brennan Toddly article on my desk.

"Don't tell me he's going to use that Iraqi gentleman's argument . . ."

"Yep, I have a call in to his office."

He puts his knuckle under his chin, in thought.

Am I going to appear too precocious? Am I about to overstep my bounds? I mean, who am I to suggest any ideas? I'm a twenty-two-year-old former intern, a researcher and an occasional fact-checker.

"Oh, I'm sure you'll come up with something to say," I say. "Like, no one has made any American historical arguments for the war yet."

He looks at me, eyebrows up, as if he's considering humoring my suggestion.

"Hmm. And Hastings, if you had a column, that's what you'd say?"

"Uh, well, I mean, President James Polk has some good thoughts on these kinds of issues."

Sanders Berman smiles and starts to walk away. I think he's regretting even talking to me. He has his head down and I hope he's not regretting it, but that is the sinking suspicion I get. If I were a female intern, at least his ego could have received some flattery, but "There's never a reason to talk to a young male intern" is probably what he's thinking. I should have kept silent, mouth shut.

No time to worry or beat myself up over it.

The phone rings.

It's Kanan Makiya.

"Hi, uh, thanks for calling. Yeah, so, like you said in Brennan Toddly's piece—"

"Mr. Toddly took me out of context."

"No doubt, um, really, hunh."

"Have you read my book?"

"Um, no, it's on my list."

"Hmmm."

We go back and forth a few more times, until, twenty minutes later, he says more or less what he said in the Brennan Toddly story. I thank him and hang up.

My phone rings again.

Kenneth Pollack is on the line.

"Have you read my book?" he asks before we begin.

"Um, no, sorry. It's on my list, though."

"Hmmm."

"But I did see what Brennan Toddly wrote about it, and it sounds like a really great book."

"Yes, thanks, but that was taken out of context."

"Right, sure, no doubt."

"I mean, how do you summarize a five-hundred-and-three-page book in a single page?"

"Very carefully?"

"You lose the caveats."

Pollack starts in on his theory and doesn't let up for a good twenty-three minutes. Nuclear programs. Weapons of mass destruction. Biological, chemical. UN reports, broken resolutions, aluminum tubes, uranium enrichment, Israel's reactor strike in 1983. Secret mobile weapons labs. I'm feeling good about it, because it's the stuff that Nishant Patel wanted him to say, and all I have to do is keep typing what he's saying.

I spend the next three hours correcting typos and condensing my conversations with Kanan and Ken into a single page, taking the best quotes and putting them up top.

I grab a quick dinner and come back to my desk after eating. Agonizing over each sentence. This is the first time I've been asked to do research, and I don't want to fuck it up.

While I'm proofreading and figuring out the best way to write it up in an email to Nishant, another email appears.

From: Sanders Berman
Subject: James Polk

Mike, per our conversation, could you send me the Polk citations you were talking about?

Regards,
SB

This really, really is the big time now.

I'M VERY SORRY

I think it's about time for me to apologize to all of my colleagues.

I'm sorry.

There, that's out of the way.

I don't want to hurt anyone's feelings. I'm a nice guy, at heart, and I have to say it weighs on me whether or not to write about everything that happened at *The Magazine*.

Thomas Jefferson said something once: "Don't mistake the facts for truth."

Actually, I said that, not Jefferson, but attributing my thoughts to him gave it more authority for a second.

It's true that without *The Magazine*, I'd never have gotten a platform. *The Magazine* gave me my start. Biting the hand that feeds and the like.

In my defense, I'd like to point out that we at *The Magazine* are always doing unseemly things, always taking other people's experiences and actions and desires and totally mangling them for our purposes. An intellectual journalist once wrote a book about it—I think she was working for the same magazine as Brennan Toddly. She said that what we do is morally indefensible. Yeah, probably, but who does anything that's really morally defensible these days? Politicians? Lawyers? Janitors maybe? Should we all be janitors? Construction workers? Cops? EMTs? Teachers?

Okay, maybe they are doing morally defensible things. Regardless, other people's experiences sell ads, make good copy, the usual. We're always sticking the long knife into someone's back, and with the right editing, we always manage to give that knife a little twist—we're professionals, after all.

Maybe I'm giving myself too much credit. Maybe my colleagues will read the excerpts (very little chance they'll buy the hardcover) and think, yes, that Hastings kid, he got it exactly right. Does anyone ever read something that's been written about them and think, "Yep, that motherfucker nailed me—all my faults and hopes and insecurities and dreams and all"?

Maybe they'll think, "What an asshole. Look at this, selling out his employer to make a quick buck." (Trust me: I make more working for *The Magazine* than writing a memoir about working for a newsmagazine. We're not Condé Nast, after all.)

Maybe some co-workers will read the book and think it's okay. And others will think it's shit. That's what I guess is called "a mixed critical reaction." My guess is that I won't have much future at the magazine once word gets out that I'm trying to publish this—which makes me a little sad. They have feelings, and I have feelings too.

So really, I'm sorry. Mr. Peoria, Mr. Berman, Mr. Patel, Jerry, Sam, Gary, Anna—it's not personal, or at least it's only as personal as anything else.

It's snowing still, December 2005. I've switched to drinking bottles of San Pellegrino mineral water because I like the feel of the weight of the bottle in my hand. Almost like I'm actually drinking.

I just got an email from Human Resources saying that the magazine is about to lay off one-third of its staff, thanks to the difficult economic climate and "the rapidly changing nature of our industry." So if the general thesis of the book is true, encapsulated in the title— that this could actually be the last magazine of its kind—it's hard to jeopardize a future if the place you're working for has none.

Which reminds me of a speech Henry the EIC gives to the new interns. He says he keeps a cartoon in his office that's from that middle-highbrow magazine, published in 1981. It's a dinosaur reading our magazine. We're a dinosaur, get it? Ready for extinction. The point, he told us, twenty years later, is that critics and naysayers have been heralding the decline of *The Magazine* forever and it's never come to pass.

There's that other saying, too. I think Harry Truman said it: "If you've worked in the kitchen, you won't eat at the restaurant." But if it's a five-star restaurant, with a couple of celebrity chefs, wouldn't you want to hear about the rats from a rat himself? The chefs might think it's an unfair attack, because, if you *really* know restaurants, you know rats are a big part of the business. All sorts of unsanitary shit goes on that you wouldn't ever want the customers to know.

All that being said, I do and always will love *The Magazine*.

Approximately three hours and forty-eight minutes left.

PART II

Why We Fight

"There is no doubt that Saddam Hussein now has weapons of mass destruction."

—VICE PRESIDENT DICK CHENEY, AUGUST 2002

"Hard-liners are alarmed that American intelligence underestimated the pace and scale of Iraq's nuclear program before Baghdad's defeat in the gulf war. . . . The first sign of a 'smoking gun,' they argue, may be a mushroom cloud."

—*The New York Times*, SEPTEMBER 8, 2002

"The debate about whether we're going to deal with Saddam Hussein is over, and now the question is how do we deal with him."

—PRESIDENT GEORGE W. BUSH, NOVEMBER 2002

"These liberal hawks could give a voice to [Bush's] war aims. . . . They could make the case for war to suspicious Europeans and to wavering fellow Americans. They might even be able to explain the connection between Iraq and the war on terrorism."

—GEORGE PACKER IN *The New York Times Magazine*, DECEMBER 8, 2002

"Barring a dramatic change of behavior by Saddam Hussein in the coming weeks . . . a military intervention to disarm Iraq would be justified."

—*Washington Post* EDITORIAL, FEBRUARY 5, 2003

"The president will take us to war with support . . . from quite a few members of the East Coast liberal media cabal. . . . We reluctant hawks . . . generally agree that the logic for standing pat does not hold. . . . Mr. Bush will be able to claim, with justification, that the coming war is a far cry from the rash, unilateral adventure some of his advisers would have settled for."

—*New York Times* COLUMNIST BILL KELLER, FEBRUARY 8, 2003

"The humanitarian case for war is strong enough on its own."

—BRENNAN TODDLY ON *Charlie Rose*, FEBRUARY 13, 2003

"We have to save the Iraqi people."

—NISHANT PATEL ON THE SAME BROADCAST

"What I'm suggesting is that if our goal is to bring democracy to the Middle East, there are better ways to do so then invading and occupying a country."

—JAMES FALLOWS ON THE SAME BROADCAST

"That's Munich talking."

—SANDERS BERMAN, *The Magazine*

"Every statement I make today is backed up by sources, solid sources. . . . What I want to bring to your attention today is the potentially much more sinister nexus between Iraq and the Al Qaida terrorist network. . . . As with the story of Zarqawi and his network, I can trace the story of a senior terrorist operative telling how Iraq provided training in these weapons to Al Qaida."

—SECRETARY OF STATE COLIN POWELL AT THE
UNITED NATIONS, FEBRUARY 2003

"The detainee was not in a position to know if any training had taken place."

—JANUARY 2003 CIA REPORT ON POWELL'S SOURCE,
AL QAEDA OPERATIVE IBN AL-SHAYKH AL-LIBI, WHO PROVIDED
THE INTELLIGENCE AFTER HIS RENDITION TO EGYPT

"Yes, [Iraq] could be an incredibly dangerous war for journalists. But then, you know, we're in a situation that's fairly dangerous for those of us who live in places like New York and Washington."

—JOE KLEIN ON ABC'S *This Week*, MARCH 9, 2003

"This is really bold. . . . Mr. Bush's audacious shake of the dice appeals to me."

> —*New York Times* COLUMNIST THOMAS FRIEDMAN, MARCH 2003

"The question is, is Saddam Hussein a threat to the world or not? I think he is. We should do it with or without the UN."

> —PETER BEINART, EDITOR OF *The New Republic*, MARCH 2003

"Iraq is a part of the war on terror. Saddam Hussein is a threat to our nation. September the 11th should say to the American people that we're now a battlefield, that weapons of mass destruction in the hands of a terrorist organization could be deployed here at home."

> —PRESIDENT GEORGE W. BUSH, MARCH 2003

"One Arab intelligence officer interviewed by *Newsweek* spoke of 'the green mushroom' over Baghdad—the modern-day caliph bidding a grotesque bio-chem farewell to the land of the living alongside thousands of his subjects as well as his enemies. Saddam wants to be remembered. . . . It is up to U.S. armed forces to stop him."

> —*Newsweek* COVER STORY, MARCH 17, 2003

"I believe that the Bush administration is right: this war will look better when it is over. . . . Weapons of mass destruction will be found. . . . Iraq is surely producing weapons of mass destruction."

> —FAREED ZAKARIA, *Newsweek* COVER STORY, MARCH 24, 2003

"Iraq is going to be a cakewalk."

"We'll be greeted as liberators."

"U.S. officials expect there to be less than 20,000 U.S. troops left in Iraq after the initial invasion phase of the war is over, anticipating a drawdown by December 2003."

"They'll be home by Christmas, I can tell you that much."

"We need to demonstrate the good intentions of Americans, but also our power. Shock and Awe, I dare say, did that beautifully."

"We forget, or pretend to forget, or convince ourselves that this time, this time it's going to be different, this time it really is evil versus good, good versus evil, this time, we swear it, the war is going to follow the script, even though in the first scene of the movie, you always have a savvy general ready to give a warning, ready to foreshadow what we all know, who says, wars never go as planned, wars never go how you want them to, wars unleash things— those dogs of war—that we have no control over, ripple effects and whatnot. But there is also the other general in the first scene, the fool to be sent up, ready to say, don't worry, it will all be over by Christmas."

—Very Important Thinkers from Very Important and Well-Funded Think Tanks

PART III

The Invasion

13.

Wednesday, March 19, 2003

The desert, the steaming dry desert.

No, that image doesn't work. Deserts don't steam.

A fog, then?

Ten details.

If I force myself to write ten details, then I will always be able to paint word pictures for each scene.

A.E. Peoria leans back against the Humvee, thinking about the system of description he had devised, systematic, rigid, a format he could repeat. A disciplined way of reporting. He didn't want to rely on his memory as much as he had in the past—was it black or blue, three cars or six, a sparrow or swallow. He would write everything down.

He'd marked his notebook, spiral, with numbers 1 through 10. Page after page of 1 through 10.

A.E. Peoria stretches, shakes his head, wonders how bad his breath smells.

1. I lean back against the Humvee.
2. Humvee is tan, sand-colored.
3. Five Humvees, parked in a row.

4. *8 soldiers. 3 smoking.*

5. *Desert fog looks like steam.*

6. *Two soldiers in chemical biological nuclear suits.*
   Astronauts. Scuba?

7. *One soldier pulls off glove.*

8. *Shit, he says, my wedding ring flew off.*

9. *Other soldiers search for wedding ring.*

10. *Wedding ring glimmers in dirt.*

"There it is, sir," A.E. Peoria says, then immediately regrets saying it. Shouldn't have put myself in the story; now if I use that anecdote, I can't be in the objective third-person voice of *The Magazine.*

A.E. Peoria is holding his digital tape recorder under his notebook. Along with description, he wants to work on listening, or if not listening, recording.

The digital tape recorder is picking up this dialogue.

"That's fucking gay, dude," says Lenny.

"Ball flaps aren't fucking gay," says Tom Yelks, a twenty-three-year-old from Akron, Ohio. "I want to start a family when I get back, not just give fucking blow jobs like you. I'm keeping mine on."

Ball flap: a piece of Kevlar with Velcro that fastens onto the bottom of the flak vest.

Yelks holds it up, examining it under the early light.

"You gotta ask yourself, you know, will this actually stop a bullet? If a fucking bomb explodes, you think this will actually stop the shrapnel? Look at this piece of shit," says Lenny, waving it around. "It's thinner than a fucking pantyhose."

By this time, others in the squad have gathered around.

"It's better than nothing," says Staff Sergeant Gerome Phelps, twenty-six, from Midland Springs, Texas. "And all you guys are going to wear it. Captain's orders."

Lenny walks up next to A.E. Peoria and confides, "If you haven't noticed, the Army is a twenty-four-hour gay joke."

A.E. Peoria writes in his notes, "twenty four hour gay joke." That clicks with what he'd been observing. The gayness is everywhere: bursting, ironic, warmly comforting, a way to deal with the homoeroticism of hanging out with a bunch of dudes.

Peoria divides men into two categories: those who like to shower with other dudes and those who don't. Peoria is very much in the those-who-don't category, but it has been his experience that athletes, frat types, golfers, and now soldiers fit in the showering-naked category, the ass-slapping, dick-hanging, towel-whipping category. This is not to say anything homophobic—god knows Peoria is against any kind of talk like that at all. He's had to deal with it his entire life.

When he was twelve years old, his father came out of the closet. When he was fourteen, his mother came out of the closet, a lesbian. Father was a professor at Harvard, mother taught at an elite all-girls college in New York. He didn't reveal this to the soldiers, though each brain cell, genetically wired by his compulsive disclosure disorder, wanted him to blurt it out. He resisted shouting: Stop with the gay jokes, my parents are gay. It's not cool. His therapy must be working. Was he betraying his roots and his parents by keeping silent? By letting words like "faggot" and "butthurt" slip by without comment? Should he explain how that kind of language might cause offense?

"Let's ask the reporter," says Yelks.

"Ask me what," Peoria says, realizing he hasn't been listening, only recording.

"Is wearing a ball flap fucking gay?"

This would be the moment to protest.

"Not if you care about your dick, I guess," Peoria says.

"Fucking Lenny loves dick!" says Yelks.

The argument continues, and Peoria starts to compose in his head something he can send back to New York. He is supposed to, according to his editors who are preparing a big package on the ground war, look for "examples of fear."

Soldiers afraid of gay men wouldn't cut it. But the fear of getting your balls blown off was something he could work with.

The soldier's number-one fear, Peoria writes in his mind, throughout the history of human warfare. An ancient anxiety, as large as death. Writings from Genghis Khan's time show that the Mongols were worried about a saber to the groin, putting a crimp on the raping. A legion of Romans in A.D. 23 refused an order for battle near the Sea of Galilee because the bronze cups they had requisitioned from Carthage—which all the other legionnaires from competing formations, even the African slaves, had been given—hadn't arrived yet. A near armed mutiny. On sea, conscripts in the British fleet under Nelson described a phenomena called splinter cock, the result of a cannonball crashing into the wooden deck, sending shards of handcrafted timber ripping through hammocks and pantaloons. Letters home from the Civil War—letters that aren't talked about too much—mentioned how Confederate soldiers had competitions to take aim "a smidgen lower south from the goddamned Yanks' belt buckles." In World War I, a French general famously gave a rousing speech, urging the young Frenchmen, already ravaged by two years of back-and-forth in slaughterhouses like Verdun and the Somme, to advance over the trenches *"avec courage,"* helmets *"sur la tête."* In the hush following the speech, one private, sick with louse bites and scarlet fever, quipped, "That's not the head I'm worried about." (*C'est ne pas cette tête qui me préoccupe!*)

Weapons manufacturers explicitly exploited this anxiety in the second half of the twentieth century, designing explosive charges that jumped from the ground to hip level before they exploded—the

Bouncing Betty, named after Betty Boop, the first hypersexualized female cartoon of the postwar era. The chant that Marines out at Parris Island introduced in 1966: "This is my rifle, this is my gun, this is for fighting, this is for fun." Lose either, and the fun ends.

The fears: soldiers spent a lot of time not really thinking to avoid them, and when they did think, it was about home and girlfriends and fiancées and sex, and after that, when they thought about the future, which seemed to loom in the country overheard to the north, it was about their balls. True fear and the language of courage. Testicles, *cojones*, testosterone to stand up under fire and not be a pussy.

Since arriving in Kuwait, Peoria had spent more than twenty days in the Humvees with the soldiers—mostly men, mostly nineteen to twenty-eight—prepared for the invasion. We need color, the editors had said, and maybe find a scandal too. War crimes are always good.

Peoria has assigned each of them a place in the group hierarchy. Characters, all of them. The staff sergeant is someone you could say is straight from central casting—is there a central casting anymore? The men are stereotypes with legs and animated mouths. They have affected their roles in the unit almost cinematically, so much so that Peoria feels like he has watched this scene before, certainly he has read about it in all the war novels, heard the banter, or a variation of it, in the dispatches from the front from every other war reporter he has ever studied. Chicken/egg, egg/chicken. What comes first: the drill sergeant or the drill sergeant in *Full Metal Jacket*?

Phelps is the badass, can-do NCO, a veteran of four deployments who has seen it all, no sweat, regularly abusive. Yelks is the typical private: talkative, youthful, running at the mouth in an ongoing and evolving profane banter with his buddy, Specialist Lenny. Yelks is always anxious to explain and make sweeping judgments on Army life and on his fellow soldiers, like "problem in the Army is that most of these guys didn't have friends in high school. I mean, they were picked on in high school. I mean, if they had friends, you know, they were fucking losers, to be honest, and now they've got guns?"

There's the large southern redneck, with a neck red from the sun, from Arkansas. A pair of black kids from Brooklyn and Jersey, who even today make jokes about the white man, though there is the double irony that they really don't feel very oppressed. The young lieutenant, an intellectual sort from one of the Ivy League schools who went against the grain and signed up to learn about war because, as he puts it, "it was such a part of human history, the human experience, and to understand myself and the world, I need to understand war," with whispers that he is thinking about a career in politics.

And then there is the quiet loner, non-aggressively awkward, effeminate, near pretty, always a half step behind, not on the ball, with a silent mystery hinting at some hidden depth, some sensitivity in a very insensitive environment—and in this unit, that soldier's name is Justin Salvador. From what Peoria has gathered, he's Puerto Rican, though he's often called Mexican or Honduran or Panamanian, and his nickname—as most in the unit have a nickname, just like soldiers in the movies—is Chipotle. He is the soldier the conversation seizes on in moments of silence. Rather than talk about the weather, a joke thrown Salvador's way acts as the icebreaker.

Salvador, slight and fair-skinned, is fumbling with the ball flap.

In the silence, the velcroing and unvelcroing can be heard.

Yelks turns to Salvador.

"Now Chipotle over there, he being a Mexican, it might not be a bad thing for him, you know, since his race breeds like field mice. We don't want your spawn taking over the country now, do we, Chipotle? New order—only the Mexicans don't need to wear the ball flap."

Everyone laughs, and Salvador mumbles a "Go fuck yourself" or something to Yelks.

The lieutenant walks up.

"Okay, guys, we got the word. We're gonna be going first. The convoy is gonna stay a couple klicks behind us. We're clearing the way. I remind you we are about to enter hostile territory, but we are liberators. As such, we will kill, but we will kill only those who are trying to kill us. Shoot if you are shot at, shoot if you are threatened. Make sure you get a positive ID. The S-2, the intel that we got, says there are unfriendlies. No shit, right? Sergeant Phelps will brief the ROEs and EOFs. All that being said, it is a free-fire zone, meaning, if you feel yourself threatened, do not hesitate."

Peoria is in the first vehicle, sitting on the hard metal seat behind the driver. Yelks is driving; Salvador stands on the .50 caliber machine gun; the lieutenant sits shotgun. The engine starts, the trucks roll off, kicking up dust.

The invasion is under way.

At the border, over the radio, the lieutenant announces, as hundreds of others did, "Welcome to Iraq." He smiles as he turns to Peoria, marking the time.

Two-thirty p.m., March 19, the year of our lord 2003.

The Humvees follow a main highway for a few hours.

There is dust, hundreds of vehicles, armored machines, loaded up, snaked out, rolling, churning a magnificent storm, choking, eye-irritating. Brown dust, and of course the dust is brown, brown dust hit by light particles, particles of sand and light, and the sun is rising up, the sun rising up in the east, and the dust becomes less brown and the dust becomes a big vocabulary word: *translucent*.

A road sign: BABYLON, 312 KM.

And over the radio, the redneck from Arkansas, who is also a Baptist, who also studies the Bible and knows it by heart, starts to recite:

"Thus saith the Lord, Behold I will rise up against Babylon, and against them that dwell in the midst of them that rise up against me, a destroying wind, And will send unto Babylon fanners that shall fan her and shall empty her land, for in the day of trouble they shall be against her round about and spare ye not her young men, destroy ye utterly all her host. . . . I will bring them down like lambs to the slaughter, like rams with he goats. Her cities are a desolation, a dry land, and a wilderness, a land wherein no man dwell, neither doth any son of man pass nearby. And thou shalt say, Thus shall Babylon sink, and shall not rise from the evil that I will bring upon her: and they shall be weary. Thus far are the words of Jeremiah."

A.E. Peoria is taking notes, thinking he needs to check that passage, or have someone in New York check it for accuracy. He doesn't want to interrupt the poetic moment by asking an intrusive journalist a question, but he does.

"That's, uh, Old Testament?" Peoria says over the net.

The redneck doesn't answer directly.

"And he cried mightily with a strong voice saying, Babylon the great is fallen, and is become the habitation of devils, and the hold of every foul spirit, and a cage of every unclean and hateful bird . . . And the light of the candle shall shine no more, and in her was found the blood of the prophets, and of saints, and of all that were slain upon the earth."

The Humvees are so enveloped in the dust that they can keep an eye only on the vehicle in front of them, staying a safe three hundred feet apart.

"He's fucking playing you, sir. Redneck can't even do a fucking briefing and he's saying he can say all that from the Bible by memory," says Yelks. "He's reading that fucking Bible of his, I bet."

The dust clears.

The lieutenant's five-Humvee reconnaissance convoy has put enough distance between itself and the main route of hundreds of vehicles that Peoria can now see clearly, and what he sees is shocking. He sees blue sky, an overwhelming blue above the desert.

He has a strange tingling sensation and a sentence goes through his head that takes him a second to place.

"Beware of blue skies and open horizons."

And A.E. Peoria remembers 9/11. 9/11 was a blue-sky day. In New York, he grabbed his notebook and jumped in a taxi and went down there to Chambers Street, and he stood next to a woman, a stranger, who had grabbed his arm as the two of them watched dark figures, one after the other, jump, fall, and the woman saying, Oh my god, oh my god. The woman gripped his arm tightly, but he didn't notice or didn't say anything, because he felt like he should be feeling pain. A terrifying rumble. Let's go, let's go, and that's when he started to run through the canyons of Lower Manhattan, and the dust was coming, the dust was coming. A man in a coffee shop kept the door open and yelled, "Get in here, get in here!" Everything was dark for forty-three seconds. Car alarms and coughing. Light came back in. He saw fingernail marks on his arm, deep cuts. He looked around for the woman, but the woman was gone.

Pearl Harbor, Hawaii, December 7. A passage from *From Here to Eternity*, something about the skies not showing any hint of clouds over the Pacific, clear blue.

He recalls an eyewitness at Nagasaki. A clear day. The city was the second choice—the first, Kokura, was covered in clouds. The bomber commander said he headed toward the blue skies. You could drop the atomic bomb only on a day that had excellent visibility.

Exterminate all the brutes, he thinks, remembering his Conrad. Exterminate all rational thought, he thinks, remembering his Burroughs. And between those two lines written sixty years apart, you have the entire canon of Western liter . . .

Dozing off.

Awake again.

Wake up, wake up, Peoria thinks, though nothing is happening. Here he is, in war, on the frontline of history, and there is just the dull engine noise that puts him to sleep, the helmet on his head, the body armor, the heat.

His senses are heightened and he looks around and the air seems much clearer, and he feels there should be ringing in his ears, an acute ringing in his ears, all the alarm bells in his mind, his senses overloading, like one of those hearing tests, an invisible high-pitched sound, as the truck bumps up and down. He has his helmet on; he has his body armor; the standard blue issue with the word PRESS across the front; he has his digital recorder, which he fumbles with as he forces himself to take notes and he feels so clumsy. There he is in war, fussing around in the backseat, with his seat belt, with his sunglasses, with his tape player, with a pen—why doesn't his pen work? The ink is not coming out of his pen, and he scribbles, and scribbles again, finally sticking the dead pen in his pocket and fishing out a new pen from his black shoulder bag—his larger backpack with his equipment is in the trunk of the Humvee. His shoulder bag, which has his satellite phone, computer, and extra pens, is at his feet. He finds another ballpoint, hits the record button, and writes down, "Welcome to Iraq, two-thirty pm, march 19, the year of our lord—" He realizes he has taken only a few notes since the invasion started, he didn't keep up with his system, he is far behind. He looks out the window and he sees dead cars and a dead tank from the previous war, and he sees shitty little mud huts with threadlike power lines, and he notes more road signs—BAGHDAD 400 KM, NAJAF 220—and tunes out the voices over the radio. He thinks to himself, Man, I am glad I'm not leading this convoy. I am glad all I have to do is watch. I am already disoriented. I have no idea where I am. I'm just along for the ride, and then he looks at his watch. Five hours have passed.

It is almost dark.

He feels something nudge his shoulder.

"Sir, excuse me, sir?"

It is Salvador, tapping him with his boot from his position in the machine-gunner slot.

"Sir, could you pass me a Mountain Dew? The cooler's behind you."

He looks up at Salvador, taking a few seconds to shake off the sleep. So he has been sleeping again. Dozed off in the back of the Humvee. It is hot, for sure, and with the weight of the helmet on his head, and the fact he's been awake for, like, twenty hours, it all keeps putting him to sleep, sleeping right through the story.

"Yeah, no problem."

He unstraps himself, turning in his seat to open the metal panel that divides the backseat from the trunk. He puts his notebook and tape recorder down on the floor. He uses both hands to pull it open. There is a red cooler in the back, the kind at every Fourth of July picnic. The ice hasn't melted yet, and he plunges his hand in, bobbing past water bottles and searching for a soda can.

"I think we're lost, sir."

It isn't Salvador speaking, but Yelks, to the lieutenant.

"This fucking GPS is shit."

Peoria doesn't know if he's heard correctly—he's not too concerned, after all, these guys are professionals. He feels the soda can. He succeeds in the small task of finding it, and is proud how quickly he did—prying open the sliding metal door to the trunk, having to find the right bolt to pull. The small satisfaction of accomplishing a simple physical action. He takes the soda can out of the cooler.

"Salvador, here you go."

Peoria doesn't get an answer.

The war is no longer silent.

"Engage, engage, engage," the lieutenant yells.

The machine-gun fire opens up three feet above his head. He sees the tracers flash, slanting down from the side window. There is a loud crash and a scream. He is thrown against the front seat, and because he is facing the wrong way, he feels the back of his helmet knock heads with Yelks, the driver. He is facing backward. The Humvee, he notices, is no longer moving. The other new sound is spinning tires in dirt.

Then the *ping*s start.

PING, PING, PING.

"That's fucking incoming. That's fucking incoming."

Scrunched up on the floor of the backseat, Peoria looks around for his tape recorder and notepad. They are somewhere on the floor. He finds the can of Mountain Dew. Where the fuck are they? *WHOOSH.* The Mountain Dew explodes; there is wet stickiness all over his hand.

Oh shit, hunh. So this is what combat is like.

He realizes the lieutenant has opened the front door, sticking his M-16 out. He is firing, and saying, "Yelks, you okay, man? Yelks, you okay?"

Peoria finds his notepad. Next to it is his tape recorder. He fumbles with it, pressing Play, then Stop, and then finally hitting Record in time to hear the lieutenant scream to Salvador, "Yelks is hit. Keep firing. I'm going to drive."

Peoria watches the lieutenant get out of the Humvee. He sees him run around the front, the truck's headlights lighting him up before he suddenly falls out of view and on the ground, the bullets passing through his body and shattering the windshield of the Humvee.

That is when he hears the first shriek. It is not human: it is the shrieking of explosives, in a shell, dropping down from the sky and dangerously close to the truck. Again, he is surprised about how accurate the movies really are in terms of sound effects. There is another shriek, and another. Peoria judges the situation, he assumes, rationally. He has heard that the Iraqis have poor aim, yet he senses that whoever is flinging those mortars his way knows what they are doing. It feels to him like he should get out of the Humvee. The engine has gone silent, but the headlights for some reason are on. They were supposed to tell him what to do if something like this happened, but no one is telling him what to do. He senses too, and then sees, that Yelks is dead, and he hasn't heard anything in a few seconds from the lieutenant either.

Then Salvador's machine gun stops, and the Puerto Rican is inside the truck, very close to his face, and telling him they have to get out, they have to get out of the Humvee now.

"Push in, then pull the handle, push in, then pull it toward you."

Peoria stuffs his tape recorder in his pocket with his notepad, and keeps trying the door, but it isn't budging, not giving as easily as the sliding metal one he had successfully opened to access the cooler.

"It's not working."

The Puerto Rican leans over him, the muzzle of his rifle hitting Peoria in the mouth, cutting his lip. He yanks on the door handle and pushes it open, almost falling out of the truck.

"Sir, we have to move, we have to move, come on."

There is another shriek. Peoria is outside, on his feet and running, or he is following, quickly following Salvador, down an embankment of pebbles and sand, moving through what feels like bushes, away from the road, and the next shriek he hears—he is losing track of how far he has run—seems far away, and the firing also seems distant. It is quiet again, until all he can hear is swearing in Spanish.

"Hey, hey, Salvador, where are we, man?"

"Shut up, shut up. We'll stop here."

There is no moon, or any stars. What happened to the blue sky at night? The two men are lying next to each other. Salvador is aiming his rifle in the direction they came from. Peoria looks at the Puerto Rican closely and sees that something is a little off. He isn't lying on his belly in the normal prone position, but off to one side.

"Where did the other guys go?" Peoria whispers.

"What?"

"The other Humvees. Where did they go?"

"They're gone, they're gone. You didn't see them? They kept driving."

"What?"

"Shit . . ."

Salvador has dropped his rifle, is clasping his hand across his belly.

More shooting starts. Peoria thinks the bullets are coming toward him. He finds it funny that his life actually does flash before his eyes. As if there is a chemical in the blood that is released only at certain moments in life, an endorphin with the flashback function. He sees things, collapsed, in seconds. Toddler. Graduation. Cambodia. Chambers Street. Dad and Mom.

He doesn't understand why they are shooting at him. He wants to stand up. He feels this urge to stand up and explain himself. He wants to tell them to stop shooting. You've got the wrong guy. There's no need to shoot at me. This is silly, you trying to shoot at me. This powerful urge to stand up and explain to the attackers that this must all have been some gigantic, enormous misunderstanding to have brought us to this point in time. It is counterintuitive—self-preservation would suggest hiding, but then why the desire to ask them to stop, to give up, to surrender?

But he sees Salvador lying there, and he knows that he can't stand up. If I stand up, he thinks, they will shoot me. So I must not stand up. I must stay here, down, hidden, and hope that they will go away.

Five minutes? Ten minutes?

No more shooting.

"The flashlight, get the flashlight. It's in my pocket, on my jacket."

Peoria inches closer to the Puerto Rican, placing his hand on his chest. He can feel his heart beating fast and is comforted by how warm the body feels. He touches a hard, round piece of metal through the cloth of the shirt. He unbuttons the pocket and pulls out the flashlight. Salvador makes a gurgling sound and wheezes.

"Sir, man, sir. I think I'm bleeding. I think I'm hit."

Peoria flicks the flashlight on, making sure to aim it down. A coffee-stained circle appears on the Puerto Rican's chest. As he moves the circle lower, the beam becomes darker. The beam lights up the top of a stain on the tan, desert camouflage uniform, right above the belly button. The beam follows the stain, which gets bigger, and he stops on the belt buckle. He doesn't want to look farther down. He knows it is blood. He knows there is a lot of blood.

"Sir, what's wrong, am I hit?"

Peoria nods.

The flashlight is now on Salvador's groin. The buttons on the pants are wet, and he catches the sight of flesh. It looks disfigured. He frowns. He starts to undo the buttons on the pants. Salvador groans.

"Oh god, not there."

"I need to administer, uuh, first aid."

Peoria's mind goes through the procedures he'd studied. He remembers the class he took in Virginia. An Australian special forces instructor, six-foot-four with a blond crew cut, saying: First, make sure there is no danger. Yell, "Clear." All clear, Peoria says to himself. Second, do a sweep of the body to make sure there are no other wounds and to find out where the bleeding is from. Peoria figures he's already done that. In his mind, he sees the instructor's PowerPoint presentation flip to the third slide—something about a tourniquet.

The fourth slide has a picture with it—a picture that was jarring at the time, as it was shown in such a clean and peaceful conference room, usually reserved for marketing presentations, and learning about war in that environment did feel a little odd. But that fourth PowerPoint slide and the Australian accent are coming back to him now, as big letters, big letters that say STOP THE BLEEDING. How do you do this, mate? You apply pressure. Does he have his first-aid kit? No, of course not—it's back in the truck. Salvador doesn't have one on him either.

The facts come to his head: Most deaths are from massive trauma and blood loss. With no bandages, he needs something else, anything. Perhaps his shirt. Okay, my shirt. He undoes his helmet, and unvelcros his body armor, slips off the North Face parka he's been wearing, and then the sixth slide pops into his head—don't let your patient lose consciousness.

"Hey, hey, Salvador, are you awake? Stay with me, man, stay with me."

"I'm with you, am I okay?"

"Yeah, I think so. You're bleeding and a little fucked-up, but you're okay, sure."

"What do you mean, I'm 'a little fucked-up'?"

Fuck. Peoria wishes there had been a seventh or an eighth slide that told him, When patients ask for their condition, lie. Tell them they are fine. Perhaps they figured that was common sense, and therefore unnecessary to teach, but if there was one thing Peoria had been told over and over again, it was that he lacked common sense.

"You're fine, you're fine. There's no bleeding. There is bleeding, but it's not bad. I think I've seen worse. I haven't, but I've seen worse on TV. Me, personally, I haven't seen worse. I'm taking my shirt off. It's clean, and I don't have any other bandages. It's not clean, actually,

I sweated like a bitch today. But once I get my shirt off and on you, I'm going to press it against your crotch and . . ."

"My crotch? My crotch? Is it gone?"

"I don't know. I haven't checked. I'm not a doctor, so I better leave it for them to check that. I'm just going to stop the bleeding. It's slide number four, you know. I learned all that from my first-aid class at the security training course in Virginia. That was a good time. There's a girl in the class who was really hot, you know. Fuck, I should really email her."

Peoria takes off his undershirt, and with both hands, presses it up against Salvador's crotch. He holds it there with both hands. He has to keep him awake. He has to talk to him. Peoria starts to talk.

"I'm thirty-four years old, and what do I really have to show for it, you know? I have a bunch of magazine articles to my name. I've been on TV a few times. I guess I've had some cool experiences, the kind no one else has had, or very few, but when you think about it, so what? So what that I've done things other people haven't. What does that really mean in the end? I haven't been able to write a best-seller, you know, and that's depressing, because I see so much that gets published that really is shit, and I'm like, Fuck, I could write shit like that. Really . . . I can't really believe this is fucking happening to me, you know? Here, you hold on to the T-shirt, just hold it tight against you."

Peoria searches his pockets. He freezes for a second—is his wallet there? Did I lose my fucking wallet? And then he goes anxiously through a checklist, out of instinct. Wallet, keys, gum, cigarettes. He checks his pockets to make sure of all his possessions. Wallet, keys, gum, cigarettes. Laptop, the laptop is gone. Recorder and notepad, okay. He takes out his wallet and finds a picture—six orgasms he had given this girl in one night—and he stares hard at the picture and asks himself, Is this it, is this her? It depresses him to think he could die in the desert with some mediocre girl as his love, a third-tier girl. He'd dated in New York for years, and he'd gone from relationship to relationship, some lasting six months, a couple lasting a year or more, and he didn't much see his family, and he didn't really have anything. He had his career, and that was about it; he'd spent the last ten years on his career, in the office, at work, all the time, and here he was going to die at work, on the job, for his career. Not even a country. To die for a 401(k) and health insurance and a vague idea of success. He could feel the spleen, a fucking mediocre career too, not like his bosses—not like fucking Nishant Patel and Sanders Berman—some of his bosses were legitimate media superstars. He remembers once, when he was on an assignment in Richmond, Virginia, doing a pro-file of a NASCAR driver, and he was sitting in the airport and watch-ing CNN when Nishant Patel was being fawned over by a fake-blonde anchor with nice tits, who was just pretty enough and had something a little off-kilter about her mouth, which made her unique enough to be on TV. He realized in Richmond that he had so far to go, and wondered if he'd ever even get there. Richmond itself, a third-tier city, and he was shocked when he saw people in Richmond go to work—as a New Yorker, he had forgotten there were other cities put there on Earth to live in, and he saw a guy with a suit and tie head to a glass skyscraper and realized there were other lives he could lead. It didn't have to be in the Big Apple, Gotham, formerly New Amster-dam. Of course he didn't do anything about it; he did not make any big career change or life choices. He went back to New York on the 727, back to the office, back to the dimpled plastic sheets hanging over his head, shining that hard yellow light, convincing himself he loved his job. Who could ask for a better job? His investment banker and lawyer friends all hated their jobs. (Actually, does he really know any investment banker friends, or is he just choosing that profession as an East Coast resident chooses the town of Boise, Idaho, or his namesake, Peoria, Illinois, to score an easy point about the cultural backwardness of certain states?) I get paid to have new experiences, to do things no one else has done, and I get to do it for, like, two weeks, or a few hours, and I never have to get stuck with the grind of doing the same thing over and over again. It all became the same thing, it all was a grind, this whole life thing, the steady nasal drip of paychecks and bills and late nights and dinner dates that depressed him.

Peoria doesn't know if he has been saying these things out loud or just to himself, and he continues talking to Salvador.

"What the fuck . . . I think I'm depressed a lot of the time. I was going to show you a picture, but really, it's not even worth it."

It is getting cold. Another factoid from his security training class pops into his mind: People freeze to death in the desert. Despite the popular myths of deserts as sweltering death traps, they are just as likely to transform, once the sun sets, into freezing death traps, with temperatures dropping to near zero Celsius in the middle of the night. And now he doesn't have his shirt on, though he did put his parka back on. That brings another first-aid fact back to his mind: He needs to keep Salvador's body temperature up. He moves in closer to him, putting his hands over Salvador's hands to apply more pressure to the wound.

"Yes, yes," Salvador says.

He has never been in this position before, spooning with a dude whose balls were blown off, but he figures his best bet is to wait. He starts talking again.

"This is a little awkward, right, but it's best because we need to keep warm. We really do. I'm not gay. I don't have a problem with that or anything. I guess you would, because the Army does really have a problem with it, but I don't. My father's gay. So is my mother. Pretty fucked-up, right? I never really understood it. Freaked me out. I was twelve and I remember thinking, Does this mean my father wants to fuck me?"

Peoria goes on talking through the night. The bleeding appears to stop, though he is certain at times that Salvador is going to die.

14.

Wednesday, March 19, 2003

The countdown clock is running on the cable news stations, ticking away in the bottom right-hand corner of the screen, synced to President George W. Bush's final ultimatum to Saddam Hussein.

What's the ultimatum?

To hand over weapons of mass destruction. No one believes that Saddam is going to do that. Nobody wants him to do it either. It's too late in the narrative for anyone to back out now.

Back home after a long day, an exciting day at the office.

I can't sleep.

I don't want to sleep.

I have my television set on.

I have ordered *Double Penetration Sluts #4* on the Time Warner Adult Video on Demand. A twenty-four-hour rental. Channel 304.

From channel 304, I punch in the number for CNN, channel 35.

Then I hit the Last button on my remote control, so I can bounce back and forth between my two choices.

Stop, fast-forward the digital television, rewind, see it again.

I'm hammering away, touching myself, and it's onto the next scene. Waiting for the right moment. It used to be easier, but I've developed a strong resistance to pornography. As a young teen, the pages of a *Penthouse* were enough. Then old VHS cassettes, Internet, DVDs, Adult Video on Demand.

The bar for my porn watching keeps going higher. Rewind again. The man shooting his jizz in the faces of Ying and Yang doesn't do it tonight. The gaping holes don't do it. Fast-forward. Maybe the next scene with Gauge will. Gauge is dressed to look like a fourteen-year-old girl. She's earns her living the hard way—it's not fair to say just on her back, but with all different parts of her body flattened against floors, walls, designer chairs, soiled mattresses, leather couches, bent and acrobatic, ass pointed to the air, the weight of her body on her neck, knees somehow stretched backward behind her ears. I read on the Internet that she does five scenes a week in a good week.

I am waiting for what is making me come lately.

Ass to mouth—shorthand: ATM.

I watch the man, whose hair could have been styled in 1991 and never been changed, take his penis from her ass and then grab her by the waist to twist her face toward his cock. I wait for the moment when he puts his cock in her mouth, the moment of entry.

It doesn't happen. There's a jump cut.

I'm pissed. That is no good at all. I need to see the full-body motion, I need to see the uninterrupted movement from ass to mouth because I am savvy enough, my penis is savvy enough, to know that if there is a jump cut, then things could have been done, organs cleaned, wiped off, made more sanitary; my brain is trained to sense these kinds of illusions, to sense when it's not real enough—when it's too clean.

I am disappointed. I should never have trusted Time Warner Cable. They've given a nod to some kind of strange decency regulations. Is it a legal thing? Why did they edit it out? Who sets these standards? Who sat around the table, saying gaping assholes okay, assholes to mouth not okay? What does that look like in legal language? Was there a board meeting? "Non-explicit or internal visualizations of sex organs."

TWC isn't going to give me what I want to see, exactly, but I already have been charged $14.95, so I am forced to make do. I am forced to make do with the fact that I will have to settle for *representation* of ass to mouth. I will have to imagine what happened in the edit myself.

Fast-forward. Gauge is kneeling and spitting and the man's hand is on his penis, a point-of-view shot, and he ejaculates in her face. I shoot too.

Ahhhhhhhhhhhhhhhhhhhhhhhhhhhhhhh.

Okay.

I hit the Last button and jump back to a CNN correspondent with the 1st Armored Division.

The correspondent has positioned himself on a road to somewhere, and the trucks are rolling by him.

I reflect. I know I am being somewhat self-conscious. I know I am somehow, in some inexplicable way, being ironic. But I am not being ironic. This is just what life is for me. What else am I going to do when sitting in front of a TV alone? Jerk off. And if my country is going to war, I'm going to watch my country go to war.

More channels. Anchors shouting about how wonderful the technology is, allowing them to stream live video while they are riding with the troops. Allowing us to see correspondents with satellite phones in Kurdistan, waiting with exiled groups. Allowing us to see inside the Bradleys. The live images of Baghdad getting bombed.

I'm tired now, so the only fighting I get that first night is a British journalist getting shot at with Americans behind a berm.

I jerk off three more times.

I watch the maps of Iraq and the columns of soldiers and I think I'm really missing out on this. I really should be over there. Maybe I'll go over there sometime. My eyes close, and I wonder how A.E. Peoria is doing.

15.

Thursday, March 20, 2003

Next morning, in the office.

My computer takes the required few minutes to load up. Iced coffee on the table, eating a croissant. Happy to be back in the office. Happy to be sitting there at the center of things in the newsroom of a major news organization while history shits itself around me.

Gary is there and he comes up to my desk.

"Have you heard the news?" Gary whispers.

"What?"

"Peoria is missing. The convoy he was with got attacked. They found his phone, and there was blood all around it. They hit Redial and got Dave at the news desk."

"No shit, oh my god. Fuck."

"Henry has called his parents. I mean, it doesn't look good."

"Fuck, wow, I can't believe that."

A wave of seriousness passes over me. It's not ironic at all. My friend and colleague A.E. Peoria is presumed dead.

But he isn't that good of a friend. I don't really know him that well.

I'm excited by the possibility that the war is real and that I have a connection to it. I have an anecdote that I can retell. I do.

"Did you hear the news? Peoria is missing. Yeah, apparently his convoy was attacked, found his phone in blood. I can't believe it either . . ."

16.

Friday, March 21, 2003

The sun comes up around five-thirty in the morning. There is an emptiness in the desert, a silence, a chill. It is at this time, though Peoria doesn't know it, that another convoy reaches the scene of the attack, finds Peoria's satellite phone and hits Redial.

Peoria is feeling a new level of all-time discomfort. An ache in the muscles, hugging himself, rubbing as fast as he can, desperate for friction and heat. Hugging himself with the strength he has never hugged another human being with. He feels damp, though he finds this hard to believe. How is he feeling damp when the temperature on the previous day had reached 90 degrees Fahrenheit? A dry heat, a very hot dry heat, but the chill has gotten so bad that it brings a feeling of cold moisture. Eyes half open, thoughts trailing, head on Salvador's knee, begging for the sun to return to its full power. Rolling over, out of the shadow of the berm he has been hiding behind and into a rectangle of sunlight, sunlight still weak, still not hot enough, the sunlight that's promise of warmth is still an hour or two or three away.

Peoria feels he should be more afraid. A dying man by his side, but he is pleasantly surprised that he has reached that point beyond fear.

That point that those on shipwrecked lifeboats feel hours before they start to poison themselves with saltwater.

A.E. Peoria doesn't care anymore if he lives or dies and he doesn't care anymore if Salvador lives or dies and there is a relief, a letting go. He feels he has found at the bottom of this berm that Zen place he has had such difficulty finding anywhere else, where fatigue and spent adrenaline and hunger and no cigarettes or caffeine have left him. The second, third, and fourth winds have blown in and blown away, and he isn't looking for the fifth wind to stand him upright. He's enjoying this bliss, and he keeps tapping his foot, tapping and tapping and looking up for the sun to start doing its daily life-killing damage on the landscape, tapping and tapping, and he thinks, Maybe this is the first sign of post-traumatic stress disorder, this constant tapping, and then he thinks, Oh boy, my lips are really dry, and he wishes he had his ChapStick, and despite his best efforts, that sixth or seventh wind is creeping up—that nagging for survival and living and action is creeping back into his bloodstream.

How he wishes he had his fucking ChapStick.

The Zen is going away. His brain is getting activated, as if by solar power, his brain and neuroses and anxieties are beginning all over again.

At around seven a.m., Peoria decides to assess the situation—these are the words in his head, "The situation needs assessing." He asks Salvador if he can walk. Salvador doesn't answer. Salvador is pale. His light brown skin is lighter. He is in a small dip in the ground in the desert. Peoria hasn't stood up since diving to the ground nine hours ago. He stands. He can see a long line of American vehicles. Then he understands that it is the noise of engines, that dull rumbling, that must have triggered him to stand, sensing vibrations in the air like a dog.

He looks down at the Puerto Rican and tells him to stay right there, and Peoria starts to run, waving his arms.

As he gets closer, he sees there are three men with rifles aimed at him. He puts his hands up.

"Don't shoot, I'm an American, I'm an American! I'm with the press!"

A soldier jogs out to him.

"What the fuck are you doing here?"

"We were attacked. There's a guy with me. He's bleeding bad. Chipotle."

The soldier yells back to another soldier, that soldier yells to someone else, the chain of command at work. Peoria points to where Chipotle is lying; he leads a squad to get him and helps as they put Salvador on a stretcher and carry him to what Peoria can now see is a tank. He jogs at Salvador's side, saying, "You'll make it, man, you'll make it."

The Puerto Rican's eyes flutter open. He sees Peoria and tries to say something. Nothing comes out, but later, when he thinks about it, Peoria is sure the words he mouthed were "Mountain Dew."

Peoria has a blanket around him and his laptop has appeared by his side. He is in the cocoon of a tank. He's been picked up and he gets handed things. Food, water, blanket, and his laptop bag reappears. How did it get to him, all these things happening? He is handed a phone, and he knows he needs to make the call back to *The Magazine* and tell them what happened. How information is getting conveyed to him and how he is conveying information back is a mystery, but he remembers that he should be doing his job.

He starts taking notes. He only gets two words down before a soldier leads him outside the tank. Another soldier, an officer, walks up to him, carrying his satellite phone.

"It's for you, sir."

Jerry is on the line.

"You okay? Fuck! Tell me what happened. We'll write it from here, just give me the details."

Peoria looks at his notebook and sees it isn't much help. Three pages, a few words a page, written as if he had been holding his pen with a fist. He starts talking, from the unit he was with to the ambush to the night in the desert and his girlfriend with six orgasms and how he wanted to stand up and say, Stop shooting at me, stop shooting at me. What the sound of a rifle fired sounded like and hitting the vehicle sounded like, *ping, ping, ping,* and Jerry keeps saying, My god, it's good you're alive, go on, my god it's good you're alive, go on. . . . Until he gets to the last act. The rescue, the chill of the morning, running with the stretcher, looking into Salvador's eyes, when the beep of a low battery starts on the satellite phone.

"What did Salvador say to you?" Jerry asks.

"He said—"

A crackle over the line.

"Mountain Dew."

"What? 'Saved you'?"

Peoria looks at the two words on his notepad.

Mountain Dew.

"Saved you?"

"Not him, me. He said, 'Mountain Dew.'"

Distance, six thousand miles, satellite interference.

"On the stretcher?"

The satellite phone dies.

The new convoy Peoria is with has to keep moving, so he can't make another call. He doesn't know that his story is going to be mentioned on the cover.

The headline is "You Saved Me."

PART IV

After the Invasion

17.

August 2003

To get the can of yellow spray paint, A.E. Peoria steps over the sleeping bodies of the bellhop and two other waiters passed out on the thin foam mats and wrapped in threaded blankets on the concrete floor in the Hamra Hotel's supply closet. Spray paint is a red-hot commodity in Baghdad, sales off the charts. The owner of the Hamra, Mr. Al Mansour, had been bragging that he'd bought ten cans just this morning and stashed them away for potential resale.

The collapse of Saddam's regime has brought a flood of new products to Iraq that people couldn't get before: satellite television dishes, air conditioners, extra-large flavored condoms, gumballs, new Toyotas, genetically modified nectarines from the European Union, premium whiskey, Turkish beer, and yes, spray paint—there had never been cans of spray paint in Iraq before, something to do with United Nations sanctions. All the paint in Saddam's regime had been in tin aluminum buckets that required a brush. But a shipment of spray paint had come in at the market, a few truckloads driven up from Dubai, and the stocks cleared out within hours, more truckloads ordered up.

Spray paint, A.E. Peoria has observed, was catching on like mobile phones in East Africa, the push-button aerosol technology a new blessing on the land.

The Iraqis were trying out these cans of wonder with gusto. An Aladdin's lamp of a free society: shake it, push, puff, and forty wishes of free expression granted before the hiss of an empty bottle.

In Iran, after the fall of the shah in 1979, there was an old man who made his living walking around the streets pulling down statues of the shah, with a simple noose and rope pulley device, reimbursed by the new fundamentalist government per statue. In Iraq there had been some highly publicized toppling of statues, some nice TV moments, but the real symbolism of the new era had been found in the cans of spray paint that had infiltrated Baghdad. Slogans spray-painted everywhere, showing the world that Iraq was still a literate cradle of civilization, the premier spot for poets and artists and love-sick songstresses in the Arab world, the first signs of a new age of legal vandalism and graffiti and contemporary writings. Messages, taunts, haikus, circles, squares, penises, threats, cubes spray-painted across the city in all colors—yellow, black, purple, green, blue, red—a rainbow of spray paint on the sagging corners of wounded buildings, on the stone exteriors of government offices stripped bare of copper wiring and paper products and Apple IIe computers, on the strikingly white pillars of Saddam's now abandoned ninety-seven palaces, on road signs crossing out the name Saddam with the Arabic word for "free," *ahrar*, and on the newest feature of the city, the concrete blast walls, two tons of concrete each, eight feet by ten feet, a perfect canvas for the country's new identity.

The ten cans of spray paint, as bragged about by Mr. Mansour, are there, and Peoria grabs one, jumps back over the sleeping bodies, and heads back out to the pool.

Over the past five months, the pool at the Hamra Hotel has become the central meeting place for American and British journalists, and the home of *The Magazine*'s bureau. A.E. Peoria helped set up the bureau on the third floor, a deluxe suite, converted into a place of business, with a kitchen, desks, phone lines, running water, rent of three grand a week, and bad room service. Mr. Al Mansour was making up for lost profits after thirteen years of those same sanctions that kept the country spray paint–free.

It is A.E. Peoria's last night in Baghdad. A drive across the desert to Amman the next morning, then a flight to Bangkok, and he is letting loose. What a five months it has been. A real learning experience.

He barrels out onto the patio, poolside. He starts shaking the can. The party is in full swing.

There is a tray of kebabs, a feast of hummus and chopped cucumbers and eggplants and tomatoes, there is a platter of grilled fish, *masgouf*, the Iraqi delicacy. He sees his translator, Ahmed, grabbing a plate.

"Ahmed, my haji, come here, man, I'm leaving tomorrow, we need to talk before I go."

He grabs Ahmed by the shoulder and guides him over to a white suntanning chair under the glow of a tiki torch. Ahmed sits down, and so does Peoria.

"Have you tried the *masgouf*," Ahmed says.

"You know, I have to say, Ahmed, there's a fucking reason you don't see Iraqi restaurants anywhere, you know what I mean? Thai restaurants, Lebanese, even fucking Tibetan, Indian, Nepalese, every kind of cuisine in the world is in almost every big city, there's all these kinds of restaurants, you know? But there's not any Iraqi restaurants anywhere. I think that says something, man. You can't blame that shit on the sanctions. How many times can you have fucking boiled and grilled chicken and fucking cubes of cucumbers and tomatoes before it's like, shit, enough, let's get some flavor. . . ."

"The *masgouf* is our national dish," Ahmed says. "Saddam's favorite . . ."

"Would you think I would eat a fish caught in that fucking river? A fish from the Euphrates?"

"The Tigris."

"It is the Tigris, man. I have to thank you for correcting me, because without you I wouldn't know shit about this country. There's a new regulation that Americans aren't even allowed to swim in that river."

"It is not a problem."

"No, it is a problem. Don't give me that 'It's not a problem' shit. I'm leaving tomorrow, Ahmed, I'm leaving tomorrow and I need to know what you really think. We can drop the 'I'm your boss, thing,' you know we're friends. You've told me everything, bro, every fucking thing. Can you believe it, I didn't even know what a Sunni or Shia was—or I guess I did know it because, you know, I'd done the reading—but not what it really meant, you know? Like a fucking Catholic versus a Protestant a few hundred years ago, or maybe ten years ago if you're talking Northern Ireland."

"I don't even think your president knew the difference," says Ahmed.

"Isn't that the problem," says Peoria. "Look what's happening. You can't feel good about it, can you?"

"Feel good?"

Peoria knows that Ahmed doesn't feel good about it, because Peoria doesn't feel good about it, and Peoria is partially relying on Ahmed to get that feeling. Ahmed's unease is understandable: he was a translator in Saddam's Ministry of Information. He is a Sunni, from a prominent Sunni tribe, the Dulaimi. One of the other correspondents at *The Magazine* first met Ahmed while he was an official minder on the journalist's visit during Saddam's regime. He'd been assigned, up until the bombing, to keep watch on the journalists, and translate. After the bombs started, the journalist told Ahmed he could have a job working for *The Magazine*, now that his old job had been wiped out by the war.

Peoria doesn't feel good about the war because he feels fear all the time now. After he'd spent the night in the desert, darkness started to creep into his mind. A real darkness, because for the first time in his life, he'd actually experienced a trauma. A bona fide trauma. A life-or-death trauma, not the garden-variety American trauma of parents getting divorced, or deciding what graduate program to apply to, or as in his case, the more unique but still peculiarly American trauma of having two gay parents coming out.

Over the past five months, when self-assessing his own life and how that life shaped the person he was, those two events—what happened in the desert and his parents' homosexual revelations and divorce—were the two events that explained how he felt about the world, how he saw the world, what the world meant to him. Things weren't permanent, things could always fall apart, never get too comfortable, and even those you trust, those you trust as authority figures and role models, are liable to show themselves as illusions.

Yes, those two traumas were the first stories, right off the bat, he'd be sure to tell a shrink or a therapist or a psychologist when he got home. He had much experience with mental health professionals—a long list of them, his parents believed in therapy—and he'd always started with the divorce and the coming out to explain how, exactly, he had become the gnomish ambitious person sitting on the chair beside the expert and talking as the hour passed.

Now he had another trauma to add.

The desert, in his personal narrative, had radically altered his life. And though normally, as his compulsive disclosure disorder would dictate, he would spend the time talking about the trauma, ad

nauseam, to whoever happened to be in his vicinity, he realized that
this was a peculiar trauma in that he was very scared to talk about it.
That was what was so unusual: the fear to bring it up. Unprecedented.

He had started to feel a great shame, an introspective sort of shame
that he thought he'd dealt with. How long did it take him to get over
the shame of, as he once heard a less than politically correct guidance
counselor put it, "having two homos" as mom and dad? At least until
he was twenty-three or twenty-two maybe twenty-four. But he still
would talk about it! And what solid ground or semisolid emotional
ground he felt he was on after talking about it. In his narrative, he
was sure the gay divorce would always be the pantheon of trauma,
the starting point of his life—if I survived that, I can survive anything, he would tell himself.

And then he actually—literally, with the reality of dirt—survived
a night in the desert, an attack, an ambush. Seven Americans killed,
he escaped. But how he processed this—how he processed this had
made him pick away at the other scabs in his mind. So he felt shame
(like the divorce), and he felt, on some profound level, that it was all
his fault, like the divorce.

His CDD, usually, would handle this by just talking about what
had happened—but he'd never felt so afraid of talking about anything else, so he didn't want to say a word about it anymore, but in
every conversation, he found himself talking about it, again and again,
getting more afraid each time he told his story, and he couldn't stop.

The desert—that's how he thought about what happened, as "the
desert"—became the new prism upon which he reevaluated everything else that had happened in his life, and more specifically, everything that had happened since he had set foot in Baghdad. It had
colored his views, it had made everything dark, and it had started to
really frustrate him that not everyone could see just how dark things
were, no matter how much he talked.

Peoria then did what he had always done: he threw himself into his work. He focused on the work.

Peoria had arrived in Baghdad with the convoy that rescued him and immediately disembedded from the unit and made his way to the Hamra. His story had made quite a splash—which brought attention to Peoria, an attention that he had once thought he craved but now wondered if it was such a good thing after all. He would be introduced, and the journalist would likely say, "Oh, you are the one who saved that soldier." Peoria would then have to explain that it was an editorial mistake. That no, he hadn't saved anyone, that he didn't have approval over the headline, that he was lucky to be alive and that he in fact was saved, not the other way around, that he had almost given up that night. But this didn't ease any of the suspicions. Journalists, Peoria knew, as a whole, were first and foremost suspicious of each other—especially if it was another's perceived successes, and especially if they had been writing about themselves; it was seen as cheating. Never write about your own problems, write only about the problems of others.

But Peoria started working, setting up the bureau, going out on the streets every day, looking for stories with Ahmed at his side.

Peoria had never experienced a city that had no rule of law. Rule of law had been a vague concept to him, something he didn't think too much about: parking tickets, speeding tickets, open-container laws. Even in Third World countries, where rule of law didn't necessarily live up to legal ideals, there at least were some laws at work, even if they weren't enshrined in a document that the brown-faced citizenry probably couldn't even read, or the white-faced citizenry didn't bother to read and just took for granted.

You could make sense out of corruption to the point where corruption started to make more sense than following the rules of the non-corrupt—why not take a bribe, after all? Playing by the rules means not playing by the rules. But you expected people to stop at traffic signs, or not to, or to drive on the correct side of the road, or not to, or to not just shoot you in the face because you're there, or to shoot you in the face because you're there. Other places had at least been predictably chaotic.

No consistency, though, was the problem in Baghdad, no way to guess the right patterns.

Over the past five months, he could actually feel the rule of law erode, the society's protective membrane disintegrating under the onslaught of a series of complex diseases. The attack on the immune system had sounds and smells to go with it. Symptoms.

In the first week, there was a light ringing in the ears, as if the whole city were on the verge of a stroke. As if the people of Baghdad woke up each day and tried to shake off a blood clot forming in the brain. All around the city, his inner ear would ring with too much blood and his nostrils would pick up an unidentifiable smell that might as well have been burnt toast, the telltale sign of a stroke. (Though not toast in Baghdad: What was the smell? Oil? Gunpowder? Trash? Flaming sewage?) And even walking in a straight line he would feel dizzy, as if he'd been turning around in circles, head spazzing to the right and left, trying to figure out exactly what was happening.

And like a stroke victim who tried to put his condition into words, he felt tongue-tied and slack-jawed and mildly retarded trying to explain what was happening, groans and grunts, indecipherable— "Fucked-up, this is fucked-up"—and this inability to string words together was reflected in his reporting among the general population, quotes from Iraqis that didn't get past three or four words, strung together, and jotted down with his handwriting that resembled a palsy case.

By week two, the medical condition shifted from signs of a stroke to a hypomanic episode. The ringing was still there, but now everyone had too much to say—the Iraqis couldn't tell him everything fast enough, especially those who spoke English, and notebooks filled up, three a day, filled with long passages and monologues. The smells floated in the air, but a man in the throes of mania finds joy even in the scent of wafting dog shit and bitter unchlorinated feces.

He inhaled the smells, absorbed them in his pores along with everyone else in the city, and it didn't seem to matter that the toast was still burning and the city was on fire; hysteria made all of it irrelevant. And, as is true for a small percentage of manic cases, some Iraqis and American soldiers and Western mercenaries turned to violence: rioting, looting, checkpoint killings, criminal acts, rape, and it didn't matter what you were stealing or killing—throwing a ripped mattress on the back of a truck was as good as smashing a priceless vase, ripping off a flat tire the equal of a brick of gold, a book to a crate of milk and cheese, a schoolteacher in a car to a terrorist with a rocket-propelled grenade, an ugly woman to a beautiful teenage starlet—no it didn't matter, as mental illness can give everything perceived the same exaggerated value, worth and worthless indistinguishable. It wasn't about value: it was about letting the mania take hold, allowing the mania to equalize all things considered, with the only solution for the hysteria to wind itself down, exhaustion the only cure.

Following the mania there was a depressive crash. With it came deep and profound questions that had no answers, or answers that could never satisfy. After two months of insomnia, months of only blackout sleep, and not wanting to get out of bed—just a rest, just a timeout from life is what everyone seemed to need. No timeout was coming. Such difficult questions in the morning, in the afternoon, at night. What is going on in life? What's the meaning of all this? Is there someone who can tell me?

And Peoria bopped around the city streets, windows of the car rolled down, no traffic laws still, asking these questions—asking these questions, he thought, on behalf of the Iraqi people and the American people. And the answers he was getting—what were the answers? Uncle Fadil says the answer is that freedom is here, thank you George Bush, goddamn Saddam. Another, when Peoria ran into a funeral procession, answers: What have you done to my family, my life—is this what freedom means, does freedom mean the death of my family? And the Americans, most of the Americans, they had answers, the least satisfying of them all—answers that hinted at such a lack of answers that the only possible response was to hope they were right. They could give you answers, yes, very good at providing answers— the answer is, everything is going great, democracy is going to be established, the rule of law and the new Iraqi government shall be here. Yes, the Americans were sure confident they had the right diagnosis, the right meds, the right brand of therapy and treatment—this is a traumatized country! Thirty years of brutal repression—how do you expect them to behave? Of course there is anger and violence, this is normal, this is expected, but within six months, they'll be on their feet, and we'll all be home by Christmas.

"Do you think," Ahmed says to Peoria, "your country will be home by your Christmas, as your general says?"

"I'm going to be home by Christmas," says Peoria. "Thanksgiving too."

"I've seen movies of your Christmas and Thanksgiving."

"Yeah, there are some good movies about them."

Yes, the American general in charge of American Forces in Iraq said this: we should have the bulk of Americans home by Christmas, and this was reported, and Peoria knew this wasn't an unusual comment for a general to make. Home by Christmas had been promised before. Pope Gregory VIII, setting off the Third Crusade in the twelfth century, issued a papal bull exhorting his allies to war. The bull promised that after a journey to retake Jerusalem, your men will be able to return in two years' time to celebrate the birth of Christ on our land, which will be made so much sweeter, so much sweeter knowing that we have retaken the holy city of Jerusalem and restored its rightful place. Longer travel times, in those days, of course, but getting everyone home for the holidays was a major concern—a concern that Napoleon ignored to his everlasting historical shame when he decided to invade Russia, and when one of his sultry little French advisers said, "Emperor, we might get stuck in the Russian winter, the mud, the cold—why don't we bring clothes for the winter?" And Napoleon didn't believe him. When winter comes, Napoleon wrote, our soldiers will be celebrating Noel in Paris—*Joyeux Noël pour toute la France!*—or the anterooms of Saint Petersburg. In World War I, the Brits promised the war would be done soon enough. Hitler expected a comfortable O Tannenbaum as well. In Korea, after MacArthur turned the tide, just to push the Chinese back over the Yalu River, word was that we'd be out of there by the New Year. In Vietnam, Lyndon Johnson, on tape, after making a massive bowel movement, grunted that he wanted to make sure Robert McNamara understood that no tour of duty should span two Christmases—we can't have them missing two holiday seasons, bad for morale.

The promise of Christmas was given, and it was a promise that the Americans believed, at least temporarily, that they could keep.

Peoria gets up, grabs a chair and drags it along the patio.

"Sit, Ahmed, sit," he says.

Ahmed sits.

"What do you think of this spray paint? Look at this, the stars, the tiki torch, the hummus—you and me? What is it? What do you think it is?"

"Peoria, I remember the day your country was attacked on the September the eleventh. I cheered."

Ahmed laughs, Peoria laughs.

"But I would not have cheered if I knew you would come here. You don't understand these people, these Shiites," Ahmed says. "They are no good, they are Muppets of Iran."

"Puppets?"

"Yes, Muppets of Iran. Saddam knew this. They are worse than the Kurds. We Sunnis, we are better well educated, you see," Ahmed says. "We respected the Shiites, we understood them, we knew they were not well educated. The engineers, the doctors, the lawyers, they are Sunni, not Shiite. But these Shiites, these Muqtada Al-Sadr and the Abdul Aziz and all of them, are not well educated. That is why we did not let them rule Iraq."

"Right, right," Peoria says.

"You see this now, in the government—sixty-five percent of the seats to the Shia? This is another Iranian lie—you Americans say Sunnis are thirty percent?"

"Twenty-four percent."

"Lies, this is not true. Sunnis are the majority and have always been here—how else do you think we have led Iraq?"

"Right, right."

"This is very dangerous, you see," Ahmed says. "Think of the niggers."

"You can't say that word, dude. You have to say 'blacks.'"

"Really? Why not? I have seen it in the *Police Academic* movie."

"Yeah, they can say it in *Police Academy*, but you and I can't say it, you know?"

"Okay. Think of the blacks slaves when your Lincoln let them out of their caves. He did not make them president! He did not make them secretary of defense! He did not put slaves to run your army! Because they still did not have the education. This is like the Shiite."

"I don't know, dude. That sounds like a bit of a stretch."

"You want another example? South Africa! Before the war, I worked with a white man from South Africa, a journalist, and he agreed with me. He said, 'When our government changed, we did not just give all the jobs to the blacks—they needed time, they were not educated, they were not ready.' And he says to me, 'If there is democracy here, if the Americans do come, I agree, you can't just give all of the country to the Shiite. They are not the engineers!'"

The Iraqis, Peoria knew, held engineers in very high esteem. Engineer, a sign of great respect and prestige. He'd never met a people who were so keen on engineering degrees. More engineers per capita than anywhere else, if the Iraqis were to be believed, and really, there wasn't much to show for it—shit still looked like it was falling apart, everywhere, and he didn't think the bombs changed all that much.

Click, click, click, Peoria is shaking the spray paint can with one hand, drinking a beer with the other.

"I need another drink," he says, and leaves Ahmed in his patio chair, and heads over to the bar, three wine buckets filled with ice, half-empty cans of Diet Coke, Arabic lettering and with the European openers—which don't just click and pop, like the American cans do, but peel back, leaving what Peoria thinks is a dangerous metal edge. You could easily cut your lip on the foreign Diet Coke. There are two shot glasses and a bottle of tequila.

"Is this Turkish tequila?"

"Fuck yeah," somebody shouts.

Peoria pours two shots for himself, takes the two shots, gulps them, down, done, finished, refreshing. He keeps shaking the spray paint can, turning it upside down and right side up, the noise like a sprinkler system, upper torso rotating, falling a bit back on his heels.

He sees Christine, a girl he would classify as top tier. Christine works for Sky News and has a British accent. She is blonde and large-breasted and she's right now stripping off her polo shirt to put on a T-shirt that another enterprising soul has made, a T-shirt that says BAGHDAD HOT.

Peoria walks up to Christine.

"Baghdad Hot."

"Peoooorrrrriiiiaaaaa, my hero," she says, and tosses him her polo shirt. "Do you think this fits?"

Peoria takes a step back, his foot resting on the filter for the pool, and grabs the silver tube railing on the pool steps for balance.

Christine's breasts, as Peoria has already noticed, are large. The cotton T-shirt stretches around them.

"Headlights," Peoria says.

"Headlights?"

She looks down.

"You mean my nipples," she says.

"Who made that T-shirt?"

"Crazy Dave the German," she says. Crazy Dave, a German, had driven an RV from Germany to Iraq, crossing at the border point in northern Iraq, and set up his RV like a trailer at a parking lot across the street from the U.S. embassy. He had a line of T-shirts—"Stay Classy Iraq," "I've Been Fucked in Baghdad," "Stuck Between Iraq and a Hard Cock," "Major League Infidel," "I ♥ Sunnis," and other sexually suggestive and culturally charged lines—creating his own little logo of a female by the name of Baghdad Betty. The term "Baghdad Hot" became popular about month four, when the first significant group of female contractors, soldiers, and NGO workers started to show up. If the normal scale for attractiveness in the real world was, say, one to ten, the term "Baghdad hot" meant an additional two or three or four bonus points were added, thanks to the sheer dilemma of the male-to-female ratio. A girl who was, say, a four or a five or maybe a six in Kansas or New York or wherever would become a seven or an eight or a nine in Baghdad. "Do you think I'm Baghdad hot?" Christine says.

"Yeah, I think you're top tier wherever. Didn't you go to fucking Yale?"

Instead of answering, Christine dives into the pool. The shallow end.

She skims the top and pops up.

The splash draws the attention of the other partygoers, thirty or so of them now, all watching Christine break the surface and pull back her hair.

Peoria, with his years of being trained in the art of American safety—always wear a helmet, always wash your hands, always look both ways before crossing the street, always wear a mouthpiece, even in soccer—realizes it is very dangerous, the pool.

The shallow end is five feet deep, the deep end, ten feet deep, but the way the lights bounce off the pool, in the darkness of the tiki torches and the heavy shades of booze, presents an optical illusion of the same depth.

He cringes.

The signs around the pond in New Hampshire that he visited as a kid, the stick figure with a slash through the chest, the long list of rules at the country club. (1) No running. (2) No diving. The statistics he had memorized after reading the story of a local boy in the eerie dive-accident-prone summer of 1986, a total of 757 diving incidents in New York, Massachusetts, New Hampshire, and Connecticut, two or three fatal, the others causing lifelong spinal cord injuries.

These warnings, he knows, are part of his culture, and that culture grabs hold of him.

Holding the spray paint, he steps up to where the water laps against the filter, and he stares at the concrete, water from the pool gathering in small rivulets.

He thinks of two words

NO DIVING.

There is no "No Diving" sign, no warning!

Christine swimming, the crowd getting noisier, louder.

Peoria bends over, arm outstretched, the spray paint can good and shaken.

He starts spraying, in large, yellow, sloppy letters: NO DIVING.

The next few hours: black, image, black, black, image—a face.

The face of Brennan Toddly.

A conversation—no, an altercation.

"I think," says Brennan Toddly, sitting next to Christine, Peoria sitting next to her poolside, "that what you did was disrespectful."

"Christine jumping in?" Peoria says.

"No, you. Your spray-painting. That was a sign of disrespect."

Peoria, yelling, now five months or seven months of what—of anger, of disillusionment, and thinking about the dead Americans and Chipotle without a dick and how cold he was that night in the desert and thinking of those slaughtered goats and donkeys and Iraqis he'd seen on the side of the road on the way into Baghdad, the piles of man shit in the terminals at the newly liberated international airport—is screaming: "Aren't we a little late for that, Brennan, disrespect? You're the motherfucker who said this was going to be a great idea, you're the motherfucker who advocated bombing a city and occupying a country and killing all sorts of fucking people, and you think I'm the one who is being disrespectful? I read your shit, man!"

A salsa bowl spills, a table gets turned over, crashing drinks.

"And why are you talking to her, aren't you married?"

Black, black.

In the bed. Christine without her shirt. Peoria apologizing for some reason.

The next morning.

Peoria dragging a duffel bag into the tight elevator, inhaling a sick breath of Turkish tequila, green and gilled-up and unshaven—*ding*, the elevator door opens—and through the glass doors to the pool.

There are beer bottles and plastic cups filled with cigarettes and spray paint everywhere: no running by the pool, no smoking by the pool, no minors not accompanied by an adult. A whole list of rules now spray-painted around the Hamra pool: no invasions by the pool, no English by the pool, no naked tits by the pool, no pornography by the pool, no Christians by the pool, no Muslims by the pool, the Jews run the pool, no pools by the pool, no journalists by the pool without adult supervision.

How many rules had he written? Was it even him? Fuck! There were some rules in Arabic too, written by Ahmed—yes, he remembers handing Ahmed the spray paint at some point.

What a mistake.

Peoria's fear breaks through the tequila sweat, one fear undiluted, and coming through with clarity: I need to flee. I need to get out of here.

I need to get out of here right now.

Two SUVs are waiting for him in front of the hotel.

He throws the duffel bag in the back of one of the SUVs, a drive out in the early morning, echoes of minaret calls heard through the tinted windows, before the sun comes up and the depression sets in again.

The trip to the border will take about eight hours, and he knows he'll fall asleep by the time they reach Fallujah.

THE PLOT MUST ADVANCE AT A QUICKER PACE

That's fun. That's what it was like. I'll tell you how I know later.

I leave you with Peoria on his way to Bangkok.

The plot needs to advance back in New York.

Time capsule: George W. Bush lands on an aircraft carrier. "Mission Accomplished."

No one ever accuses America of being a nation of historians. Our impressions over the long run are formed by a few vivid pictures and a tagline.

Nixon and Watergate: "I'm Not a Crook." Bill Clinton: "I Did Not Have Sex with That Woman." Gerald Ford: Tripping. Jimmy Carter: Malaise, though he never actually said that word. Reagan: Tear Down That Wall. Morning in America. Kennedy in black-and-white: Ask not what. Kennedy in color: Back and to the left.

War happens and life goes back to normal for the headquarters staff.

Michael M. Hastings, me, now one year employed at *The Magazine*. My attention strays from the war after the first summer of the invasion.

Anyway, mission accomplished.

You might forget that at the time, people took that seriously.

18.

September to December 2003

We've won the war, Hastings," Nishant tells me. "Now, how do we win the peace?"

I take notes.

"Post-conflict situations. The Balkans, Japan, Germany—those three should do for now. How long did the occupation last? How much money was spent? How did we enable the local government? How did we get them up on their feet?"

I do my research and get the answers for Nishant. We had 465,000 Americans in Japan in 1945 for the occupation, which lasted till 1952. Germany, well, we had only half of that country to take care of—luckily, it turned out, the good half.

The Balkans are a different story—we didn't fight those wars; we just came in on the end to broker a peace agreement and use some tactical airstrikes. De-arming programs, weapons for bread.

I dig up all this information and write it up in about ten pages, single-spaced.

My point, and I try to stress this to Nishant, is that these historical examples don't really apply to Iraq. That Iraq, in a lot of ways, seems sort of unique, at least in American history. The closest example is

Vietnam, or the Philippines, and that isn't an example anyone wants to bring up.

Nishant uses lots of the numbers in the final piece and takes a quote or two from the experts I'd interviewed, but doesn't seem to appreciate my analysis.

At the time, though, it is popular to say that we did it for the Germans and the Japanese, we can do it for Iraq too.

The story runs in September, and I stop paying attention to the war.

The U.S. presidential election is under way, and I start to write stories for the magazine's website. It's the only place I can get my political stories published. To work for the printed domestic magazine, you have to be a political correspondent, and I'm not that—technically, my title is still part-time temporary researcher.

In October, I write a story about a candidate for president named Howard Dean. He has basically been ignored by the media, and so when his camp finds out that the magazine is going to do a story on him (even for the website), they jump. My angle is his celebrity connections: a bunch of left-wingers in Hollywood want to support him, and because they are more famous than the actual candidate, the website takes the story. I get to interview Rob Reiner, Alec Baldwin, Ed Norton, and Ben from Ben & Jerry's, the ice cream maker.

By the end of the month, it's clear Dean's candidacy is making an impact—he starts speaking out against the war in Iraq, and a lot of people, it turns out, are willing to listen. *The New Republic* puts him on the cover, and they quote my story from the magazine's website. Then, the political correspondents at the magazine realize they'd better get on this story, so they decide to put Howard Dean on the cover. Brand X, our main competitor, puts him on the cover the same week we do.

In December, months after Nishant runs his "How to Win the Peace" story, Sanders Berman calls me into his office, on the other side of the building.

"The Vietnam syndrome, Hastings," he says.

"Yes, Sanders?"

"Don't repeat what I'm going to tell you, but that story we ran—'How to Win the Peace'—that's classic Vietnam syndrome thinking. It's bet-hedging, Hastings—Patel is hedging his bets, already. That was the problem with Vietnam—everyone in the news business started hedging their bets at the first sign of trouble," he says.

"We have to give Rumsfeld the benefit of the doubt, we have to give the president the benefit of the doubt, we have to give our military the benefit of the doubt—a few months into this thing and already we're throwing them to the wolves."

"Yes, it seems like there is a souring," I say.

"So we haven't captured Saddam? Doesn't matter. These things take time. Capturing Saddam wouldn't make a real difference anyway, tactically, strategically, or psychologically speaking. Not a lick of difference. I spoke to Henry about this, and we agreed to do a story—'Don't Let Vietnam Happen to Us Again.'

"My story was supposed to be on the cover this week. But do you know who is going to be there instead? Howard Dean! Howard Dean, a governor from Vermont—Howard Dean, the so-called antiwar candidate. The second time we'll have put him on the cover. He's calling Iraq 'Vietnam,' and we're putting him on the cover and doing a profile of him! And how does the profile begin? It begins with him crying because he lost his brother in Vietnam. He doesn't have the distance to understand what Vietnam was about. To understand what war is about. He's just playing to people who don't get why we need to make the sacrifices. And my story, 'Don't Let Vietnam Happen to Us Again'? One page, I'm getting one page, while Dean is getting fifteen, with pictures. It's bad, it's bad news for me and our country, don't you think?

"Our problem with Vietnam was our high expectations. We can't expect our leaders, in a time of war, to meet these expectations. We need to respect them more than that. That's why Patel's story really is aggravating—just weeks after the invasion—"

"Months, I think," I say.

"And he's holding the bar so high? We beat Saddam, we beat a horrible, disgusting, despicable regime, and there are a few riots and we're supposed to start saying it might not have been the wisest move. No way," he says. "Let me tell you this: it's a quote from Winston Churchill. Churchill."

Sanders Berman stands up in his office, walks back and forth, and looks out the window over Central Park, a classic pose.

"He carried on his shoulders a horrible burden, a horrible burden—he's like Bush in that way, a war leader. I've always been fascinated by war leaders. What great decisions they have to make. The burden they carry, the price they pay. Don't go wobbly! Nineteen forty-one, mid-Atlantic, the two boats meet in the dark. Roosevelt's ship blew a horn thrice. The response from Churchill's vessel: a magnificent ray of light from a single lamp, held for fifteen seconds. Destroyers, medium-class, circled the two ships, keeping an eye out for German U-boats—perhaps the Nazis had cracked their code? Perhaps they knew that these two great leaders would be meeting at dusk, mist curling up from the ten-foot swells. Roosevelt, huddled over in his wheelchair, covered in a shawl knitted by Eleanor. Churchill, five drinks into the evening. Their aides stand off to the side, trying not to get seasick—neither Winston nor Franklin got seasick. Franklin, a sailor from his younger days, Winston, permanently drunk. Didn't really make a difference if the floor dipped to the right and left—a hard drinker is always prepared for the sea. . . ."

A knock on Sanders Berman's door.

I turn to see who it is, but even before I get halfway around, I can feel a presence, feline, predatory. Delray M. Milius's voice follows.

"Umm, Sanders, can I interrupt you for a moment?"

"Sure, Milius, what's the daisies?"

"Breaking news, Sanders," he says, smiling. "We captured Saddam."

Sanders leans back in his chair. A look of intensity, betraying his casual southernness, flashes to his eyes.

"Does Henry know?"

"Not yet, I don't think."

Sanders picks up the phone and dials Henry's extension.

"Henry, it's Sanders. We got Saddam."

Delray M. Milius moves up from the door, and with the contempt of a Prada clerk, seems to look down at me in my chair. I'm moving in on his turf.

"We have to bump Dean. This changes everything about the war. Tactically, strategically, philosophically. I can write it. We were about to fall into the Vietnam syndrome, you know? But now we've really won the war."

Howard Dean gets bumped. Sanders Berman gets to write his story—"How Saddam's Capture Changes Everything." Without a leader, the dead-enders will soon reach the dead end.

19.

A.E. Peoria Goes on Holiday

After the flight attendants tell you where the exits are and how the oxygen masks drop down, most airlines don't play videos about why it's bad to sleep with twelve- and thirteen-year-olds, thinks magazine journalist A.E. Peoria. But Thai Airways is a little different, due to its clientele, and sure enough, before takeoff from Dubai to Bangkok, there is a seven-minute public service video that reminds him of his destination.

A red curtain in a back alley opens, a naked leg on a bed, hookah smoke hovering, a seductive haze. The camera sneaks in, creeps into the bedroom, and there is this beautiful young girl lying on the bed, wide eyes, and instantly Peoria thinks, that girl is fucking hot. The director ruins the erotic moment by flashing *14 ans*, right there, a chyron at the bottom of the screen to trigger what Peoria guesses is supposed to be a response of shame or revulsion, or self-flagellation. The video does the same trick, again and again, showing these preteens made up to look like postteens in very seductive settings, high production values in the brothels creating a romantic sleaziness. *12 ans, 15 ans, 17 ans,* and in small writing at the bottom, there is a message, in French, about who paid for the video, the Thai and French tourism boards, with a grant from Interpol's anti-human-trafficking division.

It was stupid of them to let a Frenchman produce that kind of video—this is no moment for edginess. But if I was on my way to Thailand to sleep with fourteen-year-old girls, Peoria thinks, would this public service announcement stop me? Or was it just an FYI to the regular old sex tourists—for your information, be careful that you could accidentally sleep with a fourteen-year-old, even if you're aiming for eighteen? Or, if you wanted to pretend it was an accident, now you have no excuse, because you were warned that a lot of the girls on the street—over two hundred thousand of them in Thailand alone, according to a statistic at the end of the video—are selling themselves.

Seven hours later, after landing and checking into a hotel, Peoria remembers the video, rather uncomfortably. He is staring at what looks like a children's playroom, a romper room. He is looking through a Plexiglas window of the kind used at a supersize McDonald's or a Burger King to separate the toddlers' play area from the restaurant. There is a carpeted floor with no sharp edges. All it's missing are a trampoline and a container full of colored balls. The room has levels of large carpeted steps, with spaceship-like oval chairs and a half-dozen oversize fuzzy building blocks to sit on.

Sitting, sprawling, in positions from prim to proper to sultry, legs crossed or uncrossed, vectors of narrow panty lines, thirty-five young Thai women, peasant dark to Victorian pale, stare out at the darker room where Peoria sits, deciding.

Can they see me? Are they looking? Does it matter?

He had told himself, upon arrival, that he was going to resist. See the temples, walk the famous streets of Patpong, get a tuk-tuk ride and a cheap silk suit, maybe a massage. Research. At the most, he'd get a blow job. Then technically, he could say that, like great American leaders before him (never wanting to rule out future career options, such as one in the legislature), he had never had sex with a prostitute, per se, and technically, he wouldn't be lying. He didn't think the press corps would push him on this point—there wouldn't be specificity in the question, words like "blow job" or "hand job" or "happy ending" would not be used. "Sex act," perhaps. Have you ever had a sex act with a prostitute? A question to laugh off, not worth answering. In a scenario that was admittedly more realistic, he doubted that any girl he would date would ever dig that deeply on the subject. It was a perfectly natural question, he believes, for a girl to ask if he'd ever slept with a hooker. His denial then would be honest and pure and he wouldn't be lying—blow jobs didn't count.

If only it would have stopped at the blow job.

From a hash-and-booze daze, his eyes focus on a white pin with a red number that says 72 hanging off the chest of one of the Thai women.

He's made it this far in life, thirty-four years of putting up the boundaries, of never breaking his own rule. Now he finds himself (because he's never *gone* to these places, he's only found himself there) telling a man that he's chosen 72.

Over the intercom, piped into the playroom, the manager says 72.

"Handsome man, so handsome," 72 says.

She takes his hand and they get into an elevator, up two floors. They are greeted by a smaller Thai woman, a maid with darker skin and two towels.

"So handsome," the maid says, handing 72 a key.

The key is for door number 11, three down the hallway on the left. Peoria feels like he is in some kind of '80s health club, catching a smell similar to that of a newly opened container of blue racquetballs.

There is a Jacuzzi bathtub and a shower and a roll futon with clean sheets, raised two or three feet off the floor.

72 takes her clothes off and turns on the water in the bathtub.

Peoria takes his clothes off.

72 fiddles with the temperatures. She asks a few questions in English.

"You here for fun?" 72 asks.

"No, business," Peoria says.

"What job you do?"

"I'm a journalist, a reporter, a writer," he says, and he pretends to write in the air.

"A writer?"

"Yes, for a magazine," he says, pretending to open a magazine.

"Oh, magazine," she repeats.

"*Time* magazine," he says.

She points to the bath. He doesn't know what she's asking.

"Go in."

He steps in, and she unhooks the showerhead and starts to spray him down, scrubbing him with soap—she scrubs parts of his body that have never been scrubbed so clean since childhood; she starts scrubbing his testicles, she scrubs his ass. She puts her hand right up there with soap and his rectum tingles as she scrubs away at it. She starts to scrub herself, too, and whenever she touches her shaved vagina, she smiles and giggles and says, "Don't look, don't look."

She hands him a towel to dry off. He lies down on the futon. She straddles him and starts to rub his shoulders.

She reaches, with great dexterity, into a small plastic water-resistant cabinet, like the kind you get at the Container Store, or whatever the Bangkok equivalent would be. She pulls out a Durex Ultra Thin condom in a yellow wrapper. She starts to jerk his penis, and he becomes hard. She puts the condom in her mouth, and, with the same kind of dexterity, 72 slips her mouth onto his penis, unrolling the condom skillfully as she goes.

Peoria has thoughts of safe sex—if her saliva is on the condom, on the inside of the condom, would that contaminate it? Could he get HIV/AIDs from that?

He closes his eyes and remembers what his doctor friend told him the last time he got a blow job from a prostitute in Mexico. He called the doctor upon returning home and asked: Should I get tested?

"She use a condom to blow you?"

"No, she didn't."

"Did it look like she had any sores or anything on her mouth?"

"No, I don't think so."

"You're probably good on herpes. You didn't go down on her, did you?"

"No, of course not."

"The rate of HIV in Mexico," his friend said, looking up the information online at the CIA *World Factbook*, "is about one in three hundred fifty thousand. The at-risk populations are gay men and intravenous drug users. I'd consider prostitutes at risk too. No track marks?"

"No track marks."

"Okay. And you didn't have any cuts or anything on your dick, did you?"

"Fuck, I don't think so."

"Chafing?"

"A little chafing, but I think that came from later, after showering too much and watching porn in the hotel."

"Okay. Now, if you were having sex with her, and she was having a full-blown HIV outbreak—just vaginal sex—if you were having vaginal sex with her, the chance of you, a heterosexual male, getting HIV would only be at like five percent. That's if she was all-out HIVing it. And since you weren't the one giving the blow job, it's not like you're ingesting any semen or anything. Were you? You can be honest."

"No, dude. Fuck you."

"So you're probably good to go."

Now, as number 72 lowers herself down on his penis, he opens his eyes and grabs her waist to stop her. He runs the calculations in his head. Thailand, he'd read, had done a surprisingly good job protecting its citizens from HIV—you want to protect your natural resources—and the rate of infection of females was one in one hundred thousand.

"Wait, wait," he says.

72 stops, half submerged.

"Do you do drugs, needles," he says, tapping his inner arms along the veins.

"No way, man," she says. He can tell he's almost ruined the mood.

"And you're clean," he asks her.

"Very clean! We just took bath. You have very nice . . ."

She looks at his face, searching for a feature to compliment— whether the size of his dick or his nose or his smile.

"Hair on your eyes," she says, running her finger along his eyebrows.

"Eyebrows?"

"Very handsome eyebrows."

And she lowers herself the rest of the way and starts to bounce up and down, move around, and it feels pretty good, Peoria admits. He thinks of his girlfriend back home, and knowing that it has been three weeks since the last time he spoke to her and that he wondered if they were actually going out anymore, and that as the days go on, he keeps getting email messages that vary wildly in length, from two paragraphs to three thousand words, explaining all the reasons why he should break up with her: that she waited for him patiently even after he almost got killed, what a stress that was for her, and rather than go straight back to New York for his break, he decided to go to

Thailand for a month. To Thailand—and so he should now consider himself to be broken up with her, unless he has decided otherwise. And Peoria knows how to respond—he knows what he needs to write back to save the relationship with the girl he gave six orgasms to, but he doesn't want to say it, he doesn't want to say it.

And as he starts to fuck 72, or 72 starts to fuck him, he realizes it doesn't matter if he just blows his load now, or ten minutes from now, or forty-five minutes from now; there is no pressure to perform sexually, and if 72 judges him, she will judge silently, or at least in a language he doesn't understand, and at least pretend to be satisfied—her satisfaction comes from the baht, his from the orgasm. What liberty! So he doesn't wait to come. In fact, with health and safety reasons lingering in the back of his head, he wants to get it over with quickly.

"Ah ah aha . . ."

She pops up. His cum drips back down the condom, a gooey ring around his pubic hair.

She hands him a piece of tissue paper. He plucks the condom off his cock, handling it like a dirty diaper covered in seaweed, and jumps up, his penis withdrawn in its foreskin. He drops the dead condom in a wastebasket by the door.

72 grabs a pack of Marlboro Lights and hands him one.

They smoke in tandem.

"Where are you from?" she asks.

"New York, but I haven't been home in a while."

Should he tell her? Yes, he has to. As he starts to talk, he knows he can't blame it on the unmedicated CDD. Mentally ill or not, he would have talked. He sees why men open up to whores, why they feel the need to share the dark and deep secrets, to water the ego, to repeat, I am a man and paying for sex will not change that. The desire to open up, to talk, to puff himself up, as well as his accomplishments, is irresistible. Peoria's view on prostitutes until now has been only a mat-ter of literature and the tabloids—he has always been surprised how call girls manage to get so much out of men, enough for $100,000 paydays. But he realizes now that they didn't even need to try to learn the secrets; the men would start divulging state secrets and profes-sional gossip as naturally as they would orgasm and roll over—because the talk was part of the process, part of the sex act, as certain as a lake level rises after a storm.

"Baghdad, I've spent the last few months in Baghdad," he says.

She doesn't understand.

"Iraq, you know, the war."

She looks at him, smiling.

"No, no, the war, you know? Boom, boom, pop-pop, pop, shoot-ing, fighting, you know, the war?"

72's face becomes very serious.

"Oh no, the war. It is bad?"

"Very bad, very bad. I was almost killed, you know—"

He's never said those words—he'd written them when the first erroneous magazine piece was published, but he had never said it like that, with such bluntness, which was so unlike him, to have gone months without saying something like that, something so obvious and self-absorbed and to the point. *I almost was killed, you know.* He has an audience, an audience that has no agenda, an audience that could just sit there and listen, and just get the emotion of it. He doesn't care if she misses the details. The details don't matter. It's the emotion of it, the fear of it, the goddamn danger of it, that's what she can understand and that's what he wants her to understand.

"The war in Iraq is very bad," he says.

"You fight?"

"No, I don't fight. I'm a writer, a writer," he says, writing in the air. "I was there during the morning of the invasion, and then . . ."

So number 72 is Peoria's number one. After one come two, three, four, five, six, seven, eight . . . Like pills, like shots, like hands of blackjack and lines of cocaine and potato chips and cheese fries.

And what number would be next? How many days has he been here, how much baht spent, how many girls? He tries all the girls, two girls at a time, upping it to three girls. The numbers keep piling up, and he thinks, Do I count whores when I count the number of women I've slept with? Do they count toward my number? Is it demeaning to them, antifeminist, not to count them as part of my total number of sexual partners? The girls: he touches and pokes and prods them because he can, because he's paid, and they giggle or scowl or blank out or look at him with suspicion. He mostly overcomes his health concerns after number three—he even makes his way back to find 72 and really fucks her, flips her around, donkey punches, doggy style, reverse cowgirl suplexes, titty slapping, truly aimed ejaculates. To really try to make her moan—making a whore moan, he'd once read, being the true test of a man, but he doesn't even really believe in things like true tests of manhood, and he has to admit, it doesn't matter.

There are occasional complications in the transactions. He learns that whores have feelings too. Who would have thought or known that these girls had feelings? That they are people in their own right, their soft skin a membrane holding blood and organs and brain and keeping the universe outside. He encounters these feelings with a thin nineteen-year-old girl who, after the ritual bathing, starts to blow him and swing her pussy around to his face, to the numeraled position, and though it looks clean and tempting to lick, he doesn't stick his tongue out. He doesn't plunge in. A few seconds pass, then fifteen seconds, and the thin nineteen-year-old takes her mouth off his cock and glances over her shoulder, a stern, confused look, and says, "You don't want me?" No, he did want her. But did she not know that he couldn't just lick her where she had snuggled hundreds, if not thousands, of cocks? He can stick his in there, sure, with the Durex for protection, but his mouth? He still has his boundaries. She is pissed. She feels rejected, he knows, and though he fucks her quickly, she isn't into it. He wants to get out of there—it's uncomfortable for him. He doesn't get the chance for conversation—they just walk out of the 250-baht-a-half-hour hotel room in Nana Plaza, and part in the night.

Jilted. He didn't get his part of the transaction, the talk. He didn't get the chance to explain how very important and special he was, how very dangerous his job was, what it means, what his emotional state means to him and them after spending all those months running around the streets with Ahmed, and after each dead condom, each encounter, he would say, "I am a writer, I am from Baghdad, it is a war there, it's now raining car bombs, don't you see it's raining car bombs? *Time* magazine!"

He has spoken only to whores and concierges and maids for two weeks now. Conversations, one-sided as was his way, but conversations with people there to serve him. Should he feel bad about that?

20.

The Frenchman and A.E. Peoria's Last Night in Bangkok

A.E. Peoria steps into the lobby of the Bangkok Mandarin Oriental. It is lit up and white and marble with hundreds of dollars' worth of white flowers arranged in vases and the soothing light tones of Orientalish music playing: *pong dong ping*. Through the glass windows at the back of the lobby are the hotel's two pools: one pool, still water, with cabins, shallow, private, more for lounging; and the other pool, for more active swimmers. Even at one a.m., there is a fleet of Thais to greet him as he comes in. Bowing and saying hello as he steps through the first doors, bowing and saying hello as he rounds the corner to wave at the check-in desk, bowing and saying hello as he gets to the entrance to the bar, and, finally, as he takes a seat at the bar, the waitress and bartender both bow and say hello.

At this bar, Peoria thinks, what history. The Oriental: the hotel of Graham Greene and Joseph Conrad and Somerset Maugham and James Michener. Did they, like me, partake in the city's number-one attraction, the girls? Or wasn't Maugham homosexual? The boys, then? Hard to know. Greene almost likely did, and had Peoria ever managed to get through volume 2 of his 3,400-page, three-volume autobiography, he'd probably have found the passage about Greene's slipping out in the middle of the night to congenially and guiltily cheat on his wife, who refused him a divorce. It is a city of blue-movie possibilities. Conrad, the failed suicide, multitongued linguist, waited—in this very bar, or a version of this bar—for his first commission to captain a vessel. Maugham rode out a nasty bout of malaria in a guest room, near dying. And apparently James Michener, whose books Peoria had never read but had seen on the shelves of his grandmother's home, in paperback, made a reputation there, too. Such a list of greats who'd stayed and slept and suffered from various tropical maladies and more typical Western guilt on the floors above him!

Would that ever be me, Peoria wonders. Or am I going to be left with that one book, that *Desperation Points West*, and that one story: the night I spent with a Mexican—nay, a Puerto Rican—who got his balls blown off.

What could he say about everything he'd done? Would the sum total of his life be conflict zones plus the peyote eaten in New Mexico plus the rim job from three nineteen-year-olds two days ago? All of it had been research. But to what end?

He had pursued the life of a great writer because he wanted to be a great writer. Isn't this what they did? Screw whores and get shot at and ingest large quantities of booze and drugs? Isn't the Oriental—this very bar—proof? These were not lightweights: the Greenes, the Maughams, and the Conrads. These were greats, men of true literary heft. They had passed through here and left with the valued and vaunted experience needed to write. But what is the point of all of it, Peoria thinks, if all his material never comes out, if all of it just stays endlessly circling in his head?

His thoughts are pressing up against his own career irrelevance—he can feel himself slipping off the escalator, getting sucked back toward the emergency stop button, no longer on the fast track.

All he has to do is look at the lives of these writers and he will know.

He'd gotten into a very bad habit, a reading block. He tried to read the classics, but the classics had failed him. Or he had failed the classics. Invariably, he failed at the preface and the introduction, at the author's biography and timeline. The writing was secondary to the life—the facts and details of what they did and why, where they slept and who they slept with captured his interest. The very fact that he could be reading a book written decades ago held more power than the book itself. The words, the sentences, the language—his mind wouldn't last past page 10. And so he has great knowledge of the life without knowledge of the art; he can guess at the art, talk intelligently about it, but he will admit that he really hasn't gotten past Queequeg's hug of Ishmael—pretty fucking weird, that!—but he does know that Melville worked on a dock in Battery Street in Lower Manhattan, that he'd been penniless, that after *Moby-Dick* he had said he'd never write a novel again (the critics hated it, the critics killed him, the critics said he was a loser, a dope, a maniac, a fool); Peoria found that anecdote comforting after *Desperation Points West* received its cold shoulder. But he was sure that almost every author, if they had the chance, would embrace the Melville example as their own—they'll be sorry in twenty years when they discover that they missed a masterpiece, that it was sitting right under their noses all these years and they were too stupid and small-minded to see it!

Melville. *Typee*. The South Pacific. Melville had visited Siam— that's Thailand—for a fortnight. Three nights his vessel had pulled into the kingdom of Siam, en route to Australia. Those savages. According to his description of Bangkok, the city was steaming, low-lying, waterlogged.

Melville, his son's suicide. Melville and Mount Greylock. Melville dedicated *Moby-Dick* to Hawthorne—and at the book's hostile reception, did Melville wonder if Hawthorne was ashamed to have his name associated with it? Did Melville worry that he had embarrassed Hawthorne by putting his name on a book massively considered at the time a piece of shit? Yes, he is sure Melville had those doubts. The personal humiliation of a failed novel, three years of his life, vanquished in a few afternoons of critical thought set in type.

Conrad—who hated Melville's *Moby-Dick* and who missed Melville in Bangkok by less than a decade—surely nursed a depressed beer right here. Conrad's life gives him hope—he bucked the mold. He didn't write anything of genius until he was almost forty, older than Peoria. Greene was something of a prodigy, so fuck him. Maugham, again, the details are blurry, but all of this happened in this hotel. He could feel it, live it, kick it around, be initiated by it, be daunted by it, and think that the task of equaling . . .

A man next to him at the bar taps him on the shoulder.

"There is no pride," the Frenchman says, "on being the best-looking man in a whorehouse. This is a shame."

Peoria looks at him.

"Here."

The Frenchman pushes over a small glass of blue liquid, his fingers brushing the top with a strip of something that looks like sandpaper.

"I've seen you at the hotel before. Where's your wife?"

"She is upstairs right now, in rest."

The Frenchman is the same height, Peoria guesses, five-foot-seven, with thin brown hair combed over on the front of his skull and dropping back below his ears, his head a few years away from accepting baldness by his early fifties. The kind of haircut that the man had probably had since he was twelve or thirteen.

"Marcel," he says, making a gesture with his hand that isn't a shake, just putting it on the bar.

"Peoria," A.E. says.

"You are here for work?"

"Because of work," Peoria says.

"We will have a drink and then we will discuss," Marcel says.

Peoria downs the blue liquid, feeling a lime taste on his lips around the glass where Marcel had rubbed the strip of sandpaper.

"I have spiked your drink," he says. "But it is a good spike, no?"

"Tastes like lime," Peoria says.

"We have twenty minutes here before we will go on a walk," Marcel says.

"That's great, it's just great to be able to talk to someone who knows English so well. I haven't had a full English conversation in three weeks, you know, and I have to say that it gets lonely. You don't think it would, but it does get lonely traveling alone."

"Yes, I will comfort you."

Peoria nods, not listening, already revving up.

"I've been to Paris a couple times. I think it really is a beautiful city, and I've never really got the sense that they hate Americans there."

"We do," Marcel says.

"And it's like, well, the taxi drivers don't like it that you can't speak French, so they can be dicks, but I didn't think that anyone else was really, you know what I mean? But it's really nothing compared to when you're in a place where they really hate Americans, you know? It's such a relative scale now because you go to places and you're a target. People really want to kill you."

"And what places are those?"

"I'm talking right now about Baghdad, that's where I've been, fuck, since March, since the invasion there. I know you guys weren't happy with the invasion, and you know, shit, you're right, probably right, you know, the whole thing was such a fucking stupid debacle, but that's the way history goes I guess sometimes."

"Ah, la guerre d'Irak."

"Yeah, yeah, the Iraq War."

Peoria launches into his story. The Humvees, the convoy, the boredom, the fear, and the massacre. Seven soldiers killed at one time, the worst incident of that day, and the only survivors were Chipotle and him, in the desert, holding a rag to Chipotle's groin. The Frenchman listens, shaking his head, looking at his watch.

"Do you know the Jewish author Elie Wiesel?" Marcel asks.

"Yeah, the Nazi hunter," Peoria says.

"No. But he tells of a story, in a novel. I do not recall the name, but it is fiction. The plot is about a man, the narrator, who has stepped in front of a car to kill himself. An attempt at suicide, yes. He had survived the Holocaust, our narrator. And we are in his coma, seeing his flashbacks. He is on a boat, crossing the Atlantic, and he is looking out over the railing of this boat. He is thinking deep thoughts, profoundly deep thoughts of why. Of why he is going to jump and sink. He longs for the sinking, for the feeling of the boat leaving him in its cruel wake. Another passenger on the boat sees our narrator, and says to him, 'Do not jump. Do not jump, *monsieur.*' '*Mon ami,*' our narrator says, 'you do not know my story, and if you did know my story, you would not be so quick to stop me.' The other passenger says, 'There can be no story that would make me say that. I can see in your eyes, in your pain, that you are a victim, and the victim's story should not end at the bottom of the sea.' So our narrator, he tells his story to the curious passenger, this would be the Good Samaritan. Of the camps, of seeing his mother and sister for the last time. Of living for three years with shit and death on his plate. All the time, of walking, on the last push, from Buchenwald to—and this is the twist—to Auschwitz. This is where our narrator ends up when he thinks he has gotten free and it is on this walk, this march. His father, still alive, takes sick in the cold and his father dies. Our narrator catches a fever as well, and somehow he finds a girl, a twelve-year-old girl, who takes his hand, who keeps him walking as the snowflakes fall. A Nazi officer approaches the girl. The Nazi grabs her by the arm and starts to pull her away from him. But the girl will not let go of our narrator's arm. She is crying hysterically, so the Nazi officer says okay, you can come too, and he brings both of them to a private room, a private house in the northeast corner of Auschwitz, almost a barn—you can visit this private house on tour, I have visited it myself. And in this private room, that is when the shooting starts. Our narrator can hear the shooting through the walls, and he understands that this officer was saving the girl because of this liquidation. The Allies are on the way, of course, the Allies are always on the way, but always too late, no? The Allies are rolling in, but that is still days later. And as our narrator hears this racket, this utter racket, this Nazi jazz jam of bullets and cocked triggers and grenades, wiping the grounds of Gypsies and Jews and Communists and undesirables—while our narrator is hearing this soundtrack, do you know what is in front of his eyes? He is seeing this Nazi pet the girl on her head to keep her calm. This Nazi is a man of strong sexual desires—he can get hard in the middle of a bloodbath. That is sexual potency. To get an erection inspired by liquidation. He starts to kiss the girl and take the girl's shirt off. If this was Nabokov describing this scene, he would talk about pale raisins on a plain pudding. He would write of the dry well that is more pure than a flooding and somewhat older spring. But our narrator is no Nabokov. He just sees the Nazi's pants drop, the SS eagle clinking on the floor, and the cot springs going up and down. The girl closes her eyes, and when the girl closes her eyes, our exhausted narrator, he closes his eyes too. Exhausted, no food, eighty pounds underweight. When he opens his eyes, it is the next day and the officer is gone. He looks around to see the girl and he does see her. She is on the bed, dead now, suffocated, or so it seems. By what? Blunt force trauma to the throat, we assume, though this detail is too horrible to make explicit. And the Nazi officer has left! He has left! Why did he not kill me, our narrator wonders, why did he not kill me then? Must he have thought I was already dead? Our narrator staggers out of the barn and all the Nazis have fled—back to their old cushy jobs in Wiesbaden and Frankfurt, to be sure!—and all the prisoners are all dead. The bodies, even these emaciated bodies have so much blood. He can't smell anything anymore and can't feel anything and so he collapses in the pile of cordwood flesh and is only woken up by an American fellow. A black man is tugging on his feet with a bandana over his face from the stench—they gave the Negros this cleanup duty; do your histories tell you that of this liberation?—the sick stench and his eyes open and our narrator is saved. Our narrator is saved. He says these words out loud. The passenger on the boat has listened, without interruption. The passenger would look seasick but anger is a cure for seasickness. Contempt cures seasickness. The Good Samaritan walks away, leaving the narrator alone, or so our narrator says. Our narrator knows why, why even the Good Samaritan is disgusted by such a story. Our narrator concludes: he was affronted by the very fact that the story was told to him."

"Wow," A.E. Peoria says.

"It has been twenty minutes. Let us walk. There is a place I'd like to show you."

A.E. Peoria and Marcel leave the hotel, and the mild hallucinogen laced with amphetamines is taking effect, the Oriental music *ding-dong*ing, sounding like the French song "Frère Jacques" to Peoria. Peoria thinks that's pretty hilarious, and they are both talking, fast, talking back and forth and over and under each other, and the blocks pass by like nothing. On Patpong Road there is a Thai teenager with baggy pants and a skateboarding decal on his shirt, handing out flyers, and Marcel approaches the Thai teenager and says they would like to see a show. A.E. Peoria says, Wait a minute, Marcel, the guidebook says never trust the touts, never go with a tout anywhere, and then they are walking up to a second-floor club. Never go up to the second floor of any club on Patpong. Marcel says that is the very reason he has chosen a tout and that he has gone up to the second floor: because the guidebook says no. You must not ever pretend the guidebook has wisdom, Marcel says.

They are sitting in the back corner and they are the only two men in this club and a horn blows when they walk in, and a woman walks out onstage and starts a performance; she takes a cigarette and smokes it with her pussy, she puts a straw in her pussy then puts a dart in, and from across the stage she shoots a green balloon and the balloon pops; she takes a Ping-Pong ball and pops it up, and then she does one that Peoria has never heard of before. Peoria is called to the stage, and there is a green bong with water at the bottom and a bowl filled with weed. The Thai woman sits on the bong and says, Light me, and he lights the bowl of the bong and the water starts bubbling up when her vagina begins to suction the marijuana in. This goes on for fifteen seconds, until the translucent bong is now filled with smoke, and the Thai woman stands up and quickly covers the bong to keep the smoke in. Then she takes her hand away and puts the bong to Peoria's mouth and he inhales the hit, takes it down, and he can feel it work inside his head and he falls backward. He can't see where Marcel went, but the girl who is onstage is now walking over to him. She has a collection jar and Peoria puts a few hundred baht in, but as he reaches in his pockets, he is swarmed by other Thai girls, and none of them are pretty; they are just female, they are the women who have been broken by selling themselves and are now in their late twenties and thirties and too old to make a good living doing straight-up sex, so they must debase themselves like this, taking vaginal bong hits and smoking Marlboros from their twats. He is getting clawed at and is nervous and he can't find any money—he knows the money is there but his hand in his pocket keeps going down and down like his arm is rubber and plastic and it could keep going through his pockets until it reaches the floor. He starts to yell, Get the fuck off me, feeling all the tentacles of five Thai girls, zombie squids with slanted eyes. They want his money, that's all they want.

Marcel and the tout come charging back to his rescue. Marcel starts slapping the girls and pushing them and kicking them like mangy dogs, screaming at them in French, *"Allons-y, allons-y."* The girls are recovering the baht notes on the floor and the tout and Marcel usher Peoria out of the second-floor club.

The street brings the hallucinations back to a manageable level.

"This is not the place that I wanted to bring you," Marcel says. "It is a few blocks more."

They start walking, this pair, and there is another neon sign that says "Farang Vilvage," which Peoria thinks is supposed to mean "village."

The word *farang* is familiar, he thinks: it means "foreigner." It is like those few Thai phrases he's learned—*soi dee kap,* thank you, or hello, one of those two, whatever one it is.

The girls inside are taller than those in the other massage parlors he's been in.

Marcel is handing over money, and then the host and a tall girl are grabbing Peoria by the arms and pushing him into another room. Water is spilling down over him now, and Marcel is in the same room with another girl. Marcel is giving Peoria a sign, the A-okay sign, and Peoria is surprised that despite the drug, he's got an erection. The girl goes down on him and starts to suck away.

It is the most amazing blow job he has ever experienced. It is something about the mouth, about the throat, about the grip of solid hands.

Marcel is laughing hysterically, and even the laugh sounds like "Frère Jacques."

"You see, you see how good this is?"

The tall girl then says to Peoria, you want to blow me now? And Peoria starts to laugh and doesn't understand, until she lifts up her skirt and there is a penis.

He remembers what that other Thai word means—ladyboy, ladyboy, ladyboy—and Peoria gets up and says no thanks.

Marcel, what have you done?

But he's not angry, because the spike is good, and Marcel says, okay, we will have them blow each other. They both sit back and watch the two ladyboys give each other blow jobs, for a good fifteen minutes, then Peoria says, I'm tired, man, I'm tired.

They are trying to wave down a tuk-tuk, and they get one. The man who steps out of the tuk-tuk is an Arab gentleman in a nice suit.

The Arab gentleman in the nice suit is not getting out of the way. He is engaged in a conversation with the tuk-tuk driver, an argument, scary tonal highs and lows.

Peoria feels an onrush of the psychedelic fear—the corners of all objects and shapes in his sights pop out, the carriage top of the tuk-tuk taking the neon colors from the signs and the puddles of dead rainwater in the streets and reflecting them back in lines and patterns that jump out at his retinas like a magical net capturing imaginary sea creatures, dancing on a slimy coral reef.

Accented English of the Arab and broken English of the tuk-tuk driver.

"My tip, my tip," says the tuk-tuk driver.

"Too long, too long," says the Arab. "In circles you've driven me."

"No, no," wails the tuk-tuk driver.

Marcel, stringy brown mane, bouncing, hunched energy of a five-foot-seven man, raises his left hand above his shoulder and, in a swooping pass with his crusty melanin-spotted and freckled paw, strikes the Arab gentleman on the face.

A bright flash on the slap's impact. A.E. Peoria knows that his pupils are well past dilated, both shallow and gaping shiny black holes, and it's as if he's watching a panel in a comic strip. Out of the corner of his eye he sees the bubble words ZAM WOW speed off quickly.

"Marcel, dude!"

The Arab gentleman, shocked, looks at Marcel, and now it is Arabic and French screaming.

"Allez-vous en!" and Marcel is shooing the Arab gentleman away from the tuk-tuk, kicking at his heels, arms now windmilling, light touches on the nice suit. Peoria hears a rumbling, a gurgling coming from Marcel's throat, as if he'd adjusted the treble dial on his own voice, and Peoria can hear the scratchy expectorate forming like angina crackling in a blood vessel, and the sound-expanding properties of the hallucinogen allow him to hear each molecule of the phlegm convalescing into a blob darkened by the red inner walls of Marcel's esophagus, up past the tonsils, and the image flashes through Peoria's mind as if he is standing right in front of the jaw and staring down the gullet of Marcel. The blob of spit and mucus flies out with a *whoot*. The Arab gentleman, arms raised in surrender, is backing away from the tuk-tuk when the loogie takes flight and lands solidly on his lapel.

Peoria grabs Marcel and dives into the back of the tuk-tuk, holding on to him. The tuk-tuk driver is laughing, and Peoria yells, Go, go, and the tuk-tuk driver starts off and speeds down the street. The Arab gentleman is running behind them, yelling and spitting and screaming, swatting the back of the tuk-tuk, its weak diesel engine accelerating to the speed of a man sprinting, and finally, to a nice twenty-two miles an hour, which leaves the Arab gentleman standing on the street corner, screaming obscenities foreign to Peoria's ear.

"To the Oriental," Marcel says, sitting up.

"Thank you, sir, *soi dee kap*," says the tuk-tuk driver. "The Arabs here are bad, very bad. They come for the Russian girls and they are very cheap. No money they give us. The girls say they smell."

"Yes, of course, my friend," Marcel says.

Regaining composure and seriousness, Marcel turns to Peoria in the back of the tuk-tuk.

"You are listening, Mr. Peoria, to what he is saying? We from the West, we say everyone is equal, that there are no differences or that the differences are a matter of ignorance. This is fantasy, this is fantasy. We have the Arabs in Paris and you must treat them like that— with spit and kicks. They talk of human rights, these Arabs, and this is the most disgusting of subjects. We are all human, *oui*, we are. But that is where it ends. The Arabs, you see, think they are better than the West, that is what they think, and like Nazis, they would enslave us all under their sultans and dashikis. They would treat us all like they treat their women, you understand this? This is how they treat other beings that threaten them, these Arabs. They treat them like slaves if they can get away with it. They come here and treat Mr. Tuk-Tuk as if he is a Pakistani servant cleaning the shit off the bowls of the Royal Palace in Riyadh. We are supposed to respect them for it? No, we cannot, we cannot respect them for it. Because we know that they are different—these are traits of humanity, and the Arab is still stupid, he is still stuck with the bedouins, with the nomads. He does not even understand how to use bombs and bullets—they say the Arab understands power only, but he does not even understand what power is today—he understands how to use the clubs, to club his goats and his women, to herd them, and his only power is making more of himself, his only power is fucking his women with their veils off so they produce more like him, they keep coming. Look, they cannot defeat the Jews, ten countries surrounding a speck and they cannot defeat the Jews because the Jews have learned the West's ways of the bombs and the bullets—the Jews invented them! The Jews have said, No we will not be clubbed like curs, like dogs from beyond the Pale, no, never again. So the Arabs have more children and more children and hope to overwhelm the bombs and bullets with offspring, and this offspring they will call democracy and human rights. Then they will win. And they will go and exterminate the Jews, if they could, with their democracy, they would exterminate them. The Jews know this—they are clever—and the Thais know this. Monsieur Tuk-Tuk, he knows this. Yet your dinner- and drinking-party friends in the West do not know it at all; they want to drown in their fantasy of the liberalism, they want to drown there."

Marcel pauses for breath, and as he inhales, Peoria, as if a teleprompter were scrolling across Marcel's face, sees the words roll by: democracy, human rights, the West, liberalism, ballot box, Israel, free speech, habeas corpus, the United Nations.

"When your war in Iraq started, we in France, our politicians and our people said: No, you should not. It is stupid for you Americans. *L'invasion est une connerie*—it is bullshit. We know this of course had nothing to do with morality, the morality of your cause. We French know that this is not what our objections were truly about. It was about the Arabs. We know from Algiers that it is such a foolish game to try to change these minds. We know it is senseless, pointless, and so we offered a warning, and your politicians said, 'Who is France, on their high horse, with their memories of Vichy, to tell us what is moral? Who are the French, who did nothing while Sarajevo died! You have no high ground!' And your politicians were correct. We had no high ground; we only had practical advice disguised as morality, disguised as the international community. And this advice was ignored and now you will learn what we have learned: that there is nothing worthwhile, that it is all savage and torture and Islam." He spat. "Islam."

"Oh, you can't say that about just Islam, dude, all religions are fucked."

"Can I not, Mr. Peoria?"

"I mean, look at the Crusades, look at the Inquisition, look at Northern Ire—"

"The Crusades! The problem with the Crusades, Mr. Peoria, is that they did not go far enough—they were not successful! That was our chance to rid the world of this Islam, and our forefathers failed at it. Now, with information technology, with such good record keeping, with silly ideas of human rights, the time has passed when you can get away with such a thing."

"I don't know, this all sounds like, I mean everybody is violent. I'm a journalist and—"

"You need a fatwa!" Marcel screams.

"What?"

"You need a fatwa against you, you need a jihad against your name. You need for the ayatollahs and mullahs to condemn you. Then perhaps you will understand, then perhaps your career, which you worry so much about, will be saved," Marcel says.

"I think you have to be Muslim to get a fatwa," A.E. Peoria says. "But that would be pretty cool, I guess."

"Cool," Marcel says. "You Americans and your cool."

The tuk-tuk pulls into the arching brick drive of the Mandarin Oriental.

"Have you looked in your dressers by the bedside?" Marcel says. "There are now two books there at these five-star hotels that cater to all the rich international clients: there is the Christian Bible and there is also a Koran. I will show it to you in my room."

The hallucinations are wearing off, and Peoria is left with a general brightening of his vision, a false sense of energy running through his system, keeping him awake as the alcohol exits his bloodstream. He can feel the high coming down and he realizes he needs a drink.

"I need a drink," he says.

"Yes, in my room as well."

Inside the lobby, Marcel hits button 16, the top floor, and the soothing music makes Peoria more anxious.

The two men walk down the hall to room 1614, the corner room, and Marcel takes out a plastic swipe card, thinks about putting it in, then stops.

He knocks instead.

A five-foot-nine Thai man, in his early twenties, opens the door. Marcel and the Thai man stare at each other. A soft voice comes from inside the room.

"C'est toi, Marcel?"

"Oui," says Marcel, and he walks into the room, the Thai man stepping out of the way. Peoria follows him in, impressed with what a few hundred more dollars a night can get you at the Mandarin Oriental. The suite is two rooms, a living room with a stylish sofa that leads to an even larger master bedroom with a view of the river and the Peninsula Hotel across it. On the couch is a woman, late thirties, lying in a hotel-supplied bathrobe, untied, left breast open to view under the light of one of the two high-definition television sets— both sets are on, and both sets are airing pornography, which in its repetitive casualness is somewhat disturbing to Peoria's now fragile mental state.

"You are standing there like a eunuch, but I know you are not," Marcel says to the Thai man. "Exit, you can leave now."

The Thai man pulls on a pair of jeans, bows, and slips out the door.

Marcel starts to hunt around the room, moving from one wastebasket to the other, before going into the bathroom.

"Aha!" he yells.

He jumps back into the living room, holding two spent condoms in his hand.

"This is all, two hours I am gone and the man has only filled up two of these? This is not our money's worth," Marcel says, throwing the condoms back into the wastebasket.

The woman, whom Marcel introduces as Valerie, sits up from her languorous film noir pose and looks at Peoria.

"You have arrived just in time. I was about to fall asleep," she says.

Marcel has disappeared inside the bathroom, keeping the door open but turning the water on in the shower, behind a plate-glass see-through stall. The steam starts to fill up the stall, and as Marcel gets naked and steps in the shower, Peoria loses sight of him.

Peoria goes to the minibar and takes out three small bottles and drinks them. He has reached a point of what might be called a moment of clarity—in the span of two hours he has had oral sex with a transvestite, taken a mild hallucinogen with an obvious non-mild amphetamine base, and broken up a shouting match on the street with an Arab. He is taking stock of the evening. It has been a clear case of one thing leading to another. Now he is in Marcel's hotel room and he doesn't quite know what to make of it all and is staring at a woman who he assumes is Marcel's wife. Marcel's wife, Valerie, has already thrown her bathrobe off, just a little bit more, and is massaging her pussy with a half-smile, seemingly enjoying watching the American's uncomfortableness.

It's all very French, Peoria thinks.

His response is instinctual—it's either fuck or flight, either slip out the door, following the Thai male prostitute, who, as the evidence in the wastebasket makes clear, had already made love (is that an appropriate expression here?) to Valerie at least twice, not really knowing what other sexual acts they might have engaged in.

Peoria, as a modern American male, had been exposed to these kinds of fantasies via the Internet from a very early age. Even before the speed of the Internet allowed users to download highly graphic pixel images and video clips of every debased act there was a market for, he'd been reading erotic stories on what was the most extensive erotic database of stories in English that he'd ever seen. It was quite a collection of stories, this particular website, and it opened his eyes to all manner of perversions by category: teen, bondage and sadomasochism, big beautiful white, groping, bisexual, lesbianism, glory holes, homosexuality, bestiality, pedophilia, gang bangs, orgies, rapes, violence, snuff, kidnappings, granny porn, MILFs (moms I'd like to fuck), GILFAs (grandmothers I'd like to fuck anally), celebrity fantasies, mind control, incest, interracial, Asian, swingers, nonconsensual, military, extra hair, no hair, smoke. In fact, with all of these stories in such a public and easily accessible venue and seemingly legal—words can say whatever words want to say—he had in his later years wondered if there were any taboos left that he hadn't seen or read about. He came up with a resounding no: other things, like vomit porn, water sports, scatological porn, fuzzies, plushies (where people like to have sex with stuffed animals or people dressed in animal costumes), had all, at various points, made their way into popular culture, usually in gross-out comedies, and he wasn't even getting into the hours of Japanese anime he'd watched, with cartoon demons and monsters from other dimensions manhandling and raping unsuspecting Japanese teenagers and children. By the time the Internet caught up to the videos, what he could now watch online didn't surprise him at all. He had examined, on occasion, the moral implications of this new industry—whether he was some kind of degenerate for consuming the product, and what the effects were on his sex life. Did they give him a false sense of what sex was? And after masturbating to what, if admitted publicly, would seem particularly heinous, he often felt like he'd just eaten a Big Mac and pre–trans fat fries in secret—instant gratification wasn't very good to the soul. But who believed in souls anymore anyway? Certainly, this trip to Bangkok would suggest a negative correlation with his sexual habits.

There was another category that he was drawn to that he would probably never admit to any of the women he dated. It was a subcategory of general male-on-female porn called "Fuck my wife," academically known as cuckolding. Cuckolding had been getting readers turned on and intrigued since Jesus' time—Joseph was cuckolded by God himself—and in more obvious ways over the next two thousand years, in *The Canterbury Tales*, throughout Shakespeare plays and other Elizabethan literature, and the like, the cuckold held particular fascination to readers. In the past decade of easily produced and distributed pornography, the cuckolding genre had taken a more explicit turn. If cuckolding was a subcategory of straight male-female sex, a subcategory of the subcategory was something called a cream pie.

It took a lot of work to be innocent, and Peoria didn't seem biologically inclined toward innocence.

"And so?" Valerie says.

Peoria readjusts his gauge of Valerie's age. Early forties. Under the high-definition glow of the 1080 pixels of Korean-manufactured

Samsung color, the Mandarin Oriental's courtesy bathrobe open to the hotel's air conditioner, he got a good look at her breasts. They sagged a bit under the weight of two decades' worth of topless sunbathing. Nude beaches in the Riviera, cigarette butts stubbed out in a pile of sand next to her beach towel. Without a bikini top, she had a body that American men would look at as they walked past on the shore, partially intrigued by the woman's attractiveness, partially by her comfort in exposing a pair of naked breasts. If she was so casual about allowing gazes to come her way, in view of running toddlers, German beer guts, Swedish Speedos, local teens hawking bottles of Coke and *croque-monsieurs*, one could only imagine what she would do behind closed doors; there was an openness to her sensuality, an openness that with a few bottles of wine might be persuaded to try anything.

Valerie slides her panties down, feet coming out carefully, sure of her balance. She hangs the panties on the tip of her finger. She motions, with that same finger, for Peoria to approach her, the panties swaying as if they were resting on a clothesline.

Peoria steps next to her. She pushes her panties to his face, her finger in his mouth. He starts to suck on her finger, mild saltiness.

Valerie touches his groin with her other hand and starts to rub his penis. He leans forward and kisses her, keeping her finger in his mouth, off to the side, like a hooked fish, lips making contact around the crumpled edges of the silk.

She takes her finger from his mouth and the panties stay in between their lips. He unbuttons his pants and unzips them and steps back and her panties fall to the floor. He pulls down his boxers and he can feel the crust from his own sperm, the stains of sexual moisture that the tissues in the brothels didn't wipe up. She kneels down and takes his penis in her mouth. Peoria closes his eyes and wishes that he will get hard, because there are a few seconds when he wonders if he has enough blood left in him to fill up.

He opens his eyes and Marcel is out of the shower, standing at the bathroom door, smiling.

Peoria feels a mild shock. His penis, which was becoming harder, becomes temporarily less so. How do I feel that he is watching me? Can I let go in this setting, this hotel room? It's not the intimate professionalism of a whorehouse, where if a friend was watching him get a blow job, it would seem okay, part of the atmosphere and ambience . . .

Valerie is squatting, mouth on his cock, with two hands free, she shakes off the Mandarin Oriental's courtesy bathrobe and places one hand back under her for balance, then with her other hand begins to finger herself.

"Look at me, look at me," she says.

Peoria looks down and her eyes are rolled back up staring at him. He moves his eyes from Valerie, at his knees, to Marcel, still standing in the shower door.

"Do not let him come yet," Marcel says, and goes into the other room, the bedroom.

Valerie gets up from her knees and takes Peoria's hand and leads him into the bedroom.

The bed is well used, the one-thousand-thread sheets pushed to the bottom of the king-size mattress, the decorative pillows tossed off on the bedside tables. It's a bed that has not been available for a turn-down service and a mint on the pillow in days.

Marcel is lying on his back, towel still on. He hangs his head down over the side of the bed, looking at the world upside down.

Valerie walks over to Marcel. The bed is four feet off the ground. She climbs onto the mattress and then puts one leg on one side of Marcel's head and her other leg outside of his shoulder, knees straddling his face. With her teeth, she undoes Marcel's towel and uncovers the Frenchman's erection. She turns around to look at Peoria.

"Doggy style, yes?"

Peoria moves up behind her and feels another hand on his cock, from below. Marcel opens Valerie's pussy for him and directs his cock in.

Peoria is not tall enough to be having standing-up sex while Valerie is on the bed and his feet are planted to the ground. He gets up on his tiptoes and holds on to her waist for balance.

He starts to move in and out of her, Valerie ducking her head down every fourth insertion to lick Marcel's cock, and Peoria can feel a kind of tingling on his alcohol-constricted testicles, the sandpaper of another tongue, and he remembers a line he'd read in a prison memoir, a mouth is a mouth and a tongue is a tongue, one brand of sandpaper the same as any other, and he lets himself go with the groans and the groans coming from Valerie's mouth ahead of him. He sees the digital clock that says 2:15 a.m. and he spaces out. He has a flight to catch tomorrow. Distracted, he slips out of her, and before he can get back in, he feels another mouth on his penis.

"I'm cleaning you off," says Marcel.

He can see Marcel, buried underneath her ass and pussy, in glimpses when she rises up off his face, and he can see Marcel's tongue flutter into her asshole and out of her asshole. She climbs off her husband and tells Peoria to join her on the bed.

She rolls to one side and Peoria moves in behind her. He starts fucking her ass quite hard, and he feels that he is going to come.

"Put it in my pussy, you want to put it in my pussy?"

Marcel is jerking off, lying next to them on the bed.

"My head is full of blood from being upside down," he says. "I am dizzy."

He holds Valerie's hand. What tenderness.

Peoria takes his cock out of her ass and finds her pussy.

There is an anticlimax before the climax because he has to ready himself again, to get to the point where he can come. He starts thinking even dirtier thoughts than what he is doing—he starts piling on the dirt, splashing the dirt in his head in scenarios that he plays out in his mind's eye, outrageous thoughts, more outrageous than fucking the wife while her husband jerks off and watches and holds her hand on the same hotel bed. He starts thinking: strange to have to imagine a fantasy when you have such a real-life fantasy right here. Odd, but he must focus if he wants to come. He focuses. He starts thinking: all the cocks that have ever been where he is fucking her now, and he sees them all, lined up in a row, Valerie, on a beach, on that beach in the Riviera, under a lifeguard chair—there are no lifeguard tents in the Mediterranean—no, he sees her between a sand dune and he imagines the line of men coming to take their turn with her, one after the other, stretching back into the waterfront restaurants, the jism dripping from her ass and her pussy and her mouth and her sunburned breasts, and then he comes . . .

Peoria falls over onto the bed. Valerie rolls to her back. Marcel gets to his knees, and starting at his wife's breasts, licks and caresses her body, moving toward her belly button, moving toward her pussy. Valerie puts her hand on his head and pushes lightly, her fingers tangled in her husband's thinning hair. Valerie puts her left hand on the top of her pussy, and in a move that Peoria has seen only on a computer monitor and television screen, she squeezes and a dollop of his sperm pops up.

Clams, seashells, mollusks, mussels, oysters. White discharge. Membranes and inverse epidermal layers. Pink jowls, a string of soy milk drool. A raw baked good, doughy, whipped egg-white batter uncooked.

Pushing himself up on his elbows, Peoria sees for the first time—in the dimming lights of the HDTV and the digital clock and the faint city lights cutting through the open drapes—what a cream pie looks like.

The sight is too organic and messy for him to find beauty in it. . . .

Peoria wakes up twelve hours later. He has a flight to catch.

PART V

Homecoming

21.

Morning, Monday, January 12, 2004

Unbundling, I sit down in my cubicle.

It's either the coldest January in New York on record, or I'm getting old. I've lived most of my life in the Northeast, and Manhattan is the farthest south I'd ever called home. But this is my fourth year in the city, and my tolerance for zero degrees Fahrenheit has disappeared. A coldness without the warm feelings of FAO Schwarz and Radio City Music Hall and Macy's window-shopping. A dead month, January is, another New Year's without a terrorist attack on Times Square, and I, perhaps stupidly, blame the weather for how everyone acts.

Seasonal affective disorder. It's a real phenomenon. The medical explanation, not enough sunlight. Depression and listlessness are the two well-known side effects, but there's another one: paranoia. Self-preservation instincts, from the sidewalk to the corner office. If the sun isn't hitting me, it's got to be hitting someone else, much to my disadvantage. The bitterness of Fifth Avenue winds, from apartment door to subway, melted slush and running noses—the lack of eye contact noticeable. It's like just looking someone in the eye lets a few degrees of heat escape from my eye sockets.

It's the worst month for office intrigue.

My computer whines and sputters on. Other bundled figures limp by, fifteen minutes or so behind the usual schedule. Everyone is feeling the cold.

My Outlook program comes to life, closing a series of warnings and updates and pop-ups. The server searches something, whatever a server searches, and downloads the crate of electronic mail that has entered my address and domain overnight.

An email from Judy Givens, subject: On behalf of Henry the EIC.

Dear Staff:

After thirty-three years at the magazine, I'm announcing today that I will retire my position as editor in chief, effective January 2006 . . .

Before I get to the two remaining paragraphs of the thank-yous and the memories, Gary's head appears over my cubicle wall.

"Did you see the email," he says.

"Reading it right now."

"Announcing so far in advance that he's leaving. Don't you find that strange?"

"Maybe he wants to do a farewell tour."

"Maybe, but the big news is what's not in the email. He didn't name a replacement."

"Really?"

"Yeah, and he says that a search for the replacement will start ASAP, once various factors are considered and weighed and everything."

"The race is on, I guess."

My computer beeps, another staff-wide email.

It's a reminder. This afternoon, at four p.m., there's a homecoming party at the Top of the Mag for the staff who have returned from covering the war. It gives the list of attendees, including A.E. Peoria, Townsend, Charles, and Lee.

Please join us to welcome and celebrate the work of our brave and courageous correspondents who are back after giving the magazine incredible coverage of our nation's most important story.

"You going to this?" I ask.

"Yeah, why not. Should be interesting—Nishant and Sanders and Henry will probably be there. Good time to do some body-language reading."

I hear the glass doors open at the end of the hallway, and rushing past in a blur is A.E. Peoria. It is his first day back in the office. I don't get a look at his face, only the top of his head as he blows by my cubicle.

I want to say hello, but I don't want to be too aggressive. I'll let him unbundle, de-thaw, and fire up his Dell before I go greet him.

"Hastings?" I hear the singsong voice of Nishant Patel.

I jump.

"Hi, Nishant, how's it going?"

"Fine. I'm giving a speech at the American Enterprise Institute in honor of the economist Milton Friedman. Could you write up about nine pages or so of research on him for the acceptance speech?"

"Sure, Milton Friedman award, no problem at all. Who's getting it?"

"Hernando de Soto—you've heard of him?"

"The explorer or the economist?"

"The economist."

"Yep, sure, I'm on it."

I always try to slip a few notes of humanity into these conversations to build my bond with Nishant.

"Are you going to the homecoming party tonight?"

"Hm?"

"For the correspondents coming back from the war."

"I don't know if that's in my schedule. Patricia, Lucy, have you scheduled me to go to the homecoming event?"

A furious exchange of recriminations and accusations.

"Henry the EIC is going to be there, I think," I say.

"Henry is going to be there," he says, his thoughts taking over, and he heads back into his office, followed by Patricia and Lucy.

I walk down the hallway to Peoria's office. The lights are off and he's sprawled in his swivel chair, eyes closed.

"My girlfriend broke up with me, bro," he says as I walk in the door.

"Hey, man, great to see that you're back."

"She broke up with me."

"That sucks—the six-orgasms girl?"

"I should never have told her about the spot, the questions just kept coming after that."

"The spot?"

"You want a cigarette?"

"I don't smoke, but I'll go outside with you."

From the elevator ride to the street, he recounts the conversation with his girlfriend.

"I got back and we went out to dinner and she asked me if something was wrong and I was, like, no, nothing is wrong," he says. "But she kept asking and asking and asking, and so finally I told her about the spot."

The spot. He'd been back in New York four days when he'd noticed, above his pubic hair, a red dot. Then, after foraging and brushing aside in front of a full-length mirror for self-examination, he noticed two red spots. He freaked out. He first called his doctor friend, who'd given him the odds on getting HIV after the trip to Mexico. His doctor friend recommended going to a walk-in clinic to get it checked out. Peoria did that, finding himself in a doctor's office out of the Third World, a doctor's office that smelled of rotting tobacco.

"Rotting tobacco. It's fucking cold out here," Peoria says. "Let's go back inside."

We go back inside and he gets to the point. The doctor, asking a series of invasive and highly personal questions, after drawing his blood and getting him tested, brought out a medical textbook and flipped it to the page with a large M in the corner.

"Molluscum contagiosum," Peoria says. "That's what I have. Molluscum contagiosum. I'd never heard of it. Toddlers get it—it's like the chicken pox. Toddlers and sexually active adults, you know. But it's not really an STD—it's, like, not really one. It's benign, you know, it doesn't do anything. It's just a spot, and there's a pretty easy procedure where they pluck it out."

"That sucks, that sucks," I say.

"Have you ever had a bandage on your dick?" he asks me.

"Not that I can remember," I say.

"I have a bandage on my dick right now."

I had thought, on some level, I was immune to conversational surprises, especially when sex was concerned. That over my approximately twenty-five years I had been told such a massive amount of personal information and sexual detail that very little would catch me off guard. I'm from the first totally coed generation. By the third grade we had textbook, graphic descriptions of sex. By middle school, survivors of herpes and genital warts and even HIV spoke as guest lecturers. I know sex is a beautiful living act between two adults; sex is something to discuss with your partner, in detail, before, after, and perhaps during. But I've never been confronted with a friend who has a bandage on his dick.

"I had to lie down on the table, and the doctor, a schlubby doctor too, the kind of guy you'd meet in AA, pulled down my pants, and he swabbed the two dots. And he found even more dots, he found five more, on the underside of my dick, and took a needle. He popped the head. They're like zits, I guess, that they have a head, and you need to remove the head so they stop spreading. There was a little blood. He put a patch of white bandages around my dick and then he snipped away my pubic hair. If you shave, apparently it can spread, and I guess that's why on gay guys it can spread, because they shave their pubic regions. Then he picked them out with a needle."

"Sounds pretty shitty," I say.

"Very vulnerable," he says. "After the procedure, he asked me if I took drugs and if I was depressed. I told him that I had been taking a lot of pills and drinking a lot since I left Baghdad. He thought I had some kind of post-traumatic stress. Had I taken pills recently? I had four Percocet and two Xanax that I got from my girlfriend that morning, and he wondered if it was an unhealthy relationship for me to be in. With her giving me pills and everything. If I was self-medicating."

We're back in his office. He tells me to shut the door and then he sits down.

"So I went out to dinner that night with her and she asked if something was wrong, and I said, yes, I have this spot, because the doctor recommended me to tell my sexual partners about it. That was a fucking mistake. Herpes or syphilis or chlamydia or something, I should have told her. But you know this molluscum contagiosum is benign. Most girls are pretty good about getting checked out regularly, so she would have found it eventually if she had it. Then she asked if I'd been, you know, unfaithful."

"Had you?"

"Not emotionally, you know, but I had a couple of run-ins."

Though I never could say that Peoria looked like a particularly healthy person, he looks particularly ill this morning. I picture him naked, bandaged dick, his cheeks not quite red enough from the frostbite temperatures. He looks like his stomach hurts, like coffee and a half quart of stale wine are swirling in his gut. He keeps talking, not stopping. He takes sharp, wheezy inhales, a two-pack-a-day cigarette habit. His teeth have a dull yellow sheen of moss. He looks like he has bad breath. He looks like he might never get up from his swivel chair again. He looks like he hasn't showered (he has, he tells me, but not completely because he didn't want to get the bandages wet).

And he details to me what he had the previous evening detailed to his girlfriend (leaving out a few things both to me and to Six Orgasms, as I will learn later): a sexual encounter poolside near the patio (Brennan Toddly was hitting on her too, and that motherfucker is married), and he refers vaguely to a number of unpaid sexual encounters in Thailand (though it isn't until a year later that I learn about the ladyboy). No, Peoria does not look very fit for the homecoming party this afternoon.

"She called me a rat," he says. "Do you think I'm a rat?"

A buzzing. His cell phone frog-crawls across his desk.

"It's her. I better take this."

He answers. He hits the mute button.

"Hastings, the thing is, I think I'm self-destructive, you know. Because I don't really want to be dating her, you know, because I don't love her. Anyway. Talk to you later."

He hits the unmute button.

I get up, close the door to his office, and go back to my cubicle.

22.

Early Evening, Monday, January 12, 2004

Gary and I take the elevator up to the homecoming party. A line has already formed, people standing and chatting along the windows, bulging out in the middle of a scrum centered around Henry the EIC, who accepts congratulations and regrets, even from the three other correspondents that had been to the war and come back.

With club soda in hand, I watch the progression of magazine dignitaries approaching Henry, saying a few words of consolation, shaking the hands of the three other war correspondents. Sanders Berman arrives, Delray M. Milius on his heels. Fashionably late, Nishant Patel strolls in, his assistants Patricia and Lucy behind him, carrying two of his BlackBerrys and his personal mobile telephone.

And as Nishant and Sanders go up the line, each working different sides of the room, they are both headed to meet at the towering figure in the center, Henry the EIC.

As the two contenders to his throne are about to meet, I move closer to listen. I feel a sharp stab in my side, then a liquid discharge, and looking down I see I've been bumped out of the way by Matt Healy, the crack investigative reporter, blue ink on my shirt leaking from his busted pen.

"Argrg, excuse me," he mumbles, timing his break in the scrum for when all three editors meet.

Henry, enjoying the moment, silences Berman and Patel, opening the floor to Healy.

"Matt, great you could make it," Henry the EIC says.

"I'm on deadline, so I can't stay long, but I want to make the case for going big on this," he says. "I've uncovered allegations of abuse by Americans of Iraqi detainees. You wouldn't believe what I'm hearing is coming down the pike."

Healy goes into some detail—blaring loud music, standing in stress positions, dogs sniffing, laughing, and other indignities that will be very well known by next summer. But, it's not well known now—the photos from Abu Ghraib aren't going to be released for months.

"Matt, it sounds like a great story, but making these accusations without having seen anything more than some government report that might or might not come out, that's dangerous. We need something more solid," says Henry.

It's always a risk for a subordinate to jump into a conversation with four elders, with four people who can make or break your career, who may not be too keen on your insight. You never want to contradict them in public or to say something unwise, but I feel I have something that they may not know of.

It's a file that A.E. Peoria had written for one of the larger Iraq stories; he'd filed ten thousand words, twenty-five pages single-spaced, and there's a good chance that I was the only one in the building who had actually read every last page. I'd come across two paragraphs where A.E. Peoria had described the interrogation of Iraqi prisoners, as told to him by an American officer at a detention facility in Baghdad. It was the kind of confirmation that Healy didn't have.

A.E. Peoria isn't here yet, so I figure I'm doing him a favor—dropping his name among the power elite at the magazine.

"Um, you might want to read A.E. Peoria's file too," I say.

The four esteemed gentlemen stop talking. Nishant Patel gives me a look that means, You have overstepped your precociousness. Sanders Berman, a fan of hierarchy, also looks uncomfortable. Healy, though, doesn't give a shit, and says, "Peoria? What does it say?"

"It quotes an American captain about some of the things they do to detainees, and—"

I catch a whiff of cigarette and vomit covered over with cologne, and Peoria enters the conversation.

"Sorry I'm late. I've had a hell of a time, you wouldn't believe what happened today—"

Peoria is lucky that Healy has another skill of the reporter—the sharp question to redirect a talkative subject back to where he wants the conversation to go. If he hadn't, Peoria probably would have started talking about molluscum contagiosum and his breakup.

"This guy says you have a detainee file?"

"Oh, yeah, I never knew why Jerry cut that out, it was great stuff. They've taken detainees, the real Islamic-types, and started slapping them around with the Koran, literally, the captain slapping, pissing on it, bringing it in the shower with them, even. I think they said they were jerking off in it, saying that Allah likes sticky pages, tossing it in the toilet, all sorts of stuff like that. Yeah, I don't know why—"

I back away, my place in pushing the story done, a role that would be forgotten by everyone (except for Delray M. Milius, whose eyes are on me, gauging the threat).

Henry the EIC, Nishant, and Sanders all agree that it sounds like a great story. It gets the cover. Healy and Peoria get the byline.

HOW A MAGAZINE STORY GETS WRITTEN

I'm around twenty-five now—I think I've said that. I feel like a relic, like an ancient. I feel like I'm a blacksmith in the days of Henry Ford's assembly line, an apprentice scroll writer in the months following Gutenberg's great invention, or a poet in 1991.

Meaning: I feel my skill set is obsolete.

This book is an insurance policy against my dying field: maybe I can write novels, and if that's not a sign of desperation, a jump from one sinking ship to another, I don't know what is.

But for the sake of history, I'll explain the soon-to-be-lost art. Take my descriptions with you into the next century for research when Disney or some other corporation decides to build a tourist trap of what late-twentieth-century America was like, like they do now with those old villages of Pilgrims and settlers in funny hats and clothes: demonstrations of manual butter churning, candle making, and typesetting in a printing press.

This is what, the tourist guide will say, is called a "newsroom"; it's where they produced information content on paper, like newspapers and magazines. (Kids will nod: Oh, that's where the word *paper* comes from in *newspaper*.)

A slice of life: the cubicles, animatronics or live action—dozens of people to put out one single page of print, how extraordinarily quaint.

This is how a magazine story gets written.

Before 1969, stories in *The Magazine* had no bylines. There's a single authorial voice, the voice of *The Magazine*, omniscient in its power of observation, a fullness of perspective that transcends individual insight to bring the hefty weight of an institution. It works to much effectiveness.

But then 1969 happens. *The Magazine* catches up to the culture. The individual man, the yippie, the hippie, the hip and the square. Voices that are too institutional and too authoritative are suspect. Institutions inherently are co-opted by the immoral status quo, all slightly to massively oppressive, all involved in the insane desire of the Establishment to keep Blacks feeling Black, to keep White Kids from smoking dope and feeling love, to make the Working-Class Man consume, to reduce all the peoples of the world to their sole human value of becoming efficient actors in our economic system, and to keep undermining the beliefs of the Vietnamese people, particularly in the northern part of that country.

The Magazine, to its credit, adopts positions throughout the '60s that start to border on the radical, at least compared with those of its main competitor, Brand X. It is, as the editors see it, a time when smart business strategy and positive social policy converge. *The Magazine* promotes Negro rights, peacenik rights, Mexican rights, worker rights, and occasionally the rights of napalm victims. *The Magazine* mourns equally for Altamont and Kent State and Watergate.

In practice, though, it is undermining the labor movement. *The Magazine* writers don't have a union. The writers live with the hypocrisy until 1971. The writers go on strike.

It is a brief moment in history: magazine writers will never have the chance to go on strike again.

The writers and reporters win an important concession: the byline. The institutional voice of the magazine is never the same again.

But the byline, too, is misleading to the laymen. A magazine story is not the work of one man or one woman.

The byline gives the impression that the name on top actually wrote and reported the story. Not true. The writer, in this ancient formulation, takes the reporting from others and weaves it into a narrative. There are also layers of editors and copy editors and fact-checkers and writers and reportorial changes.

Each paragraph and each sentence that finds its way into print, hand-delivered to subscriber homes, resting casually and arrogantly on the newsstands, takes at least eight or nine hours of close inspection: tweaking, polishing, rubbing, beautification, sullification, hyping. These hands are hidden; it is the writer with the byline who gets the glory.

Drawback: the writer also gets the blame.

Advantage: the name in bold print is treated as if the brilliant insights and omniscience are all his own.

The '80s and '90s: The byline takes on a life of its own. The byline separates itself from *The Magazine* brand. Bylines become brands. Layoffs mean that there are no more layers of fact-checkers and researchers and editors. The strategy of *The Magazine* is to enhance its many brands by making brands of bylines.

Healy is a brand. A.E. Peoria is a brand in the making.

23.

Mid-January 2004

I'm anticipating the reaction, monitoring the media waves from my cubicle.

Peoria and Healy's story is met with silence. Nothing. Doesn't crack the ether. Doesn't make *The Magazine* part of the conversation. Doesn't move the debate or get any television hits or radio hits. No responses from the White House or the State Department. Even Amnesty International and Human Rights Watch shrug it off.

The Magazine's public relations department is disinclined to touch it. Nobody wants this story. Complaining about Iraq when Saddam Hussein has been captured?

Three days, nothing.

What happens during those three days? *The Magazine* goes global. It is translated into six different languages: Polish, Russian, Korean, Japanese, Turkish, and Arabic.

By Thursday, an Islamic cleric in Najaf, a man who you wouldn't think would be in the magazine's target demographic—though, to be honest, by the year 2004, anyone who picks up the magazine is welcomed into its demographic—has a copy in his hands. It gets delivered to his mosque. (Or maybe he found it in the seat-back pocket on a first-class flight from Tehran to Baghdad, thanks to a promotional deal *The Magazine* has with Royal Jordanian Airlines.)

The cleric does what all truly holy men do when they come across an outrage, an indignation, an affront to what is good and decent in the world: he calls a press conference.

Only the Arabic-language press attends—the video shows, with the production value of a New England public access channel, a card table, and a filter of cigarette smoke in an elementary school classroom, Arabic script and loud trumpeting music on, a scratchy audio.

It's another twelve hours before what he says gets translated back into English. That's when I pick up on it. That's after the damage is done. The Internet has the story.

By Friday, followers of the cleric have taken to the streets in Najaf, waving copies of *The Magazine*, burning copies of *The Magazine*, and even mentioning things like death threats (though not taking it as far as a fatwa).

The Magazine's role gives a new theme to the usual riots and fighting following Friday prayers.

The local authorities, called in to stop the riots, are persuaded, after having the damning allegations on page 21 paraphrased for them— probably an inaccurate paraphrase, at that—to join the riots as well.

Furious excitement—religious, political, illiterate, a change of pace from relaxing though resentful unemployment—sweeps the streets outside "one of Islam's holiest shrines." It means only one thing: a trampling.

Crowd deaths follow. More deaths come after unknown guns fire bullets lengthwise.

Thirteen is the total.

It's clear in the first headlines I read from the Associated Press and

Reuters how this story is going to play: *The Magazine* is the cause of the riots.

The political fallout in America begins.

The administration in Washington goes on the offensive—an example of the liberal media, the pantywaist liberals in New York trying to undermine the war effort. Because of reckless reporting, the White House spokesperson says, thirteen people are dead.

The spokesperson pauses at the lectern.

Thirteen, he repeats.

The right-wing websites seize the deaths to attack *The Magazine*'s credibility. "The Magazine Murders," writes one blogger. "Thirteen innocents dead at the hands of the MainStreamMedia. Despicable."

There is no room in the discourse to mention the hypocrisy that in other circumstances, these same people would be cheering the deaths of thirteen Islamic extremists. But today they have taken up their cause with mourning blog posts.

I'm waiting for *The Magazine* to respond, to issue a statement.

Nishant Patel ducks by the cubicle, Sanders Berman hustles past. No time for chitchat today. I hear an "Arrgh" from Healy, notepads flapping in his pockets. Peoria, three Xanax already ingested, wearing an off-the-rack suit and tie, is the only one who stops by to tell me what's going on.

"Healy's sources are backing off," he says.

"What about your captain?"

"He's not answering emails. Fuck, he might be dead for all I know. I haven't heard from him in months."

"So what are you going to do?"

"They want me to go on TV to defend it."

Peoria says this and leaves me at the cubicle.

Choosing Peoria to go on TV? Bad idea. The two people who can offer the best defense for *The Magazine*: Nishant, a man many Americans assume to be Muslim because of his darker skin and accent, and Sanders Berman, a southerner who counts conservatives among his most devoted readers. Or Healy, whose reputation—the Pentagon Paper of Blow Jobs—could survive the blistering assault.

But Peoria, God bless him, so deranged from painkillers, war flashbacks, and the trauma of a benign STD, has been chosen to take the fall.

I hear a whispered conversation outside my cubicle.

The voice of Delray M. Milius, echoing off his hand, which he has put to his mouth. Sanders Berman stands next to him, looking panicked.

". . . stay out of the way . . . lay low . . . don't be associated with this story . . ."

I have an urge to pop up, to say, What the fuck, guys? But I don't. I just take a few notes. The time of the conversation, the words that I heard, the participants.

A door in the corner office shuts.

"Patricia, Lucy, is my car waiting for me?"

"Yes, Nishant," says the chorus.

Delray M. Milius's hand drops from his mouth. Sanders Berman stands upright. Nishant, a Burberry peacoat hanging over his arm, comes around the corner.

"Professor," Berman says.

"Milius, Sanders," he says.

"Off to CNN?" Sanders asks, a note of hopefulness.

"Oh, no, no time for television today," Nishant says.

"Me either," Berman says.

Two men who, as their reputations confirm, find it very difficult to go forty-eight hours without finding a way to a television studio, who carry makeup removal swabs in their pockets, are now both unavailable.

"I have a speech to give on Milton Friedman," Nishant Patel says. "An award ceremony. Hastings, you have that speech for me?"

"Right here, Nishant," I say.

Delray M. Milius's doughboy face flinches; he hadn't seen me, hunched behind the velvet cubicle walls.

"Lucy, Patricia, is my car ready?"

"It's waiting, Nishant," they respond.

Patricia snatches the manila folder from his hand, and Nishant leaves two of his assistants trailing.

Sanders Berman gives me a pained smile and turns the corner back to his office. Delray M. Milius follows him.

Peoria comes charging out of his office next.

"I'm supposed to be on CNN in forty-five minutes," he tells me.

I follow Peoria outside while he smokes a cigarette. The CNN studios are only two blocks away on Columbus Circle.

"Peoria, man, I think they want you to take the blame for this," I say.

He looks at me, inhaling, his cheeks turning Granny Smith–apple green in the cold.

"We have nothing to apologize for," he says. "All sorts of fucked-up shit is going on at these detention facilities. I know that, Healy knows that. We just need to stand by it, you know, and since I'm the one who was over there, I really have the credibility—that's what they told me, and I liked that, having the credibility to speak for the magazine. It shows that they really have put their faith in me, to choose me to do this, you know?"

"I don't think so, man. I think they're ducking for the fucking hurricane shelters while you're standing out there with the microphone, dodging telephone polls."

"You're a fucking cynical person for your age. You know, I was never that cynical when I was coming up. Now . . ."

Maybe it's the drugs or another hangover or the prescription meds or just the numb stressed-out feeling he's described to me since coming back. He doesn't get it.

24.

Mid-January 2004, Continued

Forty-five minutes later, I turn up the volume on the television on the pillar next to Dorothy's and Patricia's cubicles.

"A CNN exclusive interview," the anchor says, "with the reporter who wrote the now infamous story that sparked the *Magazine* riots in Iraq."

Although Peoria has gone to the studio, they don't actually put him in the same room with the anchor. He is, as he tells me later, brought down to a dark room on the second floor, behind a wall of glass, where production assistants and assistant producers and other young-looking people in headsets mill around, slamming phones down, rushing, wound-up. The anchor is on the fifth floor. Peoria is put on a chair to look straight into the camera.

They at least have given him a spray of makeup, I think, as his face flashes on screen, the green tone of his cheeks removed.

Isolated below, he doesn't have the comfort of seeing a human face—he feels trapped, cornered, staring at a camera with the words of what the anchor is reading scrolling underneath.

"In Iraq's holiest city, riots broke out after allegations in a *Maga-*

zine story offended tens of thousands of Iraqis and others across the Muslim world. The story alleged that Iraqi detainees were victims of abuse at the hands of U.S. soldiers, a claim that both the White House and the Pentagon have strongly denied. The riots have now claimed the lives of thirteen Iraqis. With us is A.E. Peoria, the *Magazine* reporter who wrote the controversial story. First, let's look at the words that have caused the deadly violence."

On screen, the offending paragraph is put up, with a number of ellipses.

According to a U.S. military official, detainees were told to strip naked . . . subjected to "debilitating noise levels" of rock music like AC/DC . . . and told to flush the Koran down the toilet. In one incident, the Koran was used to capture the ejaculate of a soldier who was reading aloud a page of *Hustler*'s letter section to the captured insurgents. . . .

I hear Peoria clear his throat.

"Do you think you owe the Iraqi people an apology?" the anchor asks, as a way to ease into the conversation.

"An apology, I mean, I'm sorry that they got so offended, but—"

"The sources in the story—everyone has backed off this. Our own CNN reporting also couldn't confirm your story. You can't really confirm it, can you?"

"I mean, we quoted—we had quotes from an eyewitness."

"But you never saw this yourself?"

"No, we had quotes from an eyewitness, like I said, uh, I never saw this myself, but I think, you know, we reported on this investigation that is going on into it—"

"But the government says that this investigation doesn't contain anything like what you described, that it is just a routine checkup of the facilities, and the claims that you make in the story haven't been confirmed by the investigation."

"Right, well, the other reporter, who wrote this, his sources told him that they saw a draft of the report—"

"A draft, so this was just a draft of a government report? And you're blaming Matthew Healy, one of the most well-respected journalists in the profession? As I know, from personal experience covering the government, the final version often has many things that are taken out, and so don't you think it was reckless to go ahead with this?"

"I don't think, I mean, you have to understand that I'm sorry that this rioting happened, but you know that cleric, that guy, he's a real jerk—he's not like a good guy, you know?"

"We have to go to a commercial, and when we get back, we'll bring in a Middle East expert to discuss the fallout. To join in the discussion, log on to CNN.com."

It is the first time I have seen a friend melt down on live television. It is a brutal experience. I want to give him the benefit of the doubt. I know the adrenaline is flowing through his mind. I know what he should say, I know that he should just say, Stop this madness, your questions are asinine. It's worse, too, when I put myself in the place of an average viewer who happens to be tuning into CNN at an airport lounge or as background noise as he makes the second pot of coffee in the kitchen, or the first pot of coffee if he's watching on the West Coast.

I know they will take one look at Peoria and think: This guy is fucked-up, this guy doesn't know what he's saying, he's not making any sense at all. Because the words Peoria says jumble together. They don't fit in sound bites. I know he needs time to explain himself, to explain the story, to have the viewers see the context. He just wants context. If he can just give the context of the story, if he can just make a few simple points—that the story is accurate, that perhaps they could have been more careful in how they reported it, but that other reporters had been digging around, hinting at similar activities by American forces. If he could have cited an Associated Press story from November, if he could have cited a Reuters story from last week, if he can just explain himself. But Peoria can't explain himself, because once you start trying to explain yourself on television, it's hard to win—you can't explain; you just have to state yourself, without hesitation.

I want to give him the benefit of the doubt—to take out the "ums" and "ahs" and how his eyes keep darting to the left and right. (He will explain later that his eyes were looking at the other television monitors, and he will swear the producers were cutting back to him at exactly the wrong moments.)

"We're back with noted Middle East scholar Daniel Tubes. Daniel, what did you make of the—"

"Can I just respond to what Mr. Peoria said first? What he's doing is classic. He's blaming the victims for his own reckless reporting."

"How is he blaming the victims?"

"He's saying it's their fault for rioting, their fault for reacting to the erroneous information he put out. And I think that's just despicable."

"Uh, no, I'm just saying—"

"He obviously knows nothing of Middle Eastern culture," Tubes continues. "I hate to be blunt, but that's so clear to me."

"Why do you say that?" the anchor asks, lobbing another softball to Tubes.

"*Hustler*? The Arabs don't have a culture of masturbation," Tubes says. "The story has so many holes in it, it's an embarrassment. It's offensive, because in the Arab world, and I don't think I can put this more politely, there just isn't the culture of masturbation that we have in the West."

"Mr. Peoria," the anchor says. "Is this true? Were you unaware of the cultural sensitivities you were reporting on?"

"No, I guess I wasn't aware of the, uh, lack of cultural, um, in that sense. I mean, the Iraqis I knew, um, they really liked looking at pictures of naked women and things. Um, I mean, they didn't even need to be naked, just like, you know, advertisements of a girl in a robe or a bra, or a girl in a dress that doesn't fully cover, you know, that was pretty shocking to them—"

"And so you thought it was a good idea to write about *Hustler* magazine?"

"I mean, I'm there to report on what's happening. I don't really—"

"This is the smoke screen that the liberal media have been hiding behind: they want to do their best to undermine the Americans. They hate the troops, they don't care that what they report actually puts American lives at risk. And by the way, a source at the Pentagon told me that pornography isn't even allowed among Americans in Iraq! It's against General Order Number 1. So how did they get this so-called *Hustler* magazine, this so-called November edition? How, I ask, did they get that? And flushing the Koran down the toilet? I spoke to another high-level source who told me that there are no flushing handles at the detention facility Peoria so inaccurately depicts as hostile. They don't even have toilets; they have little holes to squat in—and they have porta-johns."

"I mean, it is just to get at the idea they were throwing the Koran in the toilet, you know?" Peoria says.

"Oh, so he's changing his story again, right here! Admitting to another mistake! They don't flush; they throw! Next think you know, it's going to be, Well, there was a Koran that fell off a table in the room next door!"

"All right, we're going to turn to the viewer email, see what our audience is saying. Sam from Georgia writes, 'Peoria is a disgrace to

America. I'd cancel my subscription to *The Magazine* but I don't even have one.'

"Caroline from New Mexico says, 'I'm so disappointed in how the media always gets things wrong and no one holds them accountable. Kudos to your show for calling that reporter out for his bad news.'

"We're heading to commercial. Mr. Peoria, thanks for your time. Daniel Tubes will stay with us, and we'll be right back. You're watching CNN."

Peoria disappears from the screen, scratching his nose.

I turn off the television and go back to my cubicle. Within minutes, a story appears on the wires: "Journalist apologizes for erroneous story."

I click on the story and scroll down. In the second paragraph, the story says *The Magazine* has released a statement. This is news to me. The statement says that A.E. Peoria is suspended from his duties at the magazine, and the magazine is instituting new regulations to prevent this kind of mistake from happening again. The story quotes Delray M. Milius. It's clear they had the statement ready before Peoria even went on air.

25.

Mid-January 2004, Continued

I know I'm jeopardizing my job, for sure, but every once in a while, I'm supposed to stand up for what's right—at least that's what I'd absorbed from all sorts of morality tales I'd heard over the years.

What can I really do, as a cubicle slave, as a desk jockey, as a kid just one step removed from an internship?

I know what I can do, actually—I can leak the real story. I know I can go to Wretched.com.

I type in the URL, and wait for the screen to upload. I open another window to log into my personal email account, on Gmail. The Wretched.com site is coming up. It's the most popular media gossip site on the web.

The top story that day happens to be about an assistant producer at Fox News who'd gotten drunk at a party and had an accident in her pants that was picked up by a camera phone video. The editors at Wretched.com are loving that story, but I think after Peoria's appearance on CNN, they'll probably write something about him, too.

Sure enough, after I refresh the screen, there is a YouTube clip with Peoria, with the choice quotes printed below.

On the sidebar, there is a link for people to send anonymous tips to Wretched.com. I start writing up an email, putting down the real story, the cover-up.

Thirty minutes later, I see my email, name redacted, printed in full.

It would have worked, or perhaps helped save Peoria's reputation, but at almost the exact same time, the governor of Virginia got caught getting a blow job in the bathroom of the Amtrak Acela Express, DC to New York. The guy who broke the story? Healy. He must have been saving that one.

If Peoria had just waited a few hours, maybe he could have survived the damage, as the *Magazine* riots were forgotten with the new round of blow job news.

But then I hear screaming down the hall.

26.

February 2004

Reeling, reeled, rocked, slipped, sliding. What is the right word?

A.E. Peoria stares at his computer screen, sitting in his boxers, the white bandage visible through the slit for his penis. He scratched another bandage on his thigh covering up a puncture wound.

The Word document is opened up to his journal, file name wd35. When he had started this Word file during his senior year of college, he didn't want to name it something like "diary" or "aejournal," because if he ever lost his computer or if someone was looking in it—"someone" meaning a girl he was dating—then they'd know where to look, they could go straight to the source. He had transferred and resaved the file thirty-five times since that first document, in one of the early versions of Microsoft Word, and making its way from outdated laptop to outdated laptop, the journal now stretched to 1,700 single-spaced pages.

It isn't the most coherent document. There are so many spelling mistakes and typos that the red-line function, which marks a misspelled word, stopped working in late 2001.

But on the evening after the CNN appearance, it is to the wd35 that A.E. Peoria turns.

He knew that it couldn't have gone well. In the five minutes after removing the earpiece, being shuttled into the elevator by another large-breasted assistant producer, and being dumped out onto the street in the cold, he kept waiting for his mobile phone to light up with text messages and voicemails from friends and family who'd seen him on the program. Usually, after a TV appearance, he would be flooded with words of encouragement and support: great job, you looked great, excellent. He'd get notes from people he hadn't seen or heard from in years, all of a sudden impressed with him because he had managed to get onto a television screen.

Nothing this time.

When he got back to the office, the silence was even louder. He passed the security guard, and in the lobby there was a TV screen turned to CNN, and the security guard, a large African American woman, asked him for his ID.

"I was just on TV," he told her.

She looked at him.

And she waved him by. The doors opened to a crowd heading out for lunch, the clique that always seemed to hang out together, a group of assistant editors and senior editors who, Peoria had always felt, were replaying their high school fantasies of being the cool kids—and how he wanted to be among the cool kids! And Peoria thought that he had been finally making inroads into this crowd: one of them had asked him, at the homecoming party, if he would join their table for dinner Friday night, and this little group had come out in a bunch and blown past him, pretending they didn't recognize him, or at least pretending that they didn't know him well enough to say hello in the hallway.

On his floor, he walked by that kid Hastings's desk, and even Hastings just said hi, nothing special, no "Great job, man," and he knew Hastings was the kid who would have said "Great job" no matter what he had done.

And then he sat down at his desk and the email from Delray M. Milius was there, asking him to come into his office.

Peoria walked down the hallways again, and stood in front of the secretary sitting outside Delray's office.

"It was that bad, hunh?" Peoria said, fishing for at least a little encouragement. The woman at the desk didn't even smile and waved him in without answering his question.

"Alex, sit down," Delray M. Milius said. "We need to talk."

Peoria sat down and inhaled.

"We're putting you on administrative leave. We think you should take some time off."

"I don't think I need to take time off," Peoria said. "I don't think the story is getting any bigger now, I mean, what more could we do?"

"No, we think it's best for you to take time off, at least for a few weeks."

The conversation went back and forth like that for fifteen minutes, and Peoria finally agreed that he would take time off.

"Okay, Milius, I'm a team player and everything and I don't mind doing that at all, you know, so I only ask that we keep this confidential, because you know if it gets out that I'm taking time off, it's like I'm admitting I'm guilty and admitting I fucked up, and I really don't think I did, you know. I mean it was Healy's story and I just added that quote, so I don't—"

"Right, right," Milius said.

"I guess, because I don't want this to hurt my career here at *The Magazine*, so if we could keep this confidential, that would be great, you know, between us."

"Yes, of course, it won't go farther than this room."

"Thank you, I appreciate that," Peoria said, mildly shocked. Was he really getting suspended? He couldn't really believe it, and he felt like he wanted to do something—cry maybe, and if he were a girl, he probably would have started to cry, but Peoria really didn't cry when he was sober.

He got up and actually started to thank Milius for *The Magazine's* generosity, for keeping quiet about his leave, and started to convince himself, feeling the bandage on his dick and the extra two Xanax in his pocket, that maybe taking a few weeks off to let this story die down wouldn't be the worst thing in the world. And as he left, he looked back to thank Milius one more time, and saw Milius had picked up his phone.

Five minutes later, back at his office, he looked on the Drudge Report to see if the story was still getting top billing. It had been moved above the headline.

There was a new headline, which said "RIOT JOURNALIST SUSPENDED."

Healy got suspended? Strange that Milius hadn't mentioned it. He clicked on the story.

He read it. He saw a quote from Delray M. Milius, a statement that said they had grown concerned with A.E. Peoria's behavior and they were suspending him, pending further investigation.

Peoria sat back in his chair, numbed, and took out a Xanax. He reached into his desk drawer and found a bottle of whiskey and took two quick shots. There must be some mistake. He started to feel a number of uncomfortable sensations that reminded him of the humiliation he hadn't felt since *Desperation Points West* was reviled in a *Booklist* review.

It was as if he'd been kicked in the nuts—and for some reason he thought of Chipotle for a moment, Chipotle squealing and bleeding from the groin. He thought of Chipotle and knew, or had some idea of, what it must have been like to get shrapnel in the balls, to feel like the world had betrayed him with a quick and unexpected blast to the groin—even knowing that these things happened and it was a cutthroat world and reputations rose and fell. Peoria had been lied to by the best of them over the years as a journalist who had been shot at, had been rocked by explosions, but none of it had felt personal, none of it had felt like he had been betrayed—politicians lie, people lie when they talk to journalists, bad guys and insurgents try to kill you, nothing more or less should be expected of them, but there was no sense in taking it personally.

This, however, felt personal.

His first instinct was to write an email, a scathing email, but he stopped himself, remembering a line he'd read in a business memoir: Make war by phone, make love by email.

Okay, he thought, so maybe sending an email wouldn't be the right move. Then how could he get proof that Delray M. Milius had lied to him?

He would have to talk to him again, that's how. He was a reporter and he'd go over there right now and get him to go on the record, get him to admit that he had lied.

He grabbed his digital tape recorder and a notepad and a newly sharpened pencil, and holding them in his fists (the Xanax, or was it Percocet he'd been taking, made his hands feel heavy; he felt like he was in physical therapy, the way he was moving his hands around the pencil), and he took off down the hallway, choosing another route, past the cubicle area where the cool kids hung out, swinging past Sanders Berman's office, until he saw Delray M. Milius standing at his door and talking to his secretary.

And then Peoria tripped, stumbled over a man purse that had been left out in the hallway, and the strap, as if it were a bear trap, snagged his leg and he tumbled over, falling. He saw the corner of the secretary's desk and jerked his head out of the way quickly. He felt a squishy feeling on his thigh and wondered if his pen had busted, then he stood up, rocked backward, and looked at Milius.

"You said you were going to keep it confidential—"

That's when the secretary who hadn't even smiled started screaming.

Delray M. Milius had a disgusted look on his face.

"What? What are you screaming at? I want you on the record. I want you to tell me that you lied."

With his left hand he grabbed the notepad and with his right he searched for the pencil.

He put his hands in his pocket and it wasn't there.

Delray M. Milius was staring at Peoria's lower half.

Then Peoria looked down and saw that the pencil was sticking out of his leg.

Perhaps it was the Xanax that hit him, or the Percocet, or the shots of whiskey he had taken, but he all of a sudden felt both heavy and light-headed and he fell backward, this time not missing the sharp edge of the desk.

Peoria felt comfortable on the floor and closed his eyes. He heard shouts of "Nine-one-one," and he felt he could open his eyes, but thought it was better to just lie there. His eyes were closed and Delray M. Milius moved next to him.

He heard the southern drawl of Sanders Berman, and Milius saying, "We clearly made the right decision." Fifteen or twenty minutes passed, and in that time he lost consciousness and started to snore, and he woke up with a paramedic looking down on him.

"Are you Nicolas Cage?" Peoria asked.

The paramedic pulled the pencil out quickly. The secretary screamed again.

"We need to take your pants off to put the bandage on," the paramedic said.

"No, I need my pants," Peoria whispered.

"We need to take them off," the paramedic said.

"No, I already have a bandage on my dick," he said. "Let me keep my dignity, let me keep them on."

Peoria grabbed hold of his belt, as if he were protecting his chastity, and closed his eyes. He was much drunker than he'd originally thought.

"Okay, but that means I'm going to have to cut a patch out."

He felt the cold metal of scissors clipping away around his pants, and then he passed out again. He woke up on a stretcher in the back of an ambulance.

He was released from the emergency room six hours later. He put his pants back on, a large hole in the leg, and on the subway, normal businessmen and good-looking women gave him space as he sat in the car, with his legs crossed, hoping that no one could see through the large patch in his left leg and up to the bandage. He should have taken a cab, he thought.

He didn't feel well at all, and everything that had just happened seemed like some kind of nightmarish dream—that dream where you try to confront your boss and end up impaling yourself on a pencil.

So there he is, back in his one-bedroom apartment on the Upper West Side, staring at the screen at wd35.

Reeled, reeling, slipping, sliding. He starts to write about how he has ended up alone, in his apartment, and almost out of a job.

PART VI

Disgruntled Employees

QUOTES I WOULD LIKE TO HAVE STARTED THE BOOK WITH

"Never mistake the facts for truth."

—Thomas Jefferson, 1803

"Make love by email, make war by phone."

—K. Eric Walters, from his 1997 bestseller
21st Century Business: 101 Survival Tips

"They say war is hell. I disagree. War is war. Hell is reserved for the folks who start wars."

—From the unpublished journal of a reporter who
was killed in 1944 by a sniper in the South Pacific

"I had inflicted terrible violence on my body, on myself. I had only two things to show for my suffering, and both were double D's."

—From an anonymous subject in a research study
published by the *American Medical Journal*,
"Becoming Me: Plastic Surgery in Pursuit of
Gender-Based Wish Fulfillment"

27.

February 2004, Continued

I more or less forgive *The Magazine* for how they've treated Peoria. I'm not a suspect for the leak to Wretched.com, either. *The Magazine* is just relieved that Peoria's later incident—when he fell on his pencil—didn't make it onto the blogs.

Maybe Delray M. Milius thinks it might have been me, but he can't prove it. I'm starting to have second thoughts about the leak as well—was it worth the risk of getting caught just to try to defend A.E. Peoria (and my guilt is probably why I stop feeling bad for Peoria). I don't know him very well, really, and though I admire the reporting he's done—and *Desperation Points West* actually is a decent book—I also know he's pretty fucked-up.

Why so quick to risk everything to come to his defense? Especially now that I'm making some real progress in my career.

I'm working eighty hours a week, in the office six out of seven days. I've started to write a few stories a month for *The Magazine*'s website.

What I did realize about Wretched.com is that if I don't start writing online on a regular basis, I won't be very well positioned down the line as a journalist. The online editors at *The Magazine* really like what I'm doing for them, and so when an associate Web editor position opens up, I apply, and they offer me the job. The associate editor gig will finally make me a full-time staff member—I've been working full-time, but my title is still temporary researcher—and give me a salary, a job title, and benefits.

Then Nishant Patel calls me into his office.

"You're better off staying here at the international edition," Nishant Patel says.

"I'd like to, I guess, but the Web is offering me a permanent position."

Nishant Patel leans back in his chair, glancing at his monitor to see if any critical emails have popped up, and shakes his head.

"The Web is a black hole," he says. "There's not a future on the Internet."

You might think that this is a funny thing to say now. Maybe you would have expected a guy like Nishant Patel to say that in 1999 or 2000, or even 2001.

"But the Web is offering me a permanent position," I say, not wanting to get into the whole future-of-journalism debate. Maybe Nishant Patel doesn't even really believe what he's telling me; maybe he's more interested in getting me to stay so he doesn't have to find another research assistant.

"No, no, I think, for your career, you're much better off staying with the international edition. You can still write for the Web, of course, but it's much better for you to stay here. I spoke to Sandra this morning, and she agreed."

That's when I realize that I'm not really being given a choice. Sandra is the Web editor, and I had spoken to her yesterday, and she had been very excited about having me. Nishant pulled rank. I'm not going anywhere.

"We'll find a permanent position for you here soon," he says. Then he goes back to checking email, and I know I've been dismissed.

I'm pretty pissed off. On the one hand, I feel like Nishant Patel is really fucking with my career. I'd worked hard to get the job offer, and once I was in position to take it, Patel blocked it—more for self-interested reasons than anything about my future, I think. On the other hand, it's kind of a backhanded compliment—they feel I'm so important that they don't want to lose me. So I guess that's a good sign.

Sanders Berman is waiting for me at my cubicle.

"Hastings," he says.

"Oh, I was just talking to Nishant," I say.

"How is the professor?"

"He's good. I think he's doing *The Daily Show* tonight."

"*The Daily Show*? Good for him. I probably won't be able to catch it, as I'm going to be filling in for Chris Matthews."

"Oh, that's great. I'll have to make sure to TiVo them both."

"I'm due in DC in about five hours," he says.

"Taking the Amtrak?"

"No, that's what I'm here to ask you about."

I'm wondering what research I'm going to have to do. Probably something for the news of the day because Sanders is filling in for Matthews.

"Could you go pick up a pillow for me?"

"Sorry?"

"A pillow. One from Duane Reade would be fine. Just drop it off with my assistant."

I'm wondering why his assistant doesn't go buy him a pillow, and as if he knows what I'm thinking, he says, "I asked Nancy to get it for me last time, and I don't like her doing too many things like that. I don't want to get a reputation as a prima donna."

"Okay, right. Um, why do you need a pillow?"

"For the trip to DC. My car is picking me up in forty-five minutes."

Right: Sanders Berman hates to fly, and he also hates trains. He doesn't feel comfortable waiting in Penn Station, his assistant told me. Too many people who could recognize him. So when he goes to DC, he hires a car service.

Car services are the big topic of conversation around the office, especially for those editors who don't get cars all the time. Jerry got all the numbers, and he likes to recite them. Nishant Patel's car service bill: $7,323 a month. Sanders Berman's: $9,356. Sometimes they take them five blocks. Five blocks! Do you know how many reporters we could hire for that bill, Jerry likes to say.

"Sure, I'll grab you a pillow."

"Thanks."

I take the elevator down, and I'm getting kind of annoyed again. If I were an associate editor, I wouldn't have to be doing this kind of gofering anymore. As long as my title remains researcher, I'm more or less the office bitch. I have to figure out a way to get on staff, and I guess buying pillows is a step in the right direction.

I pick up two pillows at Duane Reade—one is from this foam material, another is designed for people with bad backs. I want to cover my bases, do the job right.

Sanders's door is open, and he's on the phone. I leave the two pillows with Nancy.

"I'll put this with his travel bag," she says, tapping a pile of folded sweatpants and a blanket on the desk. "Sanders," Nancy whispers, "likes to put these on in his car so it's more comfortable."

"Oh, right."

I see Sanders hang up, and I think maybe I should ask him if he'd step in to talk to Nishant about letting me go to the Web.

"Sanders, I just have a quick question. I applied for the associate editor job at the Web, and Sandra seemed really keen on having me there, but I don't know if Nishant wanted me to go for it. But I think it would be really good."

"The Web," Sanders says, like it's something he's never heard of.

"Yeah, the magazine's website."

"You mean Sandra the Web editor?"

"Yeah, that's who I mean."

"Oh, you don't want to go to the Web. Nothing good is happening there," he says.

I go back to my cubicle and I don't do much for the rest of the afternoon. I don't feel like working. What's hard work gotten me?

I leave an hour earlier than usual and take the F train back down to my apartment on the Lower East Side. I go to the dry cleaners to pick up clothes I'd dropped off yesterday.

In line at the dry cleaners, I notice a girl standing ahead of me. She's cute, and I recognize her face because her picture is always up at Wretched.com. She's the editor, and I know she lives in the neighborhood as well.

"Hey," I say to her.

She looks at me like I'm a danger.

"My name is Mike Hastings. I'm a writer for *The Magazine*," I say.

"Oh, okay, I thought you might be some crazy asshole stalking me. I've been getting a lot of that kind of email lately."

"No, I'm just a fan of Wretched.com."

"I'm sorry for you."

"Yeah, right. Actually, you guys posted something I sent in—I probably shouldn't bring this up—but yeah, I sent you guys an email about the *Magazine* riots and how they were, uh, blaming . . ."

"Oh yeah, sure, I remember that. Uh, thanks."

I give the Chinese woman my dry cleaning ticket.

"We should hang out sometime," I say.

"Yeah, that would be cool. Send me an email."

"I will."

She leaves the dry cleaners. And that's how my relationship with Wretched.com begins.

TOWARD A MORE
LIKABLE NARRATOR

The disgruntled employee—it's hard not to sound like a loser, a whiny bitch, ungrateful. Noticing it just now—rereading where we're at in the story.

What gave me the right, at twenty-four or twenty-five, to expect my goals and desires to be taken seriously at *The Magazine*? Why did I expect them to care or to give a shit? Let's get my head out of my ass here: this is a magazine, part of a company that routinely hires and fires and thwarts much bigger plans than mine. Why would I expect anything other than frustration and dues-paying?

Don't they say that nothing in life is easy, and if it's easy, it's not worth it?

Maybe they do say that.

I read this book on twenty-first-century business survival tips, written by a guy named K. Eric Walters.

Walters, see, he opens the book with an anecdote about Tom Cruise. Nothing beats the wisdom of celebrities, Walters gets that, and so he brings us to Tom Cruise talking on the Letterman show.

Tom says: "People look at me now and think that my life has been smooth sailing. That I got everything that I wanted, and that my career just happened to take off. No. It didn't. I had to fight to get my foot in the door, and every day, people tried to slam that door shut, right in my face. And finally I did get my foot in, and they tried even harder to kick my foot out of the door, to shut it tight. I didn't let them. I kept my foot there. And one day, it opened. That's my advice."

So yeah, maybe I was having a bad day back then, and I wasn't able to get the needed perspective.

What's a few years of hard work unrewarded? Sounds like life to me, says K. Eric Walters.

Anyway.

And so on.

Can you believe I've made it to page 232? Passed the halfway mark by far. It's still December where I'm at in 2005, and I'm still trying to get this over with before the new regime takes over in January. I think that's when it'll be the best time to bring the book to market—right when the new editor of *The Magazine* is taking over.

28.

Winter–Spring 2004

The darkness, the darkness, oh the darkness. His pillows off the bed, sheets crumpled on the floor, shades drawn, four stale glasses of water on the bedside table. The darkness in his bedroom had even taken on his scent. He could smell himself, he could smell his days without a shower and the trip to the laundromat that kept getting put off and delayed and delayed. He could hear the buzz of his laptop, the keyboards sticky from who knows what delivery food residue, the fan on the laptop clicking away. Cooling down, screen saver jumping in and out, breaking through the darkness in some sick technological light, a sick mechanical glow, an unhealthy light—but even an unhealthy light was better than the darkness.

A.E. Peoria had hated the lights at the office, the radiating lights, the plastic dimples parceling out the fluorescent rays, sucking the soul, draining life from the skin. But how he missed those lights now.

A leave of absence. Yes, he was given a leave of absence.

Hugging himself in his bed, he wished he could have embraced the leave of absence. And he had, for the first seventy-two hours of darkness. He thought, I deserve a rest, a break; it's not really a leave of absence or a suspension; it's a much-needed respite. It would not be held against him, it would not hurt his career, he could just ride it out, like Milius said, until that entire story blew over, until the news had moved on to the next big story and all that was left from the *Magazine* riots was a vague memory, a memory that he would remember certainly but that most people would forget and move on from, so that in the future, in conversation, perhaps the riots would trigger some association with him, but not the kind of detailed association of fresh scandal—"Oh, didn't you have something to do with . . ."— and there would be more stories for him to write, more stories attached to his name, and eventually the riots would get pushed back, another chapter, another life lesson, just one more step in his career.

And who needed the magazine, really, he'd told himself, on the third evening of his leave of absence, garbage overflowing, bathroom floor littered with cardboard toilet-paper rolls. I don't. I had a life before the magazine—I had a life and a career before the magazine, and I will have a life and career after the magazine, so fuck them.

But the darkness was creepy. The lack of phone calls, the lack of supportive email, the fact that the six-orgasms girl had broken up with him—and he didn't even love her, what did he care that she'd broken up with him—but now he had faced the darkness for three days and he didn't want to move.

When he dreamed, he would dream of his past horrors; he would see pencils sticking up along desert berms, flames, tanks exploding; he would dream of TV appearances gone bad, the camera frozen on him, scratching away at the earpiece until blood started to shoot out, as if the earpiece were like a small worm, a bug in a science fiction novel that had traveled into his brain and made his voice sound silly and his brain stop working. That made him stutter, drilling away, and behind the camera he could see his friends and family looking at him, he could see Nishant and Sanders and the intern Mike and yes, there, holding a pencil between his legs, he could see Chipotle, the Mexican—or was it a Puerto Rican he had saved?

He would dream of cell phones not working, of plane tickets that weren't good, of unavailable seats and long lines at security checkpoints. He would dream of getting drunk, shitfaced, and waking up trying to figure out what thing he had done that he should be ashamed of, then realizing he had done nothing, smelling his darkness, and that he had not moved from his bed for two weeks.

His laptop had been on the entire time, picking up a wireless signal, but he could not check his email—he knew messages and emails and voicemails and texts had been building up over those two weeks but he did not want to look at them. He could not stand the sight of them, because they would just be bringing more bad news, more blog postings and stories about how he had failed, fucked up, screwed the pooch, about how the *Magazine* riots had been his fault, that he had killed, by accident, by dint of bad reporting, seventeen Iraqis (the death toll had risen).

This wasn't true—he knew he had been the victim of a great crime, a great conspiracy, a great cover-up, and he wanted *The Magazine* to go to hell, he wanted *The Magazine* to burn.

But then, like a slave, he thought, he wanted *The Magazine* to forgive him, he wanted *The Magazine* back. He rationalized that the magazine was doing what it did best, that it was just protecting itself. That by protecting itself it was protecting him, too. That he was still part of *The Magazine*'s family, and that he just wanted their forgiveness. He just wanted to become A.E. Peoria, *Magazine* Journalist, again.

And after week three, he had said, I will get out of bed. I will get out of the darkness. I will forgive and let live. Let the bygones go their merry way—what the fuck is a bygone? I will check my email and voicemails, and I will be very Zen about it.

The three weeks of cleaning his system. Of no pills or booze, of cold turkey that had added to his general feeling of despair, of mild drug and alcohol withdrawal, shakes and tears and self-recriminations.

On week three, he cracked the blinds and saw the snow falling, and said to himself: It's not that bad, it's not that bad, it's not that bad. I'm okay, I'm okay, I'm okay.

He finally left his apartment to go down to the STD clinic that smelled like wet cigars.

"All looks okay under here," the doctor, a small man with a gray beard and yellow teeth, said. "Have you found any more spots?"

"No, I haven't," Peoria said.

The doctor tossed the bandage into a wastebasket.

"Okay, then," he said. "Your blood tests came back negative on other STDs."

"Great, that's great."

"Last time we talked," the doctor said, looking at his chart, "I suggested you go to AA."

"Oh, I haven't, but I've stopped everything. I've stopped everything, and it hasn't been easy, because I'm sort of in a tough spot vis-à-vis my employer right now. I'm sort of out of a job."

"You still have insurance?"

"Yes, I have insurance, but I'm on, like, administrative leave, I didn't even know journalists could get that. It's like something they give cops after they shoot a black kid intentionally by accident, you know. But yeah, I'm on administrative leave."

"And you haven't done any traveling, no more trips back to . . . Thailand?"

"No, I haven't really left my apartment."

"Because sex addiction, you wouldn't believe it, men, once a month, take these trips, rack up all kinds of debts, tens of thousands of dollars in debt. Disappear for a long weekend, a long weekend or five days, halfway around the world, that's what their sex addiction does to them. Like I said before, one sign of sexual addiction is if you have an STD—it's the equivalent of drunks having a blackout—and so it's prudent to look at those signs carefully."

"No, I'm not a sex addict, I don't think. I don't know if I'm really an addict at all," he said. "Not in the traditional sense."

The doctor looked at him skeptically.

"You should check out the meetings."

Peoria left the clinic, no more bandages, free at least temporarily from molluscum contagiosum, feeling, for the first time in weeks, prepared to confront his inbox, his voicemail, his backlog of unanswered communications.

He felt okay.

He went into his apartment, breathing deeply, forcing energy upon himself, forcing the darkness away—I can do this.

Then he got the last message.

He'd been fired again.

The Magazine, the message from Delray M. Milius said, thought that maybe Peoria should take another six months, perhaps a year or more, of leave of absence before he returned—before he discussed returning. He would be able to keep his benefits but he would not be getting a regular paycheck anymore.

Back to the darkness he went. Back to the darkness, for another three-week stretch, the bills and dirty laundry piling up, redux. Resorting to reusing the coffee filter in his coffee machine after running out of paper filters, ordering groceries and deliveries, ordering everything and keeping the door shut. Vowing to never again check his email, never to look at what other news it would bring—the wound on his leg had healed, the puncture wound had healed, the molluscum contagiosum had run its course, but a new wound had opened up.

The darkness didn't help him heal that wound. The darkness hid it from him, hid what he didn't want to recognize. He went over the scenarios in his head again and again. This wound was deep, cut to his core. He tried to ignore the wound, tried to pretend it wasn't there, but he knew he was burying his feelings, burying his emotions, burying the truth. I'm a journalist, he thought, and if I can't look at truth within myself, how can I see the truth out there in the world?

And the truth was he was terrified about his leave of absence—terrified and angry and dreading all social interaction. For the first time in his life, he didn't want to see, didn't want to spill.

What would he tell people he did? What could magazine journalist A.E. Peoria now say when asked what his job was?

The truth: The fuckers had stolen his identity. By firing him, they had taken away what he held dear—he didn't even know he'd held it dear, he didn't know how much his identity had been wrapped up in *The Magazine*'s brand: that for the past few years he had thought of himself primarily as *Magazine* Journalist first, a person and human being second. He felt like he was one of those kids who went to Yale or Princeton or Harvard and for the rest of their lives clung on to that as their calling card, as the most important part of their identity, even years after graduation day, years after it was all over for them—years after the rest of the world had moved on, they saw themselves as the Ivy League (he didn't get into Ivy League schools, true).

Was that now him? Would he now only be able to say, when introducing himself, that he used to write for *The Magazine*? A former *Magazine* journalist! Pathetic!

How did he allow his identity to become so entwined with some pieces of paper printed weekly? How did he fall for the prestige and structure—though he had chafed under the prestige and structure, he had fallen for it, more than he would have thought possible. He had fallen for it, and then they had taken it away, they had snatched his identity from him during the worst time of his life: Six Orgasms had broken up with him, a public humiliation on television, reputation raped on the blogs, a dent in his otherwise skyrocketing career. Yes, he had been bumped off the fast track, the people mover at the airport. He was back on the other side of the plastic barrier. Even worse, he was on his knees, on his stomach, his face getting hit by an imaginary janitor's mop, soaking the floors to make them nice and shiny for those who did have real careers and who did not stumble, who did not fall. For those on the fast track, the floors were clean, while he was licking the dirty end of the mop, drinking from the murky waters of the mop bucket, the janitor standing on the back of his neck, saying, You thought you almost made it, you thought you were almost there, but you weren't! You fool, how could you have believed that you were going to be one of them? One of the brands, one of the bylines that people recognized? How could you ever have thought that was where you were headed?

How could you have thought you were going to be your own brand?

No, you were a failure, a fuckup, a fucktard, a dipshit, a loser, a skank, a donkey-ass weak bitch motherfucker. Yes, these words and even worse passed through his mind—a cunt snorter! Yes, he was a cunt snorter, an abysmal failure, a catastrophic embarrassment, that's what he was. He could feel it on his teeth, even after brushing and flossing, he could smell the failure through the darkness, he could taste the failure on his pillows. The crust in his eyes: he would wipe it out, place it on his tongue, and he knew. The dried sperm in his pubic hair: he would reach down and touch and then taste the musk. He could taste the failure all over his body, a disgusting taste, with no career future to cleanse it away.

What else did he have besides a career? What did anyone in his peer group have besides a career? No close family, no God, what else was there to fall back on? To make sense of the world, to give his life meaning besides his career, his once promising career, his career that he had taken for granted. He had taken it for granted: the flying first class, the phone calls returned, the pickup lines—I write for *The Magazine*. What do you do?

Yes, the career had been his life. The career at *The Magazine* had been his id, his ego, and his soul. He didn't know it at the time. He didn't care enough about it. He just took pills and got drunk and passed out under his desk because he thought that he had it locked up. But one mistake—fuck, and it wasn't even a mistake! But maybe it was a mistake, the more he thought about it. Certainly running after Milius with a pencil was a mistake—maybe he did fuck up. Objectively, he had to admit, it appeared that he had fucked up. After all, he was in the darkness. He was living in the darkness while Healy went on to break more blow job stories and Delray M. Milius collected his six figures and Nishant and Sanders showed up again on television—yes, all of these things were as true as his unwashed sheets.

If only he could just allow himself to give up. To say, It's okay, it doesn't matter, life is too short. If only he could just knock off the ambition, if he could just take a deep breath and say, It's all going to be all right. Then he would be okay, then he could let go of the career, then he could fall back on something. But that wasn't in him. He knew it would be like telling a lion not to bite, an elephant not to deposit large amounts of excrement; no, there was no way the gears in his mind would stop turning over and over and over again. Why couldn't he just lie in bed? Why couldn't he just accept the darkness, postpone the heat death of the universe, still and silent? Or, perhaps, open the windows and open the doors and accept the light?

One night the buzzer to his apartment rang. He had ordered no food deliveries, so he didn't know who it could be. He hit the intercom button.

"Yes?"

"Alex, it's your mother."

He pushed the buzzer to let her in.

He poked his head out the door and saw his mother, with her partner, Amy.

"You two shouldn't come in here," he said. "It's a mess."

"We'll be okay."

Amy and his mother walked into the apartment, grimacing, almost coughing: dishes piled in the sink, cardboard containers on the kitchen counters, smears and stains on the glass living room tables, wadded tissues and toilet paper.

His mother opened the drapes and then the window. She and Amy moved aside a blanket and tossed a few empty boxes of television-series DVDs onto the floor.

"We're worried about you," his mother said.

"Well, I didn't want to tell you, but I got fired."

"We know," his mother said. "Amy read about it online."

"Ahahahfgahrh," he cried out.

"But that's why we're here. Amy, as you know, works with the dean of faculty, and they're looking for a part-time professor to teach journalism. We think you could do that, while you're waiting to go back to work."

"Teach?"

"Yes, teach journalism," Amy said.

"A professor," A.E. Peoria thought, and he had the first positive emotion he'd had in a while, the first stirring to his soul, because—as if it were the first tingling of exoskeleton, of another system of vertebrae spawning—being a professor was a career too, and that was something he could hold on to, that was something with backbone. It was as if the dendrites in some paralyzed part of his inner being that had dried up and contracted were firing again, new nerve endings flourishing, a network of new nerves that could take the place of A.E. Peoria, Magazine Journalist: A.E. Peoria, Professor of Journalism.

"Don't I need a master's?"

"No, you have a book published—that's a terminal degree, and you have years' worth of reporting behind you, so I think that should be enough."

And with his mother and Amy there, he felt the sparks of the old A.E. Peoria, the compulsive disclosure disorder persona. He started to describe to them the darkness, the darkness that he could breathe in, the loss of Six Orgasms, the humiliation on television, and three hours later, he had finished dumping, unloading, and his mother and Amy left, like angels of mercy—if he had believed in angels or mercy—but angels carrying something that could give him real meaning again, another career path. He wrote all of this down in his journal.

He turned on the TV, which he hadn't used to watch anything besides DVDs, and switched to a news channel.

On it were pictures from a prison called Abu Ghraib, naked Iraqis in a pyramid, a girl holding a man on a leash, even a picture of a soldier drop-kicking a Koran.

His story had been right after all.

29.

Sunday, May 16, 2004

I email Sarah to say hey. She emails back: Want to come to a book party? But I'm not calling it a first date.

Her job at Wretched.com is all-consuming. Up at six a.m., reading at least four newspapers and ten other blogs by seven a.m., twelve posts a day, a thirty-minute lunch, and then at night she goes to different events across the city to stay on top of things.

The book party is for a daughter of a famous writer who wrote a women's liberation classic back in the '70s. The daughter's memoir is one of those tell-alls about what it was like growing up around all these other famous writers. About all the fucked-up shit she saw at a young age, about the different men who passed through her mother's life, and how that led, inevitably, to promiscuity, drug addiction, expulsion from high-priced schools, and, finally, a career in writing, the shadow of her mother looming over her.

The shadow has its advantages, like the fact that her mom is a famous writer with a really nice corner apartment on 81st and Park, a perfect place to host a book party.

I meet Sarah in Midtown. I'm coming from work, and she takes the train up from the Lower East Side. We grab a coffee at Starbucks.

She's in sandals and a light blue dress that's pushing the boundaries of summer.

"Thanks for inviting me to this," I say.

"It sucks, I really don't want to go," she says. "This job is taking up way too much of my life. And I think my boss is going to be there."

Timothy Grove. A media mogul in training. Reputation is that he's something of a "new media" genius. He's the first person to make a business out of blogging. He found a way to monetize it. He's not considered really respectable though—maybe a step above a pornographer.

The theory behind his success at Wretched: We live in a society of assholes. The media is a reflection of these assholes. We'll show you what the inside of the asshole's asshole looks like.

It's been an effective tactic so far—nine million unique visitors a month.

Taking the elevator up, I walk into the room with Sarah. My first New York media party. I'm part of the scene. I recognize the people eating hors d'oeuvres and holding drinks, not because I know them but because I've read about them. My inspirations.

I stand halfway off to the side. Sarah works the room. The room pays its respects to Wretched.com.

Sarah introduces me to the daughter whose book is being released, Eleanor K.

"Eleanor, this is Mike Hastings," she says, and tells her the name of the magazine I work for.

"Oh," says Eleanor, "I think your magazine is running a review of my book next week."

"I work mostly for the international editions," I say.

"I don't know who's writing it, but it would be great to get a copy before it came out," she says. "To know what to expect."

Eleanor K. and Sarah look at me.

"So, do you think you could send me a copy? I mean, if it's not too big of a hassle, if it's not too big of a deal."

"Um, yeah, I guess I could look into that, sure," I say, knowing that I wasn't going to look into that at all. I do have access to the system of all the stories that are scheduled to run, but I'm not going to risk sending a copy of a story to someone I don't know.

"Mom, come over here, meet Mike Walters," she says.

"Mike Hastings," Sarah corrects.

Eleanor K.'s mother comes up, and I say hello to Mrs. K.

"Obviously, I know I'm a guy, but I was, uh, am, a big fan of your book, Mrs. K." I say. I've never read the book, but I've seen the paperback enough times to get the gist of what it's about.

"Thanks so much," she says, as insincere as my compliment.

Mrs. K. looks like she's from the '70s: ashram-chic clothes, long hair that used to flow and fit in a ponytail now dry and long and puffy. She has all sorts of bracelets and necklaces hanging off her wrists and necks.

"Mike's going to send me an early review," Eleanor K. says to her mom.

"How kind of you," Mrs. K. says. She seems spaced-out, as if she had traded in the pot and acid of the '60s for the lighter mood-stabilizing drugs of the late '90s, like Wellbutrin and Prozac. A pharmaceutical sellout.

"Eleanor, are you going to read soon?" her mother asks.

The room is filling up, getting to that point where the number of people will only go down throughout the rest of the evening.

Mrs. K. clinks her glass and Eleanor K. picks up a copy of the book that had been displayed on a small round table near the door.

Mrs. K. says something about how this is a very personal book to her daughter—and a personal book to her as a mother too.

I have a flash of envy for a second, watching the two. Wouldn't it all be easier if one of my parents were some famous writer? Who knew all the book editors and agents and could stock a room full of gossip columnists and book reviewers and magazine editors? I'd have that good material right off the bat—how Philip Roth taught me to masturbate on a grapefruit, how Bill Styron once called looking for his wallet, which he thought he'd left in the couch, how I read about one of my parents in a first-person account by Norman Mailer of an orgy where he'd sat on his/her face.

Eleanor K. introduces the passage she's going to read.

"Because you're all here, and many of you know, my mother has had this apartment since 1985," she says. "'Eighty-five was the year they turned her classic book into a movie, so she could afford a place like this"—everyone laughs, somewhat uncomfortably—"but it's also when everything came . . . I don't know. Crashing down."

She has a page marked, about fifteen pages in.

"'Early night. I don't want to go to bed. Park Avenue isn't a place for children after nine o'clock, my mother tells me. I want it to be a place for children. I am not a child anymore, but I want my home to be for me. I still take childish pride in answering her phones. Is your mother home? the voice asks. I'm proud that the voice asks for my mother. When I ask the voice his name, I can see his name in front of me on the bookshelf. Does your mother get calls from bookshelves? No? Mine does. It's like the boy in my second-grade class who bragged his father had climbed Mount Everest. That boy was lying, but I wasn't lying when I said that I had met the man who'd written a book about climbing Mount Everest. He was a friend of my mother's; everyone with a name was a friend of my mother's.

"'I climb up the stairs, running my hands along the cold metal from the spiral case to the second floor. The spiral staircase is my favorite part of the new home. It's neat.

"'I climb up the stairs and I look down. I am fourteen years old and already I know I'm a woman, my mother's daughter. I catch the eye of a Famous Writer. The Famous Writer with dark eyebrows. He catches my eye. He asks me if I want to hear a bedtime story. I'm too old for bedtime stories. He tells me this is a bedtime story that I'd never heard before.'"

Eleanor K. flips to another chapter.

"'How could you have done this to me, how could you? I scream at my mother, eighteen now, drunk on booze stolen from the cabinet. She didn't bother marking the levels of the bottles anymore. I didn't try to hide it. I knew the combination to the padlock. He had shown it to me while she was at a benefit, at a concert, at a panel discussion, a book tour, a play, a guest lecture, a talk show, a radio show, at a reading, at a book party.'"

Silence in the room, ironic laughter—this is a book party.

I start to sidestep toward the balcony to get out of the room. I haven't been out there yet.

I recognize the silhouette of the tallest man on the balcony. Timothy Grove. In all the profiles I'd read about him, the writers mention his unusually tiny head on a skinny six-one frame. Massively tiny, almost like a headshrinker, like the guy sitting next to Beetlejuice in the waiting room to purgatory. You had to think that a smart guy like Grove has a pretty big brain, and that his brain must be really pressing against his skull, trying to squirt out his ears. There are three other guys standing around him, leaning up against the balcony, listening to him.

I stand back from the circle, waiting for a break in Grove's monologue to introduce myself. I can hear his heavy British accent.

"See what they've done, the *New York Post*? Taking four items from Wretched—four items, ripped right off our pages. No credit, not a single credit given to Wretched. A travesty, innit?"

Grove looks at me.

I feel a bit strange at the party, wearing what I'm wearing. I don't really dress like the normal media type. My hair is a bit mussed—an ex-girlfriend, in one of her parting shots, told me I should keep my hair messy because otherwise I look like a dork—but I don't wear tight jeans or American Apparel T-shirts to work, or button-down shirts with open collars. A blue blazer and tie and gray flannels—I've always gotten a lot of shit from colleagues about it. They ask me whether I'm going to a job interview, or going on television, or if I'm thinking about becoming a banker. But Nishant and Sanders Berman wear blazers and ties, and most of the senior editors do too, so if I want to climb up, it makes sense for me to wear them as well.

But seeing Grove and his posse, gelled, hair product, hair fibers, hair molding, sculpturing crème, with Diesel jeans and pointy-toed cowboy boots or shoes, tight T-shirts, also designer, that probably cost fifty dollars a pop, I feel a bit underdressed, even though I'm wearing a tie. I probably look more like I belong in DC than in New York, but that's not a compliment in this city.

"Oh, this lad right here looks like he might work for the *Post*," he says, and his coven of straight males laughs.

"Hah. Nah, I'm just coming from work. Mike Hastings, nice to meet you, Mr. Grove."

I tell him I work for *The Magazine*.

"Ah? Another dead-tree'er come to say hullo," he says, and the young men laugh again.

"What's the readership of your dead tree?" Grove asks.

"I think they say it's like twenty million readership, three million circulation," I say.

"Twenty million, my arse. Three million copies for the doctor's office and dentist rooms, a whole forest chopped up for stale news, innit?"

"We definitely use a lot of paper," I say.

"See, boys, the blogs, the blogs are good at tearing things down. Ants and the like. Tearing it down. Throw it up, tear it down, break it apart, piece by piece. You get the scale, you get the ad dollars. Low overhead, scale, ad dollars, tear it down," he says. "What do you think of that, Hastings?"

"Wretched certainly seems to be where the industry is heading," I say.

"So, you here looking for a job?" he says, and his circle chuckles.

"Not really," I say.

"Well he should be, innit!"

Grove's small head shakes when he laughs, like a steamed pea rolling atop a telephone pole.

I laugh along too, wanting to seem like I'm cool with being from the old media.

"Lookie who's arrived," he says.

As a Wretched.com reader, I recognize the face of Rohan Mais, another up-and-coming media guru (also on the list of "Top 20 Media Players Under Age 38"). Grove's been directing his bloggers to post at least a half-dozen items on Rohan's own start-up print publication—he sees him as his "homo-competitor" for the crown of new media guru.

"You boys see what he's doing here," Grove says. "Might have some questions, privy like, for Mr. Hastings here."

Three of the twentysomethings fan out, leaving Grove and me alone on the balcony.

"A tad of a shake-up at your pub," he says.

"The pub?"

"Publication, the dead tree."

"Yeah, there's some readjusting going on."

"So whosit going to be?"

"Pardon?"

"Who's gonna take ol' Henry's place?"

"Either Sanders Berman or Nishant Patel," I say.

"Right, right, that's obvious, innit—I'm asking Patel or Berman," he says.

I'm tempted to tell him something—a little nugget of inside dope. I should have inside dope, shouldn't I? And part of me wants to tell him—to impress him. Am I after a job? I'm not averse to the possibility. There's something enticing about the world of Park Avenue book parties and instant New York media celebrity—a touch of power—and I can see that's why the twentysomethings hover around Grove, to get a sense of that power that comes with having a platform where what you say can shape reputations, kill reputations, make reputations. It's part of the fun, I suppose.

"Oh, I think, that at least right now, Nishant has the lead . . . I mean, he's a minority, there's never been an Asian editor, he's still riding that wave from 9/11, he's got a TV show, so his brand recognition is way up . . ."

"I hear Henry likes Berman better," he says.

"Maybe, but the last time I saw them"—and here I'm lying—"they were talking and, and you know, Henry ignored Sanders, at his own book party, and talked to Nishant, so I think that was a sign."

Spastically, his head nods up and down.

"So you think it's a lock for Patel, innit?"

"Not a lock, but if I had to say who was ahead in the sweepstakes . . ."

"Right, right, natch, right. You see the magazine stories before they hit, right? You could send us along a little peek every once in a while, do ya think?"

"I could give your name to the publicist," I say.

"Don't want no publicists, mate. I want to get the scoops before the scoops, you follow?"

I follow.

I leave the party an hour later with Sarah. We take a taxi back down to the Lower East Side. We don't make out. I probably should have made a move, but I'll leave it at that, because I hate those books or stories about guys who agonize for one hundred pages about not making a move. It's not usually my style—usually I make the move—but I don't want to complicate things, at least not yet, especially if I'm maybe going to try to get a job there. Instead we talk about her boss.

"I talked to Grove," I say.

"Oh? I'm sure he loved you."

"What do you mean?"

"He does that, he likes to surround himself with twentysomething straight guys. It's a thing he has."

"Oh."

The next morning, Sanders Berman walks by my cubicle. He's leaving the bathroom, wiping at his face.

"Hastings, can you believe the nonsense these bloggers write? I'd never even heard of a blog until this morning," Sanders says. "No standards."

"Yeah, blogging is a big thing, everyone is reading them."

A look of fear.

"Everyone?"

"Well, depends."

"Heard of Wretched.com?"

They say when you lie your eyes dart to the side. My eyes really want to dart to the side.

"Sure, yeah, it's popular."

"Popular? How popular?"

I've never heard a southern drawl reach such a high pitch.

"Pretty popular."

"They wrote some trash about me this morning, saying I wanted to take Henry's place, and then that Henry hadn't talked to me and that Nishant was going to take it over. Unbelievable."

"Oh, yeah, wow, that's horrible. Who knows where they get their stuff from."

"Milius is writing them right now to correct the record."

"That's a good idea, yeah."

Sanders continues down the hall.

I check Wretched.com. Under Sarah's byline, there's an item that, almost verbatim, though unnamed, repeats the conversation I had with Grove.

I've never been a deep-background source before. It gives me kind of a thrill, to be honest.

30.

Later, 2004

The winter and spring have vanished, and the clothing on women in the city has vanished with it. A.E. Peoria walks down the street, and he swears there must be an uptick in emergency room visits from men running into parking meters, newspaper stands, lampposts, doors, taxis, heads whiplashing at what the city has hidden in the winter months, bounciness, unfettered gravity, bare skin, and Peoria wonders if women have always dressed like this or is it just another sign of the times.

There is a determined shuffle in his steps, head up. A peppiness through his entire being that is the spiritual correlation to the perky breasts and large breasts and mountain breasts and canyon breasts and fake breasts and real breasts that rise and fall so confidently, so healthily, that like him, shout out life.

A.E. Peoria has broken out of the darkness. He is working on himself.

Self-acceptance.

Embracing the teaching gig. Embracing therapy. Embracing salads and 2,500 calories a day. Embracing friends who he felt betrayed him. Embracing emails that went unreturned. Embracing time, embracing taking a nap. Embracing sweatshop Bikram yoga. Embracing moments of solitude, meditation, clearheadedness. Embracing three hours a day of work. A tentative embrace of sobriety and a marijuana- and pill-free existence, of higher powers and powerlessness and fate. Embracing the idea that it is possible to heal. Embracing working out. A surprising embrace of the gym culture.

A.E. Peoria is on his way to see his personal trainer, part of the six-month membership he has with the Platinum New Members Package at the Ultimate Fitness gym on West 83rd Street.

"Five minutes' warm-up on the 'mill," Norm says.

Peoria, in blue and white Nike sneakers and breathable nylon-blended shorts and a gray T-shirt that hangs out over his gut—a gut that is already getting smaller—starts walking on the treadmill, four minutes, three minutes, two minutes, one minute, a sip of water at the fountain before the workout session begins.

Norm, big eyes, thick-muscled body, specializes in self-acceptance, three or four mornings a week, at the gym. Two days for legs, two days upper body, fifteen minutes of core, cardio up to Peoria. His core starts to feel better. His core is something that exists somewhere in between his legs and arms and chest, some strange network of muscles that ties his entire body together that can be reached with strange duckwalks and massive green-and-yellow ball exercises and squats.

"You better not puke again," Norm shouts, his way of encouragement.

In the sweat and the claustrophobia of the low-ceilinged workout room at Ultimate Fitness, the treadmills and all these different machines, these weight machines bending this way and that, twenty reps, twenty reps, twenty reps—"Feel the burn," Norm yells at him, feel the burn, and he feels the burn, and between sickening gasps, he explains to Norm that, wow, working out really makes a difference. It's all part of accepting himself even as he's changing himself—

he is getting into shape, and it doesn't take long before he is in some kind of shape, the fifteen pounds he put on since the age of twenty-seven dropping to only twelve pounds, but it's twelve pounds of near muscle.

"Feel the burn!" Norm says, as Peoria lies over on a reverse lateral pulley system, ass up high, knees jerking back with the weight of fifty-five pounds.

Triceps, biceps, lats, squats, thrusts, mountain climbers, steps, push-ups, sit-ups, crunches, and curls—he sees why the exercise industry booms. He's never really been a fan of gyms before, never really understood them. There are two kinds of dudes, Peoria has always said, dudes who like to shower with other dudes and dudes who don't like to shower with other dudes. Gym culture reeked of the former. He hadn't minded sports in high school, played soccer, kept fit, but then didn't go out of his way to embrace the unnatural experience of the gym—too artificial. He now sees why they've become so popular—working out feels good, right, it's supposed to feel good, with all the endorphins and such.

He can now be one of those people who say, "Yeah, just going to the gym." Or, "Man, what a great workout it was today." To talk of the natural high. It hasn't taken long for him to look at those around him, on the street, who clearly aren't working out, who clearly aren't taking care of their bodies, and feel some measure of superiority over them.

And Norm, he can talk to Norm between suction pops of oxygen. Norm doesn't care about the Internet or the front page of *The New York Times*. Norm doesn't care about scandal and disgrace.

Norm cares about the burn, about the core, about his progress, about his health.

Because, as he has told Norm, there are still wounds, still things that protein shakes and chocolate milk can't fix, torn muscles of his heart and brain that just won't go away. Things he can't face. Like newspapers and magazines and the Internet. Peoria has stopped reading them. He can't stomach Googling his name anymore. He can't stomach more than a glance at the front page of *The New York Times*. He can't stomach any magazines, because he doesn't want to know what's going on in that world, his old world. It hurts too much to think about it, and so, he believes, it's better to just accept the fact that he can't look at it.

"I get how celebrities feel," A.E. Peoria tells Norm, sweat-soaked T-shirt and face splashed with water from the fountain. "Why so many television and film stars don't watch TV and film. You know why George W. Bush doesn't read the newspapers? It hurts."

"I hear you, man," Norm says. "Let's stretch you out."

And on his back, leg bending, Norm's weight pushing into his chest, Peoria explains how a television star, career up and down, can't stand to watch a half-hour drama because he's thinking, I could have gotten that part! I auditioned! I had that part, I was once that person, and then the industry cast me aside. Or how a director whose film had bombed doesn't want to hear of other films. He doesn't want to see interviews of other directors. No, an actor who has tasted success and then has that success pulled away is not too interested in watching *Inside the Actors Studio*, of course not. It's too painful to see: the actor knows the fates of career paths, and career implosions and explosions are the only difference between why he's sitting on the couch and flipping past *Actors Studio* and why the actor is sitting in the studio basking in his actingness.

And so it is the same with him—no CNN, no MSNBC, no Fox News or *Time* magazine or *Atlantic*.

"I hear you, man," Norm says. "Like these dudes over at Crunch. I left after some bullshit, and it took me like a year before I'd set foot in a Crunch again. Any branch."

Peoria leaves in the early morning to work out; he slides on flip-flops and a Nike tracksuit, sneakers tossed in his gym bag, and he likes that. Like a doctor who wears his scrubs at any opportunity for comfort and as a status symbol, he likes his workout clothes, his workout bag slung over his arm, dried sweat at the corner deli, dried sweat at Gristedes, dried sweat while walking the aisles of Whole Foods, getting healthy drinks of organic cherry and bunches of organic bananas, and he can feel that he is part of this elite club, the club of those who have worked out, and that his dress, his comfortable tracksuit, is accepted as the sign of a man who has released all the bad energy in the gym, the sign of someone who has learned to accept himself.

Self-acceptance.

Three hours a day, that's how much A.E. Peoria works out now. Three hours a day—self-acceptance.

Or is it all work? Working on himself.

After working out, a coffee in the morning, a walk to get the coffee. An hour of writing in his journal. An hour of thinking about the syllabus. An hour or two of reading *Teaching for Dummies*, where he learns tips about how to relate to students, how to present himself, how to share his experiences and his learning in a way that is engaging, Socratic, compelling, fascinating, thought-provoking. Tips like "Treat the students like equals, but remember they aren't your friends." Tips like "To relate to students, make sure to use references to cultural phenomenon that they understand—for instance, *Laverne and Shirley* might mean something to you, but don't be surprised if your group of students reacts to dropping that reference with blank stares."

And he swears he's okay. It's true he's not going totally unmedicated. How can one go totally unmedicated and why would he go totally unmedicated? He doesn't want to go back to that darkness, he doesn't want to go there. So he is medicated, yes, a mild antidepressant, a few hundred milligrams a day, just to take that edge off a little bit, just to give his emotions some space from his brain.

The excitement, the buoyancy, of the teaching gig lifts his spirits. Barnard College, an all-girls Ivy League school. He will be teaching undergraduates at this school the art of journalism, a little subject called narrative nonfiction. He will mold and guide and show the way forward into promising careers, careers with the promise that his career once had, careers that he will not envy. No, he's now, at least on some days, accepted his fate, accepted the fact that sometimes in life you need to take a break, sometimes it's okay to take a nap.

His friends call—he realizes he does have friends, he supposes. He tells them all what he is telling himself. I'm not drinking. I'm not taking pills. I'm not even missing *The Magazine*. Life is more important than *The Magazine*. You know, it's time for me to do something else anyway, time for me to try something else. Really, they haven't totally fired me, I think, once things settle down, I probably can go back—if I want. If I want. My choice.

And he says this to Norm and to whoever will listen. He's come to embrace this summer as part of him. The summer after high school was the summer he lost his virginity, and the summer after that was the summer he tried LSD, and the summer after that was the summer he had an affair with an older woman, and the summer after that was the summer he traveled to Europe, then came the summer of an internship at the magazine, then the summer he wrote *Desperation Points West*, then the summer of Baghdad and Iraq—how far away that seems. (A quick flash of Chipotle in his mind that he shakes off.) And so, if every summer in his mind has a theme, the theme this summer is self-acceptance. I'm okay, I'm okay.

31.

Time Passes

It's like *Laverne and Shirley*," Peoria tells his class of twenty-six students. "You want the beginning of the story to grab the readers' attention, whether you're writing a nonfiction book, like *Desperation Points West*, or an article. You want to really get them into it. So, like *Laverne and Shirley*, that opening sequence—'We're going to do it!' Laverne is putting a glove on the beer bottle in Milwaukee. Lenny and Squiggy. You get the sense that it's a comedy, it's about friendship, it's set in Milwaukee—you get all of that just from the opening sequence."

Very little reaction.

"But you know, that theme song—rules are meant to be broken. That also applies to narrative nonfiction. I'm going to give you rules, but you can break them. But like that show, if you're going to break them, it better be, you know, brilliant.

"That's called, in journalism, we call that the lede. The opening paragraph is the lede.

"There can be an anecdotal lede.

"An analytical lede.

"A news lede.

"An omniscient-narrator lede.

"A lede in the second person. You.

"Most popular is probably the anecdotal lede, at least as far as magazines go."

He's scanned the list of students in his class, and there they are sitting in front of him. He knows that it's only natural for him to find the most attractive students first—he knows that he will not be able to resist that. There are three, two blondes and a brunette, and there is a fourth, a Mexican woman who makes fierce eye contact with him. She isn't really as attractive as the other three, but there is something appealing about her body language. He doesn't know if he's imagining it—perhaps it's something in Mexican culture where eye contact doesn't mean as much as it does in the States. Like in France, where women stare down men all the time and that's just part of the deal.

No, he scans his class of twenty-six, and he says what he says about *Laverne and Shirley*, and the rest of his first class is a rambling blur of handouts, stapled pages going back over back, of explanations about what he hopes to accomplish, about the different books on the syllabus, about how many papers he expects, about how he isn't going to accept just anything, he really wants reporting, about where they can obtain copies of the books on the syllabus—including, for extra credit, *Desperation Points West*, which, although out of print, can be ordered through a variety of websites for a good price: only 7 cents plus $1.35 shipping.

After the first class ends, he takes a breath and shuffles papers on his desk, finding it funny that he is the teacher, the professor. How very strange that is, waiting for the class to file past, smiling at the students, organizing, flushed, waiting to see if there is going to be anyone with questions or comments or concerns, waiting to see who is going to brownnose, who the kids are who don't care, looking for signs of drunkenness and drug abuse. He remembers college well.

He's pleased that one of the blonde girls stays behind and tells him that she has already read *Desperation Points West*. She has a copy. Will he sign it?

He smiles—"Karen, right"—and makes it out to Karen and then talks to her for five minutes, explaining how it was an important book, probably an overlooked classic, and that he appreciates greatly this kind of reader feedback. And while he's talking, he notes that his instincts were right about the Mexican, because she's also staying behind, waiting patiently for Peoria to finish speaking with the blonde.

The Mexican woman approaches his desk.

"Hi there, what can I help you with?"

"Professor Peoria," she says.

He looks at her, perplexed, and has a jolt of fear. Did he at some point hook up with this woman somewhere? She does look somehow familiar. Strong, slanted cheeks, a thick build for a woman, definitely third tier, maybe second tier. Certainly not first tier. He knows he must have hooked up with her or hit on her. Maybe he hit on her at some bar at some point during one of his periods in New York when that's what he was doing. Or maybe this woman is a friend of his ex-girlfriend's? Could that be? She would be the type that his ex-girlfriend would hang around—not quite that attractive, not much competition.

"Justina, is it?"

"Yes, Justina."

She waits.

He waits.

Does she want him, in this first class, to put a move on? This does seem like something out of a porn fantasy, something that isn't supposed to happen to a professor until at least mid-semester. No, Peoria resists the impulse to try something, and instead says, "I've blacked out a lot," he says.

She doesn't respond.

"What'd you think of the class?"

"You don't recognize me?"

"Oh, shit—I mean, excuse my language. Sure, I recognize you."

"You do?"

"You're a friend of my ex-girlfriend's, right? I met you at a slam poetry event?"

"No."

"Okay, we didn't, and I mean, this is awkward, we didn't hook up before, did we? Because if we did, I don't know what the school policy is about that. Fuck, I'm sure it's against policy."

"No, we never hooked up."

"Shit, then I'm sorry—did I interview you for an immigration story?"

"You saved my life."

32.

August 2005

'm working on the cover story when I get the email from Peoria. I figure it's one of those mass emails to all the people on his contact list. Hi all, here's my new information, just in case you want to ever reach me.

"Hey, Mike, how is everything at the magazine? I'm in the neighborhood today. Let's grab coffee if you can."

I say okay, but I think it's strange. Why would he want to talk to me?

Peoria says he'll be around in two hours. Both Nishant and Sanders are waiting on files from me, so I hurry to get those done.

It's a Monday, and the television outside Nishant Patel's office has been showing footage of a hurricane that hit New Orleans, and things seemed to be deteriorating real quick there. There's no way the story I'm working on is going to run on the cover.

Sanders walks by, on the way to the bathroom, and I say to him, "This hurricane in New Orleans looks pretty bad. Are we going to send somebody down there or do something about it?"

"Maybe a news brief," Sanders Berman says.

Nishant comes in from a television appearance. I mention the hurricane to him.

"We don't do hurricanes, Hastings," Nishant tells me.

"Okay, right, well, I'll get back to work on the files."

I go ahead on the cover story. Now, more than two years after the invasion of Iraq, it's called "How They Got It Wrong (And What They Can Do to Make It Right)." Both Nishant and Sanders are writing big pieces chastising various elements of American society and government. Nishant wants to aim at the Bush administration for being so stupid and incompetent. Nishant tells me—and this is a bit out of the ordinary for him, to make such a declarative statement—that he wants to call the decision "the most catastrophic foreign policy decision to be made in the twenty-first century."

"Do a little historical research, Mike, find examples of our history in war where we've launched an ill-fated foreign adventure then managed to settle for a less-than-satisfactory result, a result that doesn't meet our ridiculous expectations going in. Korea, perhaps. Vietnam, naturally." He pauses. "Get a few of the most outrageous examples in the media too—Robert Kagan, Brennan Toddly, that Kanan Makiya fellow—how the media didn't look critically at this case for war. But, you understand we need to be realistic here—we can't just leave. It's no use to just throw up our hands."

Sanders is going to give more or a less a historical defense too—yes, they made a mistake; what were we thinking?—but all great leaders make mistakes, and it is too early to count out Bush as a great leader. He is, after all, leading the country in two wars, one that is proving eminently successful in Afghanistan and one that is faltering in Iraq. "Historic examples, Hastings—I'm thinking here what Lincoln had to tell the American people after Bull Run, what FDR had to say to Americans after North Africa. Teddy up San Juan Hill . . .

History isn't made by losing our nerve . . . No, I don't think history is made by that, do you?"

I do my due diligence, digging up the most pertinent anecdotes for both sides of the argument. I start searching for embarrassing media examples and find a website that tracks those kinds of things. I edit out Patel's and Berman's own entries on the list before I send it along to them.

For Nishant, I find Eisenhower's decision to get us out of Korea. I get a great speech from our pullout in '75, in Vietnam. "We settled for half the country," Nishant writes in a draft. "And years later we've seen the benefits—a democratic regime, Samsung, Hyundai. Second-largest oil exporter in Asia. Second-fastest growth, beaten only by China." He wants to make the argument that by losing, we actually won in Vietnam. Look at the country now, thirty years later. Couldn't ask for better capitalists in training. So perhaps the same thing is true in Iraq—there's been enough creative destruction there that things will naturally take their course.

I send Sanders a Korean anecdote as well—a comment General Douglas MacArthur had made before he called it quits from both the military and life. "If we had pursued Korea to the fullest, perhaps we wouldn't be dealing with the nightmarish Kim Jong Il regime today," Sanders writes.

I figure one of them is going to have to lose the Korean anecdote in the final copy—we don't want to confuse our readers with contradictory historical precedent.

I send the files and go out to meet Peoria at Starbucks.

I order a large iced coffee. The kid behind the counter looks like he's been shipped in from the Bronx to fill up the minimum-wage jobs on the Upper West Side. He didn't understand what I wanted. Venti? he says. Yes, a large, I say.

I like Starbucks, but I refuse to speak Italian for them. Nothing against Italians—I'm not going to allow a corporation to rename a serving size.

Peoria arrives a few minutes later. He's wearing a blue Nike tracksuit.

"Just went to the gym," he says, after I stand up to shake his hand.

He orders a Grande iced coffee and we sit back down.

"Good to see you, man, you're looking well," I say.

"Thanks, bro."

I wait for him to fill the silence in the conversation. But he doesn't. It's odd to see him so healthy-looking; I wonder what kind of medication he's on, and how long it's going to last. There's something in his eyes, a layer of air bubbles in an algae-covered pond. Distracted. His upper lip keeps making a quick motion, like a snarl, the meds going to work on his synapses as they battle his true nature and find expression in a twitch. He's trying hard to seem calm and relaxed and to not just spaz out, right there at the table.

"We miss you at the magazine," I try.

He exhales.

"Wow, that's good to hear, man, because that's why I'm here. I don't want to get too specific, and I can't really tell you, but you should know. Because I'm supposed to come back."

I know he wants to get very specific—he wants to spill.

"Oh right, when?"

From what I've been hearing, it doesn't look good at *The Magazine* for Peoria. Some of the editors want administrative leave to mean he was basically fired and just hasn't been told yet, and they weren't officially informing him because they didn't want to seem like they would just abandon an employee that quickly if he was perceived to have made a mistake. Gary, representing the smart money, says that "there's zero chance he'd work at the magazine again."

"March. I was supposed to come back in March. A year off. But that was too soon, they said. Though now I have something, I have something real big. I'm working on something real big, you know, that might get me back there sooner, if you know what I mean."

"Right, sure, of course."

"It's a big story. I wanted to get the sense from you, as you always seem to know all the gossip, if you think I'd have a chance of coming back earlier if I had a big story."

I don't know if I should tell him the truth or even the truth about what the rumors say.

"Is, like, the coast clear?"

"There's some discussion about you, yeah."

"They're talking about me, so that means they haven't forgotten me. That's a good sign, I think."

"No doubt, like Wilde said, they haven't forgotten about you."

"That's what I wanted to hear. I mean, I can tell you, and this is between you and me, I've really been working on self-acceptance this summer, and I've accepted, you know, that the magazine doesn't really mean much to me. Can you believe that? I mean, when I was your age, I would have dreamed for the job I had, and then when I got it, I didn't know how dependent I became on it for my own self-worth. I, like, started to identify with the brand. I started to say things like I love *The Magazine*. I started to see it as family and as a place where they really, you know, cared about me as an individual, and man, I loved telling people I worked for them—it made me feel like I had some worth. I guess I took it for granted and I didn't see that if I lost that, if I lost that, I didn't think it would be that big of a deal, but it was like my whole identity got shattered. My entire identity. So I worked on self-acceptance, and I think now, you know, it's not a big deal at all. *The Magazine* isn't life. But I also realize, you know, how much it means at the same time, you understand what I'm saying? When I had my class—I'm teaching up at Barnard—you know, something really strange happened and my reporting instincts just *BAM!*, just pounced, and I said, Wow, this is such a blockbuster I can't even begin to say. I didn't get much sleep thinking about it, which really, I think, hurt my workout. I almost puked again, but then I had a protein drink and a slushy and that settled my stomach."

"You're teaching? That's great."

"Yeah, our semester just started. But that's how I got this story, or at least what I think might be a story. But I really can't tell you about it right now, I really can't."

"Okay, dude, sure, if you don't want to tell me about it, that's cool. But you can, like, trust me, you know?"

"Well fine, I'll tell you."

For the next fifteen minutes, Peoria launches into a bizarre story that I really don't believe. I think he might be having some kind of psychotic episode, or breakdown—a cousin of mine had had that once, and, as is strangely the case with psychotics, when the brain breaks down, it seems to break down in the same way for everyone. This cousin believed that evil alien ghosts were trying to do something with his genitalia and that the signals to these extra-dimensional creatures were coming from a place on the far side of Lake Superior. Peoria's story had whiffs of that, and the other signs seemed to fit: wearing a Nike tracksuit in the afternoon, talking fast, a stream of consciousness that, really, I could barely follow. Something about Babylon, a Mexican food dish, Thailand, and the GI Bill.

I don't know what to say, he's acting so strangely. I just want to get out of there. Yes, it sounds like a story, I tell him, but no, you should not approach Delray M. Milius about it.

Maybe I should tell him to forget it, that there's no rush, that I think he should think about it more. I think that's the best chance for him surviving at *The Magazine.*

And that he didn't have a chance to survive at *The Magazine* anyway.

But I don't say that, I don't, and maybe I miss a chance to save him, but I don't know that until later.

I go back to the office. Both Nishant and Sanders have responded, asking me to get a few more details, and maybe talk to a couple of historians to back up their respective cases. I'm keeping an eye on the news—all this Katrina stuff looks pretty bad—but it's a Monday and only a handful of people are in the office and it definitely doesn't seem like anyone else thinks it's a big deal.

Tuesday, Sanders runs the story meeting. He says we are going ahead with the Iraq cover, and that the "website can handle the hurricane."

On Wednesday afternoon, Delray M. Milius runs by my desk, hissing on the phone, "I know I told you not to go when you called on Monday, but we didn't realize how big this was. We need you to get down there now!"

On Thursday, Sanders runs the story meeting again. Henry the EIC is on vacation.

"Clearly, we're doing Katrina on the cover for this week."

During the international story meeting on Friday, Nishant Patel relents.

"Okay, we'll hold off on our covers and do this hurricane."

I get a frantic email from Sanders on Friday night, asking me to do some research for the editor's note.

"I want more details on how LBJ handled that natural disaster in . . . whenever that was."

I have to fact-check his editor's note on Saturday. It reads:

I, for one, have given the President the benefit of the doubt. But it's clear by his failure to realize how catastrophic the events in New Orleans were, how long he delayed before responding, how—and I'm going to use a word that the kids these days use—how clueless our President has been, I am disgusted. How could they not have seen how big this was? Why did it take them 72 hours, until Wednesday, to get into action? I have written before, that the President, a commander of two wars, is, by his very nature, a hero-prophet. After observing his reaction to this hurricane, I would be forced to admit that perhaps my estimation has proven premature.

All of this means that I forget about Peoria. I won't hear from him again until he sends me his journal months later.

THE PRE-DENOUEMENT

Okay, so the book is getting a little out of hand. I'm aiming to wrap it up at 80,000 words, and we just hit 80,000 words now. The plot is just beginning to materialize in full force, and there are all sorts of other threads and developments that, if I'm going to get to them, would add an extra hundred fifty pages to the book.

I'll spare you.

We get the joke quickly. I don't want to be tedious about the whole thing.

Most of the top media folks are a bunch of clueless assholes, egotistical, vainglorious, pompous, insecure, corrupt—you get the picture, right? Not that they're bad people—they're not out there running death camps—but it's just who they are. If it weren't them, it'd be someone else, right? And if I'd worked at another magazine, they'd be someone else too.

Like my uncle used to say—he's a priest—about giving homilies at a Catholic mass: Make it three minutes long and mention basketball.

Keep it simple. Grab the reader by the throat. A fact in every sentence.

I'm breaking these rules, and as Peoria tells his students, many of whom I've interviewed, I'm trying my best to do it brilliantly.

We're coming up on the end here—I'd say less than an hour left in the show.

33.

October 2005

A.E. Peoria sits at a table of his favorite Italian restaurant on the Upper West Side, pondering what he should call the individual sitting across from him.

Justina. Justin. Chipotle. He saw a documentary once about Muhammad Ali, and the writer was having that same problem—should I call him Muhammad Ali or Cassius Clay? Lew Alcindor or Kareem Abdul-Jabbar? The Artist Formerly Known as Prince and Sean Combs also pose that problem.

Justina is talking, laying it on heavy, dropping the wisdom. Justina is explaining the conversion.

"A belief in war," Justina says, "is like a belief in God. Comforting until you look too closely at the facts."

Peoria doesn't quite know what to say, but he does know he should write this down.

"Science," Justina says, "science is a religion that can prove its miracles."

Peoria keeps taking notes.

Ten details.

Thick bowl of pasta, penne Bolognese.

Four slices of garlic bread.

Justina is wearing a white sweater, preppy, for the fall, jeans that don't quite fit comfortably on her hips.

Black heels.

Dusky light.

Couple next to them glances over.

Table leg is shorter than the other; waiter kneels to slide a piece of cardboard underneath the dwarf leg.

Thinks: Good Justina isn't wearing a dress.

Elaborate silver jewelry.

Elaborate earrings: big hoops, bumblebee yellow.

Dark olive complexion contrasts against pale creamy sweater.

Chardonnay, lipstick trace on glass.

A.E. Peoria is surprised by the amount of wisdom she has, and wonders if that's some kind of stereotype—the wise transvestite or shemale, hard-earned packets of knowledge, dropped out, like crumbs on a trail to self-acceptance.

"I'm a miracle of science, Alex," Justina says. "I'm a miracle of fate."

It is their second meeting, not quite the third, not yet the meeting when things go wrong.

A.E. Peoria has promised that he will write about Justina only when Justina gives him permission to do so. Justina explains that she is at Barnard College on the GI Bill. But, as she explains to Peoria, there is a debate in Barnard about whether to accept transgendered students who were once male. It is a raging debate—protests, petitions, clauses in the student handbook. So, Justina hasn't mentioned her unique circumstances to anyone else. She also is fearful that the funding for the GI Bill could be taken away if it became public that it was supplying funds for the education of a transgendered individual.

Peoria knows this, has nodded and sworn the vow of secrecy, but he is already mentally preparing to back out of that promise. He hasn't quite admitted to himself that he is going to back out of the promise—he hasn't quite accepted the fact that he's ready to give Justina the major burn. He is telling himself that he should just be prepared to write about Justina now, or next week, or three weeks, in case he or she changes his mind, or whenever he has enough to tell her story, whenever he can go to his editors at *The Magazine* and say, I've got something for you, an exclusive. It involves an Ivy League school, a transvestite, and a Purple Heart. Can't beat that for a story.

Justina trusts him, as he is the man who saved his life, and especially since he agreed to the preconditions of the interview. She explains that the school has the most powerful LGBT organization in the country, so that is why she went there, that leaders of the LGBT know of her case and helped grease the paperwork, helped her in, but they are keeping her hidden, a shemale Trojan horse. She worries it could be a case that would have to be tested in court—if your gender has changed since leaving the armed forces, does your status as veteran change? She knows the conservative elements in the nation might be outraged, might say they do not want their taxpayer dollars paying for a transsexual to go to school, even a veteran transsexual with a Combat Infantry Badge. Already, explains Justina, she has lost her family and she does not also want to lose her benefits.

"So like, uh, how did you pay for the operation?"

She smiles.

"There wasn't much to pay for . . . I came back, you know, and it was gone. It was gone completely, a scar, a hole with a catheter. I was in my bed at Walter Reed for months, for months, and they would come in and say prayers and I would get balloons and flowers and even the president and celebrities would come by. One celebrity, a Hollywood star who had just tried to kill himself on painkillers and heroin, three weeks later he came by Walter Reed. Like he wanted to see how good his life was compared with people who really can complain. I couldn't even look at him. I was so angry those first months. They started giving me pills, testosterone supplements, to make up for everything that I had lost. But the pills, they made me so angry! I just got angrier and angrier. And then they would cut my hair, they would still pretend I was in the service, still pretend that I was still part of this army, and I knew that wasn't true anymore. So when they let me out, I wanted to die. I wanted to curl up and not wake up and just let myself die. It couldn't be done in the hospital—they were watching you, therapy groups, post-traumatic stress discussions, very well regulated on the pills that one could take lethal dosages of.

"They kept a close eye on me, because they say the wound I have is called, in psychiatry, is called a non-threatening terminal wound. Non-threatening, in that, physically, the damage was minimal! Minimal! Terminal in that it could lead to my death by my own hand later on. This is the wound, I have heard soldiers say, they would rather die than have. Do you know what is the best piece of your body to lose?"

"Uh, your hand?"

"No, they say, BK, below the knee, non-dominant leg—that is the best leg to lose if you have to lose something, I have heard them say. Maybe they didn't know about me when they said it, that at least they still had their penises, at least they did—because if they didn't, they would rather have died out there, on the field, in the sand. Bleed out. And where am I? What am I supposed to say to that, me with no penis, no testicles, a scar on skin? I wanted to die. I do not think I am being unreasonable . . ."

Peoria hasn't touched his pasta, and Justina hasn't really made headway on her grilled chicken salad. She's ordering like a girl, Peoria thinks, ordering a salad for a main course at dinner.

"At Walter Reed, there were reading groups. Discussion groups. A reading group, one of the books we were given was *Born on the Fourth of July* by Ron Kovic. Have you ever read this book? It is a powerful, disturbing book—it gives lie to everything that we fought for in Vietnam, in Iraq, in most wars. My fellow soldiers, they couldn't see it like that. They believed the book was interesting because it showed how bad VA care used to be, compared with what it is now. They found the positive message in the book—only in the modern-day American volunteer Army could you have soldiers find a positive message in that book, even the disfigured soldiers, soldiers with nine reconstructive operations on the face, soldiers whose arms have been sheared off at the shoulder, who cannot move anything below the Adam's apple, only among these soldiers could you have someone say, '*Born on the Fourth of July* is a book about the improvement in health care.'"

"I guess my question is, you didn't think that the book was about improvements in health care? Sorry, I've like, only seen the movie, a long time ago."

"No, it is not about health care. I found the book to be about transformation. Kovic's trauma transforms him from the soldier, born on the Fourth of July, the patriot, to an influential antiwar activist. It is about how this spirit of resistance was in him the entire time but it was not until he was shot, twice, until he lost the movement in his legs, that he realized that the surface, the patriot, was not who he really was—or no, I should say that he was always a patriot, it is just that his expression of patriotism did not fully form until the trauma. What was hidden inside him was a true patriot, his true self, a self that was prepared to go out and take criticism for revealing the government's lies. We are beyond that, we are beyond that, don't you see? We have to know the government lies, there is no shocking us— every soldier, or most, with a brain, know on some level that the government lies. So the transformation in this war, well, it is very hard to be the same—the veteran who comes back and says 'I was lied to' is greeted with a shrug—well, yes, of course you were, didn't you see Oliver Stone's film with Tom Cruise in it?"

"Shit, Justin, Justina, you're losing me—a bit. I don't quite get it—I'll rent the movie again, I have Netflix, so I can put it in my queue and everything."

"The transformation, for me, it could not just be political. It had to be more fundamental than that. It had to be a transformation of nature, my human nature, and what is more fundamental to human nature than gender?"

"Right, good question."

Peoria has this strange sense, forcing himself to listen again, that Justina had rehearsed this quite well, and he wonders how an enlisted soldier had that much education. Most didn't, most would have trouble answering Jay Leno's on-the-street stumpers: What two countries share the border with the United States? Who is the senator from Puerto Rico? Mexico City is the capital of what country? Who was the third president of the United States? You didn't get the rare intellectual or philosophizer unless you were talking to an officer.

"I don't understand, though, why you enlisted. I mean, you're obviously pretty smart."

"My family is very rich, a rich Hispanic family in El Paso. I had a very good education. I could have been an officer, I would have been accepted quickly, but I felt that if I was to understand what my family and the other immigrants went through, then I would have to join up as an enlisted man. Like Charlie Sheen in *Platoon*."

"Right, like, you would have to be rich to think like that."

"*Exactamente.*"

Peoria has been listening for close to forty-five minutes straight, and this is about his maximum attention span—this is the point where he nods and hopes that his digital tape recorder keeps capturing the seconds ticking away on the display counter so he can go back and listen to it later.

He looks down to make sure the little red light is still going, sees that it is, pushes it a little closer to Justina, making sure that it is not being blocked by the edge of a bread plate, and exhales.

"Anecdotes, do you have any more, you know, like I talk about in class?"

"Anecdotes?"

Justina pauses, and Peoria recognizes the subtle shift in the eyes— the shift that indicates the brain is about to disassociate with the words she is about to speak, because whatever it is, whatever sentences are arranging themselves in her head already have warned the brain that protective barriers of enzymes and neurons are necessary, walls must be erected on the sides of her syntax, to keep the language away from the emotional side of her brain, the tear ducts and the heart.

"Cindy Sheehan. She is the mother who camped out at President Bush's ranch after her son was killed in Iraq. You remember her?"

"Yeah, Cindy Sheehan."

"She came to Walter Reed. She was not allowed in, and I don't know if she wanted to come in, but she stood outside the Mologne House, the brick buildings, for three weeks, with a group of antiwar protesters. She stood outside the gates with her signs, and in my ward, we would come and look. Protesting outside Walter Reed. We would peek outside and see her and we would be filled with rage. With absolute rage. What is she doing here, tormenting us? The man in the bed next to mine, Lucas, he had lost his left leg above the knee. A full hip disarticulation, or FHD. He could not stand seeing her out there. He would say, 'The lying bitch! Her son did not even like her'—and he would tell me how he had heard from someone who knew her son, someone in her son's unit, that they were estranged, that she was not on good terms, and there she was, an impostor, outside the walls of the pain box, the pain house, marching to make a political point of her tragedy, exploiting her son's death, the fucking bitch, the fucking slut bitch whore. This became an accepted fact among the men of our ward, of the Army, I think. That she and her son were not close and that she should not be there. She should shut the fuck up and honor her son's sacrifice, like the rest of us. Lucas wanted to make her shut up. He would wish he had his thirty-thirty hunting rifle that he would use to bag bear and deer and sometimes to help with the local wild boar problem in Georgia. He would say to the CO, a doctor, when he came by, 'Sir, you've got to give me a shot at her. You got to let me get my rifle in here. All it will take is one, one shot. I'm a good shot and no one will be none the wiser.' He yelled this to the doctor one day, and the response from around the ward was incredible, like some kind of prison movie with the inmates banging tin cups on the bars, this steady beat of clinking and clanging started across the third floor. It was dinnertime and we had forks—men with one arm and one leg hitting against the metal bars of the hospital beds. The rhythm began, swelling up, and we all felt very good, and the shouts started, 'Sheehan, Sheehan, Sheeeeeeehhannnnnnnnnnn.'"

"That's some heavy shit," Peoria says, thinking it makes the perfect anecdote to begin his piece, one certain to spark controversy and discussion.

"That night, as it happened, she was going to hold a candlelight midnight vigil to mark the last night of her three weeks. I believe it was even on Veterans Day. Lucas believed it would be his last chance. He plopped into his wheelchair and rolled over to my bed. 'My prosthetic is working well enough, and I know you can walk, so tonight is our last chance,' he told me. 'We have to go outside and we have to take her out. It's our duty,' Lucas whispered to me, 'we must do it.'

"Did I want to take part in such an adventure? Yes! I did. I did not think twice about it, I did not have a moment of reflection. We would again be in a small unit—it was such a relief to have a mission for us to do, another high-value target for us to take aim at, as Lucas put it. At twenty-three thirty, silent, like we were trained, a whole group of us gathered: me, dickless; Lucas, minus a leg; Payton, a quiet type, no right arm; Jack, two below-the-knees—yes, a half-dozen of us. Like a crippled A-Team. We could be a black humor sitcom. We did not feel at all ridiculous. Fuck them, we had a mission tonight, and if you would have seen us limping along, down the fire exit, one floor, two floors, three floors, down to the ground level, where we would walk out the back and circle around the side of the building, leave at Gate 3, and come up the sidewalk, where we would change into civilian clothes rather than hospital garb, maybe you would have laughed or felt sympathy or started to cry or sneered about how pathetic we looked. But we did not feel ridiculous. We were motivated. Very highly motivated. We were the volunteer army of 2002, and this was not some kind of pussywhipped Vietnam veterans who were just going to sit back and take it. We were making a preemptive, Rambo *First Blood* strike. We were not going to take this kind of abuse from a lying whore like Cindy Sheehan. Lucas led the pack, around the sidewalk, and as we came closer, we could start to hear the sounds of a song, a song they were singing, and we could see lights for television cameras. They were singing for the cameras. They had been silent all night but now the lights and the sound boom were there, and so they started to sing. They started to sing that very stale song 'We Shall Overcome,' as if they were King or Chavez—they shall overcome? They shall overcome what? Who were they, when we were the wounded, missing our manhood and our dignity and keeping our head held high. They were going to tell us, what, that it wasn't worth it? What the fuck do they know about Iraq? What the fuck do they know about costs, about it not being worth it? They have no idea, and especially that Sheehan, who hated her son and whose son hated her, had no right, no right to be overcoming anything at our expense. Lucas walked with his hand out, already in a grip, imagining Sheehan's neck in his hands, ready to strangle her to death. He would strangle her—he could taste how satisfying it would be. Army hand-to-hand combat training, army grappling is based on numerical superiority. You get the enemy down, you grapple him, immobilize him, and the others come to your help to finish the beating or detention. We, the other six, would run interference, form a tight circle around him, and therefore there would be no witnesses. There would be no one to see who did it and we would all say nothing. We would all say she had attacked first, and it would be the word of seven veterans against the word of what—a hippie peace activist, a radical tormenting the wounded warriors. Radicals versus veterans. We knew that in any court of law, we would win, the troops would be supported. We turned the corner and there Sheehan was standing, at the head of the crowd . . ."

Peoria tunes out. The whole thing sounds ridiculous now, and he wants to direct Justina back on track to the more important story, the story about her. All this bullshit about Sheehan is getting tiresome.

"Okay, yeah, yeah, so it didn't happen, and when you looked into her eyes or something, you came to realize something about yourself?"

"Yes, that's right, I—"

He cuts her off. "Great. Okay, so you go back to El Paso and your family isn't like, what, supportive?"

"Oh, they were supportive. They wanted me to be a hero. They presented me to friends saying I was a hero. My mother would cut in front of lines at Applebee's or Outback and say, we should sit first, our son is a hero, a veteran, a wounded soldier. They didn't tell anyone what my true injury was. They didn't want that information to get out—they just said I was shot in the lower regions and that I was recovering."

"Right, right."

"I curled up in a little ball in my house. My bedroom that I had had as a teenager, there I was, supposed to be a man in his twenties and living in his parents' house, in his old bedroom, same posters, same desk for studying, same all of this. I acted like I couldn't walk, like I was too sore, and my parents, they accepted this. I could have walked, but I didn't want to. I wanted to stay in bed. I wanted to just wither away. I stopped cutting my hair. I stopped taking those testosterone pills. I stopped those things, and I drifted, for weeks.

"My anger, after I stopped taking the pills, my anger started to go away. Like a eunuch. At first, I missed my anger—my anger was all that I had—but I didn't want to take some pills to be a man. For three days, I shook—I shook with the emptiness of these fucking hormones to make up for what would have been in my testicles! I woke up—"

"When?"

"This was five months after my Alive Day, they call it. Alive Day. A sick fucking joke, someone at HBO must have devised it, I don't know, to make us feel good, rather than call it Blown-to-Shit Day. The shakes had stopped—I had stopped shaking from lack of anger—and no, it was no peace, but I walked by the Dallas Cowboys poster, I walked by the picture of Miguel Fernandez in his Tecate-sponsored open-wheel racing car—we had gone down to, my father and I, to watch him race and got a picture, all of us smiling, the sponsored beer, red and green in the backdrop. I went to the bathroom and I took a shower and I picked up a shampoo—my mother's shampoo, a coconut-scented flavor from Vidal Sassoon, and I cleaned my long hair, down to my shoulders, and I stepped out and tied a towel around my head like I had seen my sisters do, and I saw how much weight I had lost, how thin I looked, and I looked down at the scar and it looked like a vagina. I smiled, I smiled and I batted my eyelashes, and I inhaled, and I felt at peace, because what I had been resisting, what I had been resisting was that I was no longer a man, yes, and that I was really a woman now, I was a female. I was thin and effeminate-looking always, and perhaps it would always have been so, but if it wasn't for fate, if it wasn't for that shrapnel, I would not have seen it, or it would have taken me years to see it, to act on it."

A.E. Peoria hits the stop button on the tape recorder and thinks, Man, this chick or dude is fucking nuts. He slips the tape recorder in his pocket and realizes that he has an erection.

34.

Later

I don't expect to see Peoria back in the office so soon.

"Mike, dude, good that you're here," he says, elbows on the cubicle wall. "I took your advice—I decided to come and talk to Delray M. Milius, to make amends, you know, and to pitch that story I told you about."

"Cool, bro, that's cool."

I don't know what he's talking about. I gave him the exact opposite advice. But I suppose that's what he wants to do, and no matter what I had said, he had interpreted it as confirmation of what he had already decided.

I'm surprised that Milius even agreed to speak to him after the pencil incident—I thought for sure it was just a matter of time before Peoria got canned permanently.

"He said I could bring you in as a research assistant, you know, to help me get some background to the story. You have time for that?"

"Ah yeah, just doing a couple things for Sanders and Nishant, no worries."

"Okay, great. I gave you the details last time we met, right? About what I was sitting on? Swore you to secrecy, obviously too, as this can't leak out, you know? It's all very sensitive."

"Sure—"

The Peoria that I knew is back—divulging, disclosing, vomiting up his exclusive story. It's kind of mind-boggling to hear. I hadn't heard anything like it before. Sure, there are gays in the military stories, and there are stories over the past few years about transgendered kids in high school and college, and about how some state universities, like the University of Vermont, were creating unisex, or multisex, or transgendered bathrooms because the risk of attack on transgendered people is extremely high if they go into a men's room, and they aren't quite accepted in the ladies' room either. But never had I heard of a shemale war hero.

"Not 'shemale,' dude, that's not a politically correct term. Plus, she's got no junk anyway anymore, so it doesn't make you a shemale unless you have, like, a dick and breasts—she's working on the breasts, though. But really, what I need from you is to get me the science behind it, and some of the social context for this—talk to a few experts in the transgendered community. Don't quite tell them what we're talking about, you know, but we want to get the legal issues and everything resolved first, you know. We're really going to be doing Chipotle a favor, I think."

"So she's cool with you running the story?"

"Oh, you know, man, she doesn't really want to do a story about it, at least not right now, but sometimes the news value has to outweigh personal considerations. You can't just sit on a scoop like this because the person you know could get hurt by it."

"You don't want her to get kicked out of school and lose her benefits, though, right?"

"Yeah, that's probably going to happen, you know, but there are enough support groups and shit out there that if she does lose that, I'm sure someone will step in, you know?"

"Okay, right, maybe."

"Yeah, maybe, there's no guarantee in this business on anything, you know. Like that lady said: Anyone who does journalism and doesn't realize that what we're doing is totally immoral is a fucking clown, you know?"

"That's cool, dude, yeah, of course."

"Okay, man, I've got to run, because I'm, like, meeting her later tonight for what I hope will be the final interview—I've already got like thirteen hours' worth of audio files—maybe you can start working on transcribing those too? You have the Sony program, right? My other notes, you know, just keep them to yourself and everything."

Another assignment. If Delray M. Milius is willing to put his grudge behind him, I realize that this is probably going to be a big story to be part of, and I'm glad he thought of me to work on it. That means, including the Iraq stories, I will have contributed to more than thirty-five feature stories over the past year, which will put me way out ahead of the rest of the newbies.

Sanders strolls by my desk.

"Have my notes for the Imus show ready?" he asks me.

"Oh, coming along, no worries."

"I don't like to look bad on that show—he can throw some tough ones at you," he says.

Sanders has become a regular guest on the Don Imus program, one of the highest-rated radio shows in the country. Along with Oprah, Imus can move books like nobody else—and Sanders's book had moved, thanks to his regular appearances and endorsement by Imus. It's been a regular task for me to do, to get notes together on the possible subjects Imus might bring up on the show, maybe write a few jokes for him, or possible subjects. Not that Imus or his producers ever stick to the topics Sanders tells me they are going to talk about—a continuing source of annoyance for Sanders. I get to work writing up the notes.

35.

Sunday, November 20, 2005

Watching transsexual pornography started as research but it has become a compulsion within days. Men who are now women is the category that A.E. Peoria Googles. Full-blown transsexuals. Hundreds of thousands of links appear, safety filter off, images and video clips and paid sites. The shemales, the he-shes, the cross-dressers, the post-op and pre-op transsexuals, strap-on kings and queens—how much of this community, percentage-wise, he wonders, is involved in pornography or cabarets or strip clubs? And isn't it odd to base one's whole life around sex? Or did we all base our lives around sex, and if you could get a job focused on sex, perhaps you were ahead of the game? Perhaps the transsexuals understood something that no one else did? But what's the point of becoming a ladyboy if you aren't going to hustle on the street?

But Justina isn't a ladyboy or a shemale—she's a transsexual, and she wants to pursue a career in academia, in writing, in the arts or in advocacy, eventually. Advocacy, there's another popular profession for transsexuals. You either got a job in the sex industry or got a job advocating for transsexuals' rights. Advocacy and pornography and show tunes—the three primary industries of the transgendered community.

Peoria's morning research starts with his iced coffee and a check of the email and the list of phone numbers of experts he wants to call.

Up at six a.m., hitting his stride again, feeling for the first time since before the Iraq War that drive, that fulfilling call of work, a sense of purpose—a story to write and to tell and to understand. On his laptop, on his wireless, he streams a local news radio show—usually, the program he starts listening to is *Imus in the Morning*—but the pull of the boundless Internet, with all of its perversions, drags him back to free porn sites, and he lowers the blinds in his apartment, pulls down his track pants, and watches the explicit sexual acts.

As a young man growing up, photos in magazines were enough to get him off. First, publications like *Playboy* were good enough, but then he upgraded to *Penthouse*; the open vaginal and anal shots of *Penthouse*, still done respectfully, were the next level. Then, he discovered *Hustler*, and his masturbatorial bar was set even higher—*Hustler*, now that was explicit, threesomes, full penetration, dripping cum shots, and a new and enticing category called Barely Legal, which forever altered the way he viewed young female teenagers running cash registers at ice cream stands and in grocery stores and Japanese school uniforms and cheerleading outfits.

When he got his own apartment out of college, in the '90s, he was able to own his first VHS player and visit his first sex shops in the city, on 33rd Street: a candy store, all the different racks of various interests for sale, and all he had to do was duck in and buy the videotapes to see those still images that had worked for him for so long come to life. The sheer freedom of being able to rewind and fast-forward and pause, with no worries of parents or siblings ruining his privacy. That's freedom. He never bought another magazine again.

The Internet proved to be a disruptive force for self-abuse. With the Internet, the sheer range of digital images did the job at first—he was able to stop watching videos on the VHS and start watching, on his computer, acts that he had read about but never seen—women sucking off farm animals, women urinating on the faces of other women, women urinating on the faces of other men, men urinating in clear streams into the open mouths of women, defecating even, strapped and bound with metal and leather contraptions, penetrated with massive objects like baseball bats and giant rubber dildos, a foot in diameter, or shaken soda cans stuffed in rectal canals, and on and on. These images—who was putting them out there? Where was it all coming from? And what an amazing thing it was, all of this that previously one would have had to order via the U.S. Postal Service from a European country, now all available thanks to the spread of dial-up connections and 32-bit modems.

The Internet, he knows, had been developed by DARPA at the Defense Department, for war, but sex quickly took over as the primary innovator, from the days of the first chat rooms. Now, with DSL and cable connections and streaming video feeds, digital images of the most grotesque and enticing kind no longer worked to get Peoria off. He had to see the movement, he needed the image to be flashing at 32 frames a second, in a little box on his screen, uninterrupted—watching porn on a slow connection didn't even do it, he needed a high-speed connection or he just wasn't into it.

He was not terribly concerned about the moral implications until June 2002, when he'd gotten the fastest speed available and clicked on a link that said "vomit porn," and at that moment he had a crisis of faith, or the closest thing one who does not believe in anything can have to a crisis of faith.

A white girl, wearing a blue skiers' tuque with an embroidered golden star, had been kneeling down in front of a crowd and giving head to a black male of significant perpendicular length. Using the now ancient deep-throating technique, she worked the man's cock avidly, eyes watering, his large hands clasped around her ears, occasionally pulling out to the left or right to make a popping sound against the suction on her cheek. At minute 2:33 into the clip, the standard degradation went off course; at first, the male performer responded as if it were still part of the performance, but then she ripped his hands away and started to crawl away, a desperate move, as if she were a child with motion sickness in the back of the car trying to unroll the window, or a coed searching for a bathroom stall after expecting to come into the restroom only to touch up her makeup. She started to puke, a yellow and a watery flow, all over the ground, and the camera first zoomed in on her face as she vomited, and then the camera pulled back to get the reaction of the cheering crowd and the still-hard penis of the black performer, and then the video ended, and A.E. Peoria himself felt sick, he felt ill, and wondered if maybe he shouldn't be watching this stuff, maybe it was destroying his soul, if there was such a thing.

That didn't last long.

He thinks of it now because he'd had the same first reaction to the transsexual performers: that something was somehow unholy or desperately sick in the acts that were being performed, that it was somehow disturbing to his subconscious that the women being fucked in the ass used to be men. But as he watched, he instinctively started to touch himself, and he started to hold the images in his head of Thailand, enhancing a sexual experience that he had avoided masturbating to at all costs—he was straight after all, it was his parents who were gay—but the transsexual porn brought these memories back, and he no longer felt revulsion, and in fact, started to get off on the idea that the man fucking the woman was actually fucking a man, a dirty little secret that wasn't a secret but added a level of fantasy to the moving video clips, a level of fantasy that his own memories augmented.

After one week of research, he started to worry: In the same way that he was never able to go back to magazine porn after the Internet had evolved, would he ever be able to have normal sex again, with a normal female? Or had his fantasy wires been so crossed that he would need to keep upping the sexual illusions and delusions and confusion in order to reach a fulfilling orgasm? And then, he asked, in a rare moment of self-awareness, did he want to go back?

And then there is the issue that he tries to avoid. That he tries to sublimate with Oedipal and Freudian and Jungian rationalizations and all that—he tries to ignore that he really wants to fuck Justina.

PART VII

The Last Week

36.

Later

'm preparing the notes for another Sanders Berman spot on the Imus show. I haven't heard from Peoria. That's not too surprising. He'd dumped his notes my way, emails and journals and audio files that I haven't yet bothered to look at. I had learned at the magazine to work on deadline, and even opening the email was effort I didn't want to expend until I was sure the story was going to go forward.

I'm surprised when I get an email from Sarah, the Wretched.com editor. She asks if I'd be able to fill in and guest edit Wretched the next week. Timothy Grove runs what is more or less the media equivalent of a sweatshop—no benefits, ten days of vacation, no extra time for holidays—and Sarah needs to go home for an emergency next week. Timothy Grove had protested and said that if she couldn't find a replacement, she would lose her job. So she asks me.

I should ask for permission from Delray or Sanders, to be safe. But I know they'll most likely reject it. Nishant might be more willing to say yes, because he doesn't really pay too close attention to the day-to-day, so as long as I ask him, I'm covered. I send an email to Nishant, and I never hear back. I take the non-response as his tacit permission.

Sarah invites me to a party that night at a bar on the Lower East Side called the Dark Room.

The Dark Room is on Ludlow Street, above Rivington. This doesn't mean much to most people—but as Greenwich Village was to the '50s beatniks and the '60s hippies, the Lower East Side is to this strange and much less influential crowd of the early '00s, at least in their minds. They are important, or believe in their own importance, even if only expressed with the required self-mockery. They aren't artists, and not really a community of writers, either: they are bloggers, and their focus is each other. They are hyper-consumers; they don't write, they create content, stripping away any pretense of some larger ethos or goal except that it is somehow hip, rebellious—though they'd never use those words and they mock hipsters and rebellion too. A desire to be noticed and to criticize the criticizers of the world, to gain its acceptance by rejecting it, breeding a strange kind of apathy and nihilism and ambition, floating in a kind of morally barren world where they say, Look, here is the asshole's asshole of the world, the New York media, and we will show you, minute by minute, post by post, what the rectum walls feel and taste like, and you will know even better these sensations because we ourselves are part of this intestinal lining, and we are okay with that, we have embraced it as our contemporary calling, at least until we can get real jobs or a book deal.

On the Lower East Side, where they live, gentrification on these blocks was more or less complete—the last remaining Jews had been pushed out a decade before, the Hispanics were still found but mostly outside the primary five-block radius, hanging around in small groups and whistling outside of the subway entrance to the F train on Second Avenue. Orchard Street is filled with luggage stores and leather stores and glasses shops, run by Pakistanis, storefronts selling junk and trinkets and passport photos, a slow death before developers can come in and create a trendy boutique.

But none of this is totally clear to me at the time—it seems like a cool crowd to be part of, it seems like the new new media is a place to visit, and here they are, in the Dark Room.

Sarah meets me outside the front door, where a Cadillac Escalade–size bouncer checks our out-of-state driver's licenses under the purple glow of a flashlight.

The bar is split into two rooms, to the left and right of the entrance, eight-foot ceilings, everything black. To the right is a stage, where live bands or DJs play next to a bar; and on the left, there are couches and tables.

Sarah points to the far corner where a table has been staked out. A group of about seven males and three females, all white, age range twenty-three to thirty-five, stand sipping beers and gin and tonics.

She starts making introductions, yelling the names and the blogs that they are associated with.

There is Allan Tool, who holds some kind of deputy managing editor title for Wretched; Franklin Liu, who blogs on Mediabistro; the other Sarah, Sarah Klein, who does Gothamist; some guy named Arnie Cohen, most notorious for his ability to get mentioned on everyone else's blogs without actually doing anything of note, except hitting on Sarah Klein in the back of a taxicab and then blogging about his rejection; Jennifer Cunningham, who would later have a "crisis of conscience" and leave Wretched to focus more clearly on herself; and on and on, names with a "blogspot" and a "dot com" attached, names that I've heard of before by reading one referring to the other. The closest thing to someone from a traditional media outlet, besides myself, is a kid with short dark hair and beady eyes and a skinny tie who works for the *New York Herald* named Jonathan

Lodello—he is here, Sarah whispers, to do a story on the new new media scene, a story that will surely then be linked to on all the blogs of everyone sitting around the table, generating traffic and page views that can help with the advertisers and buzz.

Franklin runs up to Sarah.

"Let's do coke."

Sarah looks at me.

"You want to come?"

"I'm good, thanks."

"Laaaammmmmme," says Franklin.

"Yeah," I concur.

He takes Sarah by the arm and they find a spot in line at the bathroom. I sit down next to another kid.

"Kelly," he says.

"Mike," I say. "Kelly, as in Kelly Treemont?"

"That's me."

"I've read your blog. I thought you were a woman. The name."

"I get that. You don't do the powder either?"

"Nah, I used to do that shit a lot but stopped."

"Me too," he says. "I'm very boring now. I live with cats. I'm in recovery."

"Great. I work for a magazine."

"Dead tree, oh no."

"Yeah, the trees are pretty dead."

"You know, to be honest, I take a little Adderall still," he says. "It helps me in my writing. I'm working on a memoir. About my experiences with drugs and alcohol, and I don't know if you know, but I'm gay, so it's about my experiences with drugs and alcohol and being gay and everything."

"Sounds great," I say.

"You know, I think it's been out there, a little, but my experience, I think I have a really unique perspective."

"How long have you been working on the book?"

"Three years. This blogging, you know. But I found an agent. She's excited."

"Very cool. Having fun?"

"I'm waiting for Timothy. He's supposed to show."

"Timothy Grove?"

"Of course. He doesn't like these places—he prefers Balthazar, a place where he can pretend he's Anna Wintour or Graydon Carter—I think coming here reminds him too much that he's not really one of them, no matter how hard he tries. He'll always be more Larry Flynt. But you should watch out. He's a collector of straights."

"Is that right?"

"Aren't you the one they have guest blogging this week?"

"Yeah."

"There are things you could do, you know, if you want to make it permanent."

"Things?"

"Yes, things."

"Good to know. Is that how, uh, I mean, has anyone else ever done those things?"

"Me, of course, but it was brief, and I thought I loved him, though he is such a fucking scumbag."

"Yeah, sounds like it."

"Oh, watch this, this should be good."

The other Sarah, Sarah Klein, stands up from the table and grabs Jonathan Lodello's hand.

"She has such huge tits," Kelly says. "You know the backstory?"

"Uh, no."

"Franklin broke up with her three days ago. She's totally pissed about it, and she is totally convinced that Franklin is going to go and sleep with Sarah, and so she has to make him jealous by dancing with Lodello. If you want to get laid tonight, you should really talk to her, I'm mean, she is going to be ready to go away with someone cute like you."

"Oh, thanks, right."

"You have very nice eyes."

"Yeah, I appreciate that. They work okay."

I get up to get a club soda at the bar. Kelly doesn't want anything, and while I'm waiting at the bar, Timothy Grove comes in. He looks lanky and recently showered, and there are three men, all in their twenties in a semicircle, the same group I had seen at Eleanor K.'s house. He's dressed in all black—black jeans and a black T-shirt, probably a two-thousand-dollar shirt, though—with black cowboy boots and silver rings on his left and right hand and two studded diamond earrings on his left ear, new additions, it looks like. He moves—"slithers" would be tipping my hand—he moves over to the table, looking like a Persian prince from some ancient time.

The other Sarah, Sarah Klein, appears next to me.

"Do you dance?"

"Not this early. Can I get you a drink?"

"Red Bull and vodka," she says.

"Very youthful."

"I'm going to be thirty-four next week, so I do everything I can do to be very youthful."

"Right, right."

Timothy Grove has taken over the corner table with his entourage. I walk up with my club soda.

"Ah, the dead-tree'er, innit? Dead man walking. You talk to old Sanders Berman and Nishant Patel about how they are running to the ground your old brand there? Third round of layoffs coming, innit, and what are they doing? The little princes are scrambling for the top editor job, trying to be the captain of the good ship *Titanic*. Make brands of themselves over it, and there you are, still the little drooge of them, eh, while they build up their names to trampoline off the dead tree, floating on the dead tree until it goes down? That was your original sin, giving it away for free, giving all that content away for free, what a sin that was! Didn't get the Internet, they did not at all, and opened the door for the likes of me to come and give 'em a good interrupting kick. Good to see you finally get it, Hastings. Good to see that you're wanting to work for us now."

"I appreciate the opportunity."

"You even speak in the dead-tree language. We don't 'appreciate opportunity' here, there's no need for the brownnosing and suck-upping here, Hastings, no need at all."

"Okay, right, well it should be fun."

"Here's a numbers game for you, some research I just had done for my empire. Your magazine circulation ten years ago? Maybe three million, and claiming a readership of twenty-one million. Highly unlikely, but still had impact, it still mattered who you decided to put on the cover. Had that lyric in a Paul Simon song, innit? Thousand words a page, eighty-three pages on average an issue. Now you're down to 725 words a page, and fifty pages an issue. Full staff of your foreign correspondents was thirty-five a decade ago, now you've got ten, but you're still holding on to them, just to tell your little adver-tisers that you have an international brand? Isn't that right, Hastings? You know how much that international brand is worth to your adver-tisers? Seven million dollars, my sources at your magazine tell me, seven million. No domestic bureaus—no more Detroit or Miami or San Francisco or Dallas, just DC and New York and a woman in Los Angeles. The dead tree, they didn't get it—and they laughed at me at first with my nonpaper. They said, 'Oh, there's no future in that,' but they weren't looking too closely, were they? They were blinded, stuck, a bunch of arrogant fools on the good ship *Titanic Lollipop*. I think you've seen the light, Hastings, seen the darkness, more like it, and you've become one of us. If, that is, you do a bangers job this week."

"Right, right, yeah, I'm looking forward to it."

Franklin rushes to the table, Sarah behind him, laughing, eyes darting, nostrils cherry red. He whispers something into Sarah's ear, and a few minutes later, when I look around to see if she wants to leave, she's already gone.

I walk outside the Dark Room. I feel a brush of long leather jacket charging inside.

"Whoa," I say, moving to the wall.

"It's you," Sarah Klein says.

We're standing in the dark alcove in front of the exit. The bouncer holds open the door, and in the light from the streetlamp, I can see her face.

"In or out," the bouncer says.

"Out?" I ask.

Sarah follows me out onto the street.

"I was about to leave too," she says.

"Sorry to hear about you and Franklin, that sucks."

"Fuck him, he didn't mean a thing to me. I was only out here looking for him because I forgot to tell him something about this post I'm writing."

"You were out here looking for him?"

"No, like I said, I just wanted to tell him something. I can't believe it. He's such a fucking asshole. Where's the other Sarah?"

"I think she left too."

"With him?"

"So it would seem."

There is the inevitable awkward pause.

"You're upset."

"Yes."

"If you want to talk about it, my apartment is just around the corner."

We start walking down the street, and I notice that Jonathan Lodello of the *Herald* has left the Dark Room at about the same time and sees us before we turn the corner.

37.

Later Still

A.E. Peoria tries to get comfortable in his bed, but he is lying on a hard object, buried beneath the sheets. He moves around restless, still can't figure out what it is, until in frustration he grabs the sheet and throws it up in the air.

"What's wrong?" Justina asks him.

"Oh fuck, I didn't mean to wake you."

"Does being with me make you nervous?"

"Ah, here it is, fuck," A.E. Peoria says, holding up the object. "The jar of Vaseline."

Justina laughs and rolls over, putting her head on his chest. Peoria places the Vaseline onto the nightstand, next to a cruddy box of condoms that he had purchased three years before, when he had moved into his apartment, but hadn't really used very much; the box just kept getting buried under papers and other junk that found its way into the nightstand drawer. His girlfriends were usually on the pill, so he hadn't had a need for them.

Did being with Justina make him nervous? Yes it did. Did he want to tell her that? No, but would he be able to stop himself?

What he really wanted to do was to call his doctor friend, and ask what his percentage chance of catching an STD is from sleeping with a transsexual. Have there been any studies done on that? What are the percentages? How many partners had Justina had before him? Does anyone really get infected with HIV from just one sex act? He supposes it's possible, but how unlucky would he have to be for that to happen? And really, he hasn't heard much about HIV in recent years, and he'd never had sex with African prostitutes, or gay men, or heroin users, so he had felt quite well protected and secure until now. Even the fear he'd felt in Thailand had been put to rest by a Reuters story saying that the Thai sex industry had really nipped the HIV problem in the bud, thanks to a public information campaign, symbolized by a cartoon figure named Pac Con-Dom-Dom, a lively semi-transparent condom with a red sash and googly eyes, who would, like a Japanese spirit, swoop into brothels and teenage bedrooms moments before penetration, to say, at least in translation, Please remember to be safe. The cartoon worked, and practically eliminated that disease from the Southeast Asian nation, protecting its sex industry for at least another generation or two, until some new fucked-up supervirus came out that could kill every fornicator around.

But Peoria starts worrying about this midway through the second time they are having sex, after remembering that you aren't supposed to put Vaseline on condoms or something because the Vaseline eats through the rubber. Shit, there's even a Pac Con-Dom-Dom public service announcement about it on YouTube! But maybe that's inaccurate, referring to some outdated Vaseline in the developing world. Maybe Vaseline has gotten rid of that glitch; maybe it's now closer to the K-Y line of products, but it was the only lubricant that Peoria had available in his apartment—he had picked it up after broaching anal sex with his now ex-girlfriend, but when they finally did have anal sex, it was at her apartment, and she had K-Y.

Then there is the fact that he signed a contract with the school that said he wouldn't sleep with his students, at least while he was teaching them. He didn't ask about it at the job interview—he didn't think it would be a wise question—but he had read the paperwork carefully enough to see that professors were given a loophole that meant that as long as the student wasn't getting credit that semester and complied with other state and local laws, there was some room to maneuver. Finally, he started to feel a strong attachment bond, as his mother's partner would say.

"Yes, I think I am nervous. I mean, you are a student and I've never slept with a man before."

"I'm not a man."

"And what if the Vaseline ate through the condom?"

"What?"

Peoria pauses. He gets out of bed. He goes into the bathroom, closes the bathroom door, and turns on the hot water and starts to scrub himself.

What was it with this strong attachment bond anyway? She understood, Justina understood. She understood what it was like to be out there in the desert, and he had never really dealt with that. The I-am-going-to-die-amid-loneliness feeling, the absolute trauma of helplessness—no one had understood that, no one had gotten that, and maybe he had pretended that it didn't really matter to him that he had shrugged it off like the wannabe war correspondent is supposed to do. But it did affect him, and it was an experience that—despite his ramblings, despite throwing hundreds of thousands of words at it in conversation—that defied all conversation and writing and one that just required you to be there: you had to be there, and the only person close to the trauma of that night was Justina, and this is what is so powerful.

The door to the bathroom swings open slowly.

Peoria peeks around the shower curtain.

Justina stands there, flat belly, just thicker than a rail, tiny flat breasts with artificially puffy nipples, hairless vagina, if that was the right word, that even with reconstructive surgery resembled crushed Silly Putty wedged into an inverted ant hill.

She pushes the curtain aside and steps in, kneeling down. She starts sucking his cock.

A mouth is a mouth, a hole is a hole, Peoria remembers . . . Peoria gets hard.

He closes his eyes and rests his hand on the soap dish, knocking over a bottle of Gillette 2-in-1 shampoo-conditioner.

He usually has a hard time coming in hot water—he never masturbates in the shower, for instance—but he lets his imagination go, and his imagination goes back to the memory, the first time he had touched Justina, while he was still Justin, his hand warmed by blood, bodies pressed together, the absolute fear and excitement of death enveloping him, a memory so powerful he had pretended it didn't exist, and with the warm water falling off his short, five-foot-seven frame, splashing to the top of the long black hair at his knees, he lets the memory wash over him, maybe even washing it away however briefly, and he comes.

Swallowing, Justina looks up.

"I know what you were thinking about," she says. "I was thinking it too."

They both start to cry.

38.

Monday

Whoosh. I'm pulled into the blogosphere.

I'm at my cubicle at *The Magazine* at 6:45 a.m., a copy of the *New York Post* and the *Daily News* on my desk, scanning the papers for items that I can't find online. I'm hooked into Wretched's email system, where all the tips from readers come in, naming names, hinting at layoffs, leaking details to fuck somebody over. Wretched's slogan is "Envy is a beautiful thing," and it's apparent from the kind of correspondence that envy is the grease of the Wretched Empire.

I don't want to use my real name as a guest editor, so I come up with a pseudonym. I settle on K. Eric Walters, the name of a little-known and short-lived Irish revolutionary who had accidentally punched out a Brit in a drunken brawl, sparking a rebellion that Michael Collins would later take credit for. There is also a K. Eric Walters who spends his time as an amateur bass fisherman—the perfect name, one that gets plenty of Google hits, seemingly legit, and would cause a bit of confusion for anyone trying to figure out my identity—food critic? Bass fisherman? Molecular scientist at UCLA? Film critic for some site called Rotten Tomatoes? Yes, there were plenty of K. Eric Walterses to choose from.

Grove emails me.

Specting 10 posts a day? Use IDs.

I forward it to Sarah, with a "?"

Oh, he's obsessed with IDers. I don't know why. The guy is a freak. Something from his FT days I think.

Ten posts a day. Where to find them?

I check the story-tips email box. There is a forward from a publicist at a publishing house, a press release announcing that Stephen King's son has just published his first collection of short stories. "Think he deserves this on merit?" the emailer asks.

Okay, that works. Nasty potential there. I copy a chunk of the press release then write a few lines about how Stephen King's son got a book deal because he was Stephen King's son. Scathing.

And then I'm off, and I get a full sense of the power of the blog, like I'm walking a tightrope, a live piece of performance art. Hundreds of thousands of readers out there are responding within seconds and minutes to what I am writing, and I sense this sensation and the only thing I can think of is that it's like crack. This is a powerful drug, having the ability to communicate so freely and widely and instantaneously, and to get a response—yes they are reading my snark, hurrah.

The next few items are simple. A reporter for *The New York Times* has written a book about the three weeks he spent in Iraq at the paper's Baghdad bureau and has made up names for some of the Arabs they spoke to—probably true, and that is the problem with it, and Wretched is able to tee off, getting three posts out of it, until finally, one of his allies from the *Times* stands up for him in an email and says, Hey, if you want to really start talking about inaccuracies for the *Times*, try writing about our television critic—she has more corrections per story than any other *New York Times* person currently on staff. And with a bit of LexisNexis fun, I do a post on the television critic and how many mistakes she makes per column; by this time, I'm done, it's noon, the rush hour is over—the highest traffic is usually in the morning—and I go grab a sandwich at the corner store.

The subject heading of the email says: "Imus Racist comment."

"Hey, did you listen to the show today? Imus called the Rutgers women's basketball team a 'bunch of nappy-headed hos.' That's racist!"

The emailer is Sarah Klein, the other Sarah, who left my apartment earlier this morning. I know that she could use a link from Wretched. It would really drive the traffic her way. She has posted a partial transcript on her website.

I don't think much of posting it. It's one of many. It takes off.

39.

Tuesday

Like wildfire—cliché. Like flesh-eating bacteria? Closer.

The new new media, the new media, and the old media, go into action.

Again, at my desk, at 7:30 a.m. I'm not alone.

Sanders Berman, looking ill, leaves the men's room and walks by.

"What are you doing here so early, Hastings?"

"Oh, just working on some extracurricular stuff," I say. "Yourself?"

"Some silly thing with the blogosphere. Apparently Don Imus said something racist on air yesterday. I was on his show, and now the *Times* is doing a story on it, so I'm going to talk to their reporter in a few minutes. Have you heard anything about it?"

"Um, yeah. I saw something on Wretched.com."

"Wretched? Who reads that trash?"

"A lot of people, I think."

Berman leaves me at the cubicle.

Throughout the night, the Imus comments, the "nappy-headed hos" controversy, has swept away all other news. Bloggers on the East Coast and West Coast and in the American Midwest have listened to the show, in full, and started to dissect the entire transcript; the cable news networks are playing the audio recording, and "Is Imus a Racist?" columns are already being prepared for tomorrow's papers.

Fifteen minutes later, Sanders Berman comes back down the hall, his face greenish. He goes into the bathroom again and then comes back out.

"They said I laughed, Hastings."

"Laughed at what?"

"The reporter, the *Times* reporter. They said that Imus called the Rutgers team a bunch of nappy-headed hos, and I was on the line, doing my weekly interview, and they said I laughed at the joke."

"Wow."

"I cleared my throat, I recall, and unfortunately it happened to time with his comments. Have you seen Milius? Where is he?"

Berman disappears down the hall again.

Within minutes, the *Times* has posted a story on its website, including the Sanders Berman comment: "'I don't think we want to rush to judgment,' magazine editor Sanders Berman said. 'We should wait to see how it plays out.' Mr. Berman, a regular guest on *Imus in the Morning*, can also be heard apparently laughing after Mr. Imus's remarks. Mr. Berman said he was 'clearing his throat.'"

By noon, human rights groups, media watchdog groups, civil rights organizations, and the majority of mainstream media outlets are calling for an apology from Imus. Former guests on Imus's show, many of whose books had become bestsellers after their appearance there, are also demanding an apology. Imus refuses at first and strikes back at his critics, saying they are acting like "rats on a sinking ship. Not that this ship is sinking."

Nishant Patel, back from a meeting with European advertisers, strolls in around one p.m.

"Mr. Hastings, hope you are well, sir."

"Yes, Nishant, doing great, thanks."

"What have I missed?"

"The Imus controversy. He called the Rutgers basketball team a bunch of nappy-headed hos. They're black, so everyone is saying it was racist."

"Ah, I would visit Princeton when Yale played them, in American football."

"Sanders was on the show when he said it."

Nishant nods, then goes to his corner office.

"Dorothy, call Henry, tell him we should talk very soon."

"Yes, Nishant. You know, of course, that Henry is away, and Sanders is acting . . ."

Nishant nods and turns away.

Dorothy stands up and scans the room.

"Patricia?"

Patricia pops up from her cubicle, startled.

"Yes, Dorothy?"

"Call Henry the EIC and tell him Dr. Patel wants to speak with him."

"What is the EIC?"

"Not what, who—Henry, the EIC."

"Henry from the copy desk?"

"No, not the copy desk, the editor in chief."

"You want him to call you?"

"You won't get him, you'll get his assistant, and tell her to tell him to call."

I turn back to my cubicle. I've already posted three items on what is being called a "growing controversy." I'm getting a little nervous. Glad I have a pseudonym. I'm thinking that it might be smart to resign my position at Wretched for the week. That's when Grove pings me.

"Great job so far, keep this up and there might be a position for you here. Leave the dead trees once and for all."

I hear the hiss of Delray M. Milius, walking two steps behind Berman. They stop on the other side of the cubicle wall.

"Send another statement to the *Times*," Berman says. "Tell them *The Magazine* is no longer going on the show. Tell them I found his comments reprehensible—I scoffed at them on air! And let's get one of those staff meetings together. And make sure to invite all the . . . we need to get their input . . ."

Delray M. Milius sends out a company-wide email, calling for an emergency staff meeting to discuss the new policy in relation to the Imus show.

An hour later, the conference room on the fifteenth floor is filled up with staff. I'm about to sit down when Delray tells me that these four seats are reserved. I say okay and stand in the back of the room, by the door.

Charlotte, the youngest African American woman on staff, comes into the conference room.

"Sit right there," Delray tells her, pointing to the empty seat that I was going to sit in.

The three seats next to her are filled by the remaining three African American members on the magazine's staff.

Sanders Berman comes in, second to last, beaten in being fashionably late only by Nishant.

"Ladies and gentlemen, I'm sure you've all heard of the growing controversy surrounding Don Imus's appalling comments," Berman begins. "First, I'd like you to know that I had no idea that Imus would say such things."

Berman looks around the room, his eyes stopping on Janet, the woman who runs the magazine's public relations department and who regularly books the magazine employees for media appearances.

"Janet, I'm really disappointed that you never told me Imus ran this kind of a show. I'm really disappointed that no one warned me that he would say such horrible things."

Janet starts to respond, "You've been on the show for three years and—"

Sanders cuts her off. "Let's make sure it doesn't happen again."

He sweeps the conference room.

"So, our new policy. We're not going on *Imus* anymore. And we're going to address the issue of his comments in the next issue. I'd like you four," he says, pointing at the four African Americans on the staff who are sitting at the table, "I'd like you four—Charlotte, Sammy, John, and Lucas—to take the lead on this reporting."

"I don't cover media," says Charlotte.

"It's okay, and I think we really need your perspective. And if you have any problems, or would like to discuss this further, Delray is going to talk to each one of you individually. Obviously, this is not how I wanted my time as acting EIC to go, but Henry supports, and the Dolings support, my position to boycott Imus completely, and I support all of you to do the best damn story we can about it."

I go back to my cubicle. I figure I'd wait an hour before posting anything about the meeting on Wretched. Things are getting way too close to home. I have to tell Grove that I can't be guest editor the rest of the week—he has to take over the site himself.

I send him an email.

He responds.

"That's fine, but you did sign a weekly contract with us, but I see how you are in a bind, so just give me updates on what's going on inside your magazine. You don't have a choice, otherwise I'll do a post now saying you were the one who started this whole controversy."

Fuck.

"Mike, Nishant wants to see you," Dorothy calls out to me.

Shit.

I walk into Nishant's office. He's sitting there, reading the new issue of the *New York Herald*, its distinct pink paper standing out against the other papers on his desk.

"Have you read the *Herald* this week, Hastings?"

"Not yet, didn't know it was out yet."

"You're in it. I didn't know you were friends with these bloggers."

That Jonathan Lodello. He'd put me in his story. I wonder if he's mentioned that I'm guest editing under a pseudonym. If so, my career at *The Magazine* is about to end, and fast.

"Oh yeah, what did he say?"

"Nothing, except that you are dating a girl named Sarah Klein. Wasn't she the blogger who started this whole controversy?"

"I'm really sorry, Nishant. I'm no longer having anything to do with that crowd. It was a mistake being there, and it was a mistake guest editing this week—"

Nishant isn't listening.

"So, your girlfriend, don't you think she might find our meeting this afternoon with Sanders interesting?"

I suppose she would, but I don't know what Nishant is getting at right away.

"She's not my girlfriend, but—"

"I mean, to have the four African Americans reporting this story, doesn't that also have the faint stench of racism? After Berman laughs—scoffs—it seems rather clumsy to then have four blacks at *The Magazine* do the black story. You don't think so? Perhaps I'm mistaken."

"Oh yeah, I guess that could look bad."

"Hastings, you sent me that email, I don't think I ever responded, about you guest editing Wretched. Is it this week you're doing that?"

"Nishant, yes, but I'm not doing it anymore."

"And I never gave you permission, and you didn't ask Berman or Delray about it either?"

"I thought you knew, you were cool with it, no news is good news, and everything—"

"I would suggest you not doing it from this point on. That being said, I would not object to any further communication that you might have with Ms. Klein."

He turns back to his computer. I'm dismissed.

Back at my cubicle, I compose an email to Sarah Klein. I cc Timothy Grove. This is all I can give you, I tell them. He writes back, "Perfect."

This is how the scandal is propelled to the next level, wishing for another victim, full saturation, because this is a scandal that has started to drag others down with it, amplifying speculation, its tentacles grappling more boldface names into the abyss, into that area that got other boldface names to start speculating and hiding and focusing on survival—somebody is going to have to pay for Imus's comments, and if it is more than just Imus, all the better, as long as it isn't you.

There doesn't need to be any official words or messages; the instinctual calculations have been made—to risk a career and a family and a paycheck and a well-crafted brand name and status to defend Don Imus? Not likely. The indignation that can be found in the talking heads in the media elite is not so much over Imus's comments—after all, who truly gives a shit—but the indignation of almost getting dragged down too by his careless remarks. This feeling of a near-miss sparked the true outrage, which is expressed in comments about racism and demands for apologies, but it is truly just a cover for the outrage over Imus's misstep, and while making that gross misstep, to have threatened their own careers.

Danger looming, the momentum building up, an epic fall approaches. The knives are unsheathed, incisors sharpened, and enemies and targets of his scorn in the past are making phone calls, remarks on television, coming out of the media landscape, electronic specters with Rolodexes and grudges and access to editors, nudging the story along. Silently building, it expands and expands and by nightfall, the name Sanders Berman is on every Movable Type page and every gossip columnist's screen—will he go down too?

40.

Wednesday

I pick up the slow mumble of Berman's drawl as he leans up against the wall down from my cubicle. Delray M. Milius stands with his arms crossed. I figure they would have learned not to talk important business in the magazine hallways by now, but the crisis has made them more unsure of themselves, and they fall back into old patterns.

"Who's the leak? Who's the leak? . . . I can't even talk in my office because it could be her, my assistant . . . Lawsuits . . . I don't hate African Americans . . . You're right, we can't say that in a statement . . . All the advertisers have boycotted his show . . ."

"We need to change the subject," Milius says. "We need to change the subject soon. We don't want this to go on another week."

"How are they taking it?"

"Not well. Charlotte has offered her resignation, citing racial prejudices."

"Christ. This, this is bullshit—this is reverse racism. Just because I'm from Alabama, I'm a racist? Just because I laughed at a joke? And now that I've seen the clip of that basketball team, I can't deny that they do look like nappy-headed hos, one of them even has a tattoo that says 'ho,' I mean, this is just so incredibly unjust—"

"Sanders, Sanders, please, this isn't the time. Stay on message, and we'll change the message soon. We'll change the conversation."

"How?"

". . . A.E. Peoria . . ."

I'm surprised to hear A.E. Peoria's name.

Should I warn him? But warn him of what?

Three hours later, A.E. Peoria rushes in.

"Mike, fuck, hey. I'm meeting with Milius. They don't want to run the story this week, do they?"

41.

Wednesday, Continued

A.E. Peoria sits for a full five minutes without saying a word. He's sworn to himself that he is going to do a better job at listening. Receive mode. He is in receive mode, sitting in a chair across from Delray M. Milius. It is an accomplishment that he is even back in this office after the mistakes. At first, he wants to start apologizing for the pencil incident, to tell Milius about his transformation, to tell him about Norm and his iced coffees and self-acceptance, to tell him again about how he has changed and learned to love himself, somewhat, how it's a struggle he's working on every day. But then he thinks, No, I won't apologize, no need for me to bring up old news, he's probably forgotten about it anyway. I will just sit and listen and absorb and show that I have changed, that I am reliable, that I am a good citizen of the magazine.

"So, can you give us a draft of the story by tomorrow night," Milius says.

"The story?"

"About the transvestite."

"Transsexual."

"Right."

"Of course I can, no problem at all."

A good citizen of the magazine, he does not want to express any reservations; just say yes, agree to anything. Yes, that is his new philosophy of success, and this is the first time since his suspension that he is able to test it out.

So he says yes, I will do the story.

"All I have to do is get permission from Justina, you know, and then we should be okay."

"Permission?"

"Yes, need to get her approval, you know, so I can write the story."

"You haven't told her you're going to write a story about her?"

"No, not yet, you know, I was waiting, you know, but it's helped because I've gotten really good stuff, you know."

"Get her permission. We need this story. I don't have to mention that this is really your last chance."

A.E. Peoria leaves the office and walks out onto 57th Street. He has thirty blocks to go to his apartment on the Upper West Side. It is a fall day in New York, a beautiful fall day, and passing by Columbus Circle he nods happily at the immigrants waving laminated maps of the park and offering guided tours and he feels the need to walk. A walk in the city, what a pleasure, what a time to think, how amazing he feels, a man in the big city with a sense of purpose, with a renewed life. Is there any other street to have been walking on than Broadway with a view of Central Park, life, hustle, neurosis, energy, and attractive people? And it is only twenty minutes later that it sinks in what Delray Milius had actually said; he had said it so softly, with a strange inflection, that the offense wasn't processed at the time.

This story is his last chance. A threat, really.

Of course, he tells himself, Justina will be happy to help me tell this story. She'll be totally psyched about it, you know, I think she is going to be totally psyched. He has a date planned with her that night—he'll tell her after they see the movie.

He goes back to his apartment and starts to write. Where to begin?

No, I won't make this about me, he says. I will start with her, with Justina. I will start the story where it all began, back in Iraq at the invasion.

From memory he writes, chronology his friend, starting with the anecdote of the ambush, then her descriptions of her stay in the hospital, then her recovery process—the surgery, the day that she sat in her bedroom and realized looking downward that she was no longer a man and didn't want to be a man—then he writes about the GI Bill, and how it doesn't cover sex changes, and how that is unjust, and that she got into Barnard even though the documents on the GI Bill said she was a male. But that kind of subterfuge is for civil rights, heroic, and previously never disclosed—this is breaking news you are reading here people, this is a test case, this is a story generated and produced and distributed underneath a great brand by the great A.E. Peoria, Magazine Journalist. This is the story that will spark debate and conversation and change policy—yes, this is a great story.

All he needs is his last step. To tell Justina.

He emails Mike Hastings. He sends him what he's written so far. I need your files, he says, by tomorrow morning, the story is due tomorrow, and I need your files and you need to be ready to fact-check this fucker by Friday.

He closes his laptop. Tomorrow he will wake up and crash the rest of the story. The hours had disappeared as he'd entered his writing space, they'd just flown by, and the film he is scheduled to see with Justina starts in fifty-five minutes. He hopes they can still get seats.

He waits for her outside the theater on 68th Street, a massive Loews Cineplex, and he stands in front of a movie poster that has the tagline "Sometimes, it's only once." Apparently a love story, and this makes his eyes wet on the edges, thinking of Justina, the gift that has been brought into his life. He saved her life, and now she is going to save his career. An equal trade in his world. He got tickets out of the electronic kiosk—two adults for the film, a romantic comedy, that year's installment about a holiday get-together gone horribly wrong, dinner sequences with turkeys and cranberry sauce and accidentally offensive remarks and humorous, lighthearted, hilarious violence.

It is New York, so other pretty girls pass on the street, but he doesn't watch them with desire, which is his usual fallback position. He doesn't compare them on tiers or rank them with numbers; he feels no need to do that anymore. He has accepted himself, and yes, when he sees her, he thinks, Wow, this is the first time that I have waited for a girl out-side the theater and felt lucky when she actually appeared. How strange is that? What am I to make of the fact that this feels so right?

Justina appears in a navy peacoat over a dress, her thin legs in black stockings coming out underneath. She has, out of self-consciousness, kept her female style quite simple, wearing knee-length skirts, pearls, peacoats, one season's worth of outfits from J.Crew—and yes, for a former man, she looks quite good—you can't tell.

"Popcorn?"

"Put extra salt on it."

After the film, they go to the Italian restaurant, only five blocks away, where they had their first date not long ago.

"I have really big news, so big I can't believe I was able to keep it in this long," he says.

"I can't wait to hear it," she says, squeezing his hand, in between a dish of olive oil and a brass candleholder.

"The magazine wants me to do a story for them this week," he says.

"That's so amazing. I'm so proud of you."

He waits. This would be the moment.

"I'm going to tell our story, your story," he says. "Isn't that great?"

"What do you mean?"

"I think we can get the cover, you know, I'm writing it, it will be your picture. I mean, it's going to be huge. You're going to be famous, and maybe we can get a book deal and a movie out of it too. I mean, I think it's that big, you know?"

Her face does not change into the shape he expects. It does not glow. He recognizes a kind of pained anger, and for a moment he sees the same face that had rested beneath the Kevlar helmet years ago, in Iraq. A masculine face, a face of rage.

"You can't do this. You can't write about me. I'm not ready, I'm not ready for it."

"But I thought you'd be cool with it. It'd be doing me a huge favor."

"Not yet. Can't you wait?"

"No, it really can't wait—the magazine asked and I said I would deliver. I mean, I'd been talking about it with them for months, you know."

"You've been talking with the magazine for months about this? And you haven't told me?"

"Uh, yeah, I mean, didn't I mention it?"

"I'm a fucking story to you," she says. "I'm a fucking story." She stands up from the table.

"If you do this, if you do this story, you will lose me."

"No need to be so dramatic—I know you're Latin and all—"

"Latina! A story! Throw our love away for what, for printed pages!"

She leaves the restaurant.

"But I saved your life," he yells.

"Fuck you!"

"Don't get in the cab."

"I'm getting in the cab, get away from me."

"Don't get in the fucking cab."

"I'm getting in the cab."

He withdraws his hand before the yellow door slams on it, and he looks to see her through the window, but she has turned her head away. The only face he sees in the cab is on the small and newly installed video monitor, the face of New York City mayor Michael Bloomberg, reciting a public service announcement.

Relapse. Seven months of sobriety gone, just like that.

A.E. Peoria, magazine journalist, turns and walks into a bar, puts his credit card down, and starts to drink. Sober, yes, only drinking wine, which doesn't count, and now he knows that the only response is to get totally fucked-up, totally wrecked, to embrace that abyss that had been missing from his life. Justina's rejection has brought it back to him in full—oh, how good it feels, the beer and shot then another beer.

At 123rd and Lexington, three hours later.

"Put your fucking shirt back on, motherfucker," the drug dealer says.

"I saw the shoes up the telephone line, and I know that that means you sell crack, right?" A.E. Peoria says, putting his shirt back on. "See, I don't have a fucking wire."

"Shut the fuck up, man! Give me the cash."

"Give me the stuff."

"Shit, hold on."

The dealer goes over to a payphone.

"You still have payphones? That's so strange—isn't that, like, bizarre? I guess it's a class thing. But it's strange, I mean, even in Africa and shit, everybody has cell phones—they call them mobile phones, you know, because 'cell phone' isn't really accurate. They took the cells out of the phone a long time ago. And it's strange that only in America they still call it a cell phone."

A teenager runs down the street. He hands a small packet to the dealer, who goes up to A.E. Peoria and slaps his hand. Peoria takes the packet and kneels down.

"What the fuck you doing?"

"Oh, I keep my money in my sock when I come up here, but I guess I shouldn't have told you that."

"Man, just leave that shit on the ground and get the fuck out of here before I beat your ass."

"Okay, okay."

Peoria starts walking blindly down the street, crack secured. All he needs now is a way to smoke it. He threw out his crack pipe months before, during his self-acceptance and healthy-living phase. Which put him in a dilemma.

"Hey, handsome," a woman in tight black latex pants says. "You holding? Want to make a trade?"

"You have a crack pipe?"

"Shhhh, you're a crazy man, aren't you. Come with me."

"What do I get out of it?"

"I suck your dick for a hit."

She grabs his hand, and she presses a buzzer on an apartment building, where rent is clearly paid late each month and with cash.

A.E. Peoria stumbles into a room with a white mattress in the corner, three people passed out on the floor. He unzips his pants.

"Let's get high first."

He hands over the crack, and she takes a few minutes to stick it in a glass pipe. She sparks a Bic lighter, and he stares at her callused fingertips.

She exhales and passes the pipe to him.

He inhales and falls back.

She starts sucking his cock.

"Let me just finish my way," he says, looking at her and masturbating. She starts to push her breasts together and moan.

He stares at her breasts, but he isn't getting closer to ejaculating. He closes his eyes, and opens them, and closes his eyes again, fixing his mind on Justina, then opening them to get the image of the fat whore, then closing his eyes to fix on Justina, then reaching out and touching the breasts of the fat whore, and finally, thinking of Justina, coming.

He takes another hit from the crack pipe.

Fifteen minutes later, he jumps up.

"What the fuck am I doing here? What the fuck am I doing here?" he screams.

He sees the street sign—89th and Columbus. He's near Justina's place. His mobile phone says it's 5:45 a.m. He looks across the street and feels an agitating emptiness, an emptiness that stretches back years and years in his life that he can never quite fill, not with crack or with booze or a yearly gym membership or even with his career. No, this emptiness does not just reach across to the piled-up garbage bags and the trickle of yellow cabs crawling by in the empty streets— the only time of day when they travel under the speed limit, when the drivers drive cautiously, which is strange because it would be the safest time to go fast. The newspaper delivery trucks, and the neon sign promising the world's greatest coffee, and the other neon signs promising the world's greatest slice of pizza, and the emptiness of a metal grate pulled down over a fast-food juice and hot dog joint, or the emptiness of the Yemeni clerk in the twenty-four-hour bodega, guarding the stocks of booze in the back from drunks, having to say over and over again that he can't sell again until noon. This emptiness that he sees stretches everywhere and far back into his own past.

His own life. That he knows that there is no hope and no god, and nothing at all, and he knows that the story won't save him either, and he feels the crack leaving his nervous system raw and dry, and he knows the crack has abandoned him to life, and he wants to cry, and he wants to yell out, "Look, here I am world, on the corner of 89th and Columbus, coming down off crack, drunk, a magazine journalist, a New Yorker, a failure, and all I want is to be held."

She answers the buzzer on the third obnoxious ring.

42.

Thursday–Friday–Saturday

I don't have a good feeling about the email from Milius, summoning me to his office.

"Hi, Delray, what's up?"

"It's three p.m. and we just lost the writer on our cover story," he says.

"What happened?"

"Peoria isn't doing it. He won't write it. He's fired."

I nod.

Milius opens a drawer and pulls out a copy of the *New York Herald*, placing it on his desk.

"You're aware you were mentioned in association with these bloggers this week?"

"Oh, yeah, that was funny."

"You're aware that the magazine has had a series of leaks this week that have done a lot of damage to our brand?"

"Yeah, I saw something about that online."

Delray stands up, clasping his hands behind his back, and stares out the window.

He sighs, as if he had practiced the entire sequence of movements in front of a mirror, a corporate executive ballet.

Delray turns back around and sits.

"You have all of Peoria's files. What else?"

"His journals, his interviews, yeah, I have that."

"You've also done reporting, yes? He sent you pictures of Justina too?"

"I've talked to all sorts of experts, yes."

"Okay, you're going to do the story."

I don't say anything.

"You don't seem very excited, Hastings. This is your first cover."

"Oh, I am very excited, but you know, it's Peoria's story, and I'm sure if he doesn't want to do it, it's probably for good reason, right? Like that he doesn't want to screw over Justina."

"Do you know a blogger named K. Eric Walters?"

"Hmm."

Milius homes his eyes on me, stretches his face back, a flake of facial moisturizing cream falling onto his desk.

"This isn't ideal for anyone. But I promised Sanders this story, and so we are going to give Sanders this story. You're going to do it, you understand?"

"I understand."

I'd like to say that I agonized over the decision, that I thought twice about it—because I know by taking Peoria's story, I'm putting the last nail in the coffin of his career, and I know that I'm also jeopardizing the privacy and future of Justina. Who knows how the military is going to react to this? Most likely they'll strip her of the GI Bill benefits. Who knows how the liberals at Barnard are going to react to having been deceived? Maybe they will support her, maybe not.

But I don't agonize over it. I don't want to lose my job, and if Sanders finds out that I'm the leak, then I'm done for too.

Plus, this is a great opportunity. My first cover story for the magazine.

I go back to my desk, call up the half rough draft that Peoria had sent me the day before, and start to write, just like I had learned how.

EPILOGUE

You should feel like the story is over, like you're walking out during the credits, waiting for a few deleted scenes or bloopers. Like you want two or three more screens of text to explain what happened to who and how. Maybe then you'll watch the sequel, if one is made.

The next week, Henry the EIC decides who his successor is going to be. The decision doesn't become public until a few weeks later. They don't want it to have the taint of the nappy-headed hos scandal.

Henry offers the EIC job to Nishant Patel.

Nishant turns it down—he's just gotten his own cable news show.

Henry then decides that Sanders Berman, after all, is the right man to lead the magazine into the twenty-first century.

A.E. Peoria gets fired from Barnard.

Justina doesn't get expelled. She becomes a cause célèbre on campus.

There is talk of court-martial—defrauding the government—but the charges never go anywhere. The ensuing controversy outrages the LGBT community. A young woman is temporarily blinded by pepper spray during a protest. A defense fund is raised.

After the spring semester, A.E. Peoria and Justina get married in a civil union ceremony.

He sends me an email from their honeymoon in Thailand. He wants my notes and reporting, he says, because he is working on a book proposal. He doesn't seem very angry at me.

It's now 2008. I'm finished writing—finished three weeks ago.

I'm about to go into work at *The Magazine*. I should be hearing back about this book soon. I want to get mine out there before Peoria finishes his draft.

It's a story I should be able to sell.